SHEER
CHANCE

SHEER CHANCE

Suzanne Goodwin

St. Martin's Press ❧ New York

Library of Congress Cataloging-in-Publication Data

Goodwin, Suzanne.
    Sheer chance / Suzanne Goodwin.
        p.   cm.
    ISBN 0-312-15654-5
    I. Title.
PR6057.0585S48   1997
823'.914—dc21
                                          97-8210
                                          CIP

First published in Great Britain by Little, Brown and Company

First U.S. Edition: July 1997

10   9   8   7   6   5   4   3   2   1

SHEER
CHANCE

PART ONE

Chapter 1

Keith Waring stood framed in the doorway against a skyful of stars.

'Here's the rescue party,' he said, stepping into the cottage. 'My God, Avril, it's freezing! Shall I dump my coat here?'

He took off a huge overcoat and a scarf of the kind men used to wear with evening dress. He rubbed his hands.

'Aha. You've lit a fire. That's what we needed to brighten up the old place you thought you were saying goodbye to for weeks. And here's the medicine prescribed by your doctor.'

Avril smiled as he unwrapped a parcel produced from a plastic bag, and waved a bottle of champagne. She murmured how extravagant. Keith, who liked admiration, preened. He confessed the bottle had been given him last month for his birthday, and his wife did not like champagne.

'I thought you and I could share it. We'll drink to celebrate the very first evening I've spent with my assistant.'

3

He talked like that. My managing director. My colleagues. Avril had been 'my assistant' since the day he'd hired her as his secretary.

He opened the bottle with a practised twist; it smoked and scarcely popped. They drank amicably, sitting by the recently lit and noisy fire.

Keith was the right man for an evening of disappointment. He was big and cheerful and hearty, with a mop of thick blond hair, a round face and an engaging grin. He had the deceptive air of being a forty-year-old Mr Pickwick, but with none of that gentleman's naïveté. He was one of the directors of a successful firm of Bridport solicitors. Optimism radiated from him like scented after-shave, but he was too shrewd to be annoyingly cheerful with his clients; nevertheless they subconsciously felt he looked on the bright side.

He was married to a don at Exeter University. She specialised in the Italian Renaissance, gave many lectures abroad, and was rather a grandee.

Sitting beside Avril he sipped his own champagne.

'How's Sally?' Avril felt bound to ask.

'In Hanover again. They make a big fuss of her in Germany.'

'She does get around.'

'More invites than she can cope with. She enjoys being in demand.'

'Do *you* enjoy it?' Avril said after a moment.

His looking-for-a-joke face became quite solemn.

'No. It's a bore. It interrupts the flow of our life together. And she sleeps badly in strange hotels.'

'She could turn down some of the lectures,' suggested Avril. Keith was least fun when droning on about his wife.

4

He always spoke as if she'd taken vows for the religious life instead of standing up on platforms and – Avril remembered an office party – showing off.

'She couldn't do that. She's dedicated.'

The solemnity disappeared. He grinned.

'I don't like my own company, Avril. That's why I was disgustingly pleased when you rang and said your trip had been cancelled. A chance for me to come over and see you.'

He gave her a look of innocent conspiracy, faintly coloured with admiration.

His assistant, as he would call Avril, was attractive. She was thin and had a rather wasted look; you might have described her as fragile, although physically she was quite strong. She had a mop of curly black hair and unexpectedly dark brown eyes, as well as the physical attribute desired by actors: good bones. A frail-looking girl with uncared-for hands.

She and Keith talked office shop, she cooked an omelette, and they finished the champagne. They were easy with one another and Avril enjoyed his feeble jokes. When he finally looked at his watch it was well after midnight.

'What a selfish hog I am, keeping you up.'

She walked with him to the door and out into the garden, bringing a torch. It wasn't necessary, for the night was light and the stars sparkled. The frost seemed to make them glitter, and Keith pointed out the Plough. She wasn't surprised when he put his arm round her shoulders. They had scarcely shaken hands in the five years she'd worked for him, but now in the starry dark he looked down at the thin face, ghostly in the strange light.

'You're lovely,' he said, pulling her close.

Avril liked the sensation. Knowing he was attracted gave

her a moment of sexual confidence. He kissed her, delicately opening her lips.

'Brilliant, your trip being cancelled.'

'Now you won't have to pay for a temp.'

'How did you guess?'

Next morning Avril thought about Keith almost before the drama of her cancelled trip. Staring up at the time-gnawed beam over her head, she no longer felt angry and disappointed that she wasn't going to St Vincent to join her husband. She had looked forward intensely to the trip and had been quite furious at the sudden cancellation. It was absurd, but Keith's company, Keith's goodnight kiss, had given her a kind of solace. He had made her feel she mattered. She had sometimes imagined he was interested in her sexually when she was working for him, but had never been confident about herself and had pushed the thought aside. Now she was sure. Keith was an uncomplicated man. He was what he was.

So was Hugh. When they had married, Avril had not actually seen the man she had taken on. She had not been blind, as love is supposed to make you, but blindfolded. For the first year of her marriage she had gone around with her groping hands stretched out in front of her, feeling only the muscular figure, the outline of a handsome face, the set of fine shoulders. Eyeless, she envisaged a god. Little by little the scarf knotted round her head became loose; finally it tumbled off and she saw the man she'd married. Hugh was not unfaithful, but faithless. He could no more stop climbing into bed with a woman than a canary could stop its song. He'd walk across a room of people to seek out some new woman, always beautiful and usually, though not necessarily, young. Returning home with Avril, he would talk about his new acquaintance a good deal. It was the sign. Avril had no divorce-court proof of his promiscuity. Instinct was enough, and his later manner, relaxed and self-satisfied. Sex with another woman also stimulated his desire for *her*, and Avril noticed that Hugh at his most passionate was often Hugh straight from another woman's bed.

She saw that he had a curious gift: he was sexually irresistible. Not because of conventional good looks, height, classy manners; certainly not from any originality of mind or imagination. What Hugh Brett had was an aura of desire. Whenever he wanted a woman, he got her.

An Indian girl at art college had once told Avril about the god Krishna. When he played upon his flute and a woman heard his music, she was, that instant, enslaved. No woman on earth could refuse Krishna's call. She would leave her palace or her cooking pots, her throne or her children to lie with him. Hugh was like that.

Avril was still excited by him sexually but she did not love him now. She despised him for a vice as permanent as drink or drugs or gambling; she disdained his pathetic lies. But she'd become accustomed to betrayal; it did not hurt the way it ought to do. Her heart had grown cold towards him.

There was something else about her marriage which was far worse to bear and which gave Avril at times a pain so excruciating that when it came over her she felt she would faint.

He refused to let her have children. Neither he nor Avril had said a word about this before they married. Even had they done so, she was too far gone then to have believed him. *I can do anything with him.* She had been certain of her magical power.

When he first told her how he felt about children she was sure he would change his mind. She was affectionate and persuasive and logical. Later she became wild and sad, and in the end she was desperate. Nothing had the least effect on him.

As far as Hugh Brett was concerned, children were for other people. He was like a man at the sea's edge watching the crowds frolicking in the water and never even wanting to go in because he could not swim.

His mother had died when he was young; he'd been palmed off on relatives who were not much attached to a moody, difficult little boy. His father, in the Royal Navy, was posted abroad a good deal and never considered taking the child and a nanny. He only returned, to upset his son, on long leaves.

When Hugh grew into his teens his entrance to Dartmouth was a matter of course. His good looks were now noticeable, and even mean-spirited aunts and great-aunts who had never loved him began to flutter and flatter Hugh in uniform. A swan indeed. With the undeserved and unexpected gift of beauty came Hugh's pursuit of and success with women.

This was the man, with his self-confidence and ancient wounds, who had married Avril, refused her children, and, as stupid as most adulterers are, constantly cheated on her and believed she didn't know.

She loathed her childless state. Her friends in the Navy, married friends in the Dorset village, spent their time and talk on their young families. Children ruled. Mothers drove them on the shared school run, weaved back again through the country lanes to collect them at teatime. Mothers consulted about uniforms, new or second-hand, and agonised over coughs and temperatures, chicken pox and other schoolroom plagues. They went to toddler group together, telephoned each other about teething, sleepless nights, and the floods of tears when a child went to school for the first time. Everybody caught each other's colds.

Hugh was free of the drama, totally unaware of it, though not of the sexier-looking mothers. As for Avril, she baby-sat. Some of the children even loved her, but nobody belonged to her. No weighty six-year-old threw herself sobbing into Avril's arms, no baby gave her a knowing grin through a mask of wet cornflakes. Her days did not burst with love and worry. She simply drove into Bridport to work for Keith. And pretended not to notice Hugh's boring affairs.

There was an escape. Avril was a closet painter.

There hadn't been a time when she did not paint. Flat on her stomach, she had covered sheet after sheet, not only with Mummy, Daddy, and Our House, but with anything which took her fancy. People or animals, bicycles or cars, planes or seagulls. Once her father found her sobbing because the cat had walked out of the room.

'I only got to his tail.'

When she was seven she began to paint what she called 'nachur'. Her mother – at the teacher's suggestion; Susan Vincent was impressed by teachers – allowed the child to have a nature table, and Avril went plant-hunting. The table was seasonal. Catkins, buttercups, grasses which made her parents sneeze. And as the year ended, spiky conkers and the transparent wings of sycamores. One summer her mother offered a spike of delphinium.

'Look, darling. So blue!'

Avril glowered from under her school fringe, and her

brother Rick pityingly explained:

'Av only paints things that are sort of wild, Mum.'

'I've told you before not to call me Mum,' said Susan, who had vainly demanded 'Mama'.

The nature table did not last; everything died and water in tumblers full of dead flowers or weeds turned green. Avril's brother, intermittently interested in a sister four years younger than he was, treated her painting like a husband whose wife is a secret drinker.

'You've been at it again. Did you spill the turps?'

It was not her mother's idea to send Avril to art school. She'd hoped for a debby daughter who would go to naval dances and to a royal garden party among visiting Australians. Avril's father Gerald Vincent decided his daughter should go to college. He'd seen her expression when debs were mentioned, and her happy face when she'd been painting for an hour or two. He sent her off to enrol.

Suddenly Avril was in a new, noisy world of men and girls the same age and with the same interest as herself. Voices echoed, feet clattered, the air smelled of paint. In the many studios and classrooms students attended lectures, drew, painted; they sat down to matey and deafening canteen lunches. There were rave-ups and indignation meetings, and Avril's passion for painting slowed down because she was having so much fun. She hadn't completed the three-year diploma course when, a diver from the highest Olympic board, she plunged straight into love. She left college, married and stopped painting altogether.

It was sad, it was soon, when she needed to pick up her brushes again.

At first she didn't hide her work, and when Hugh came back from naval barracks he found her working on the kitchen table. His irritation that she wasn't smartened up, with dinner cooking in the oven, and all set to concentrate on him, took the form of a paternal condescension.

Coming up behind her to look at what she was doing, he drawled, 'How sweet.' When she propped a finished canvas on the windowsill, he picked it up and chuckled. Something unreasonable, something violent, happened to her just then. When he left the room, she hid the canvas in the broom cupboard. After that she used a deep drawer in the kitchen where, when they were safety dried, she could stow her canvases like so many guilty secrets.

In the seven years since she had floated up the aisle at the Brompton Oratory, a soul in bliss, her painting style had strengthened. She chose still life. The same apples, leaves, sycamores. There were no human figures in her paintings. She tried to put something eloquent into the natural objects, something beyond definition.

On the morning after her promised trip to join her husband in St Vincent had been so summarily cancelled, she had a sudden desire to talk to her brother in London. With coffee on the kitchen table and the telephone on its long lead in front of her, she rang him. It'd only be his bloody answering machine.

But his voice answered. As surprised as she was.

'Av? Are you at the airport? I thought you were going yesterday.'

'I got put off.'

She told him about Hugh's last-minute call. Rick laughed.

'Poor old Av, bags packed and the milk stopped. But why did he cancel?'

'Boring. Some naval VIP decided to visit the island at

short notice. So Hugh's got to be there running about after him. I was really sick about it, having fixed everything.'

'The island isn't going to go away,' he annoyingly said. 'And I might remind you the Navy is paying and the trip isn't costing you or Hugh a bean.'

His habit of piously pointing out when she was being ungrateful or unreasonable – he himself was far more selfish than she was – made her sigh loudly. He got the point.

'I do realise it's disappointing. Poor old Av. Imagining the islands in the sun and finding yourself still in the Dorset mud.'

'It isn't mud. It's a hard frost.'

Then, as he guessed she would, she asked if he'd like to come down for the following weekend. Rick had already decided this would suit him, and when he accepted she exclaimed with pleasure. He was pleased. He enjoyed a plateful of sisterly affection, and though she saw through him, Avril adored him almost as much as his mother did.

No one but Hugh and a couple of his Service friends had approved when Avril decided to leave art college after she married. Rick was rather angry.

'At least finish what you're doing before you start ironing shirts.'

'I won't iron shirts.'

'Want to bet? Anyway, as I was saying, get your diploma first. You never know when you might need it.'

'Oh, sure.' He knew she was not listening. He was fond of his young sister in his way, and in any case downright stupidity, and out-of-date stupidity at that, riled him. Avril was drifting about as an engaged girl, behaving, Rick thought, like a character in an old thirties movie. He tried again. He might as well have argued with the wall.

His own career was going well. He had begun as a runaround on a provincial newspaper, and had risen steadily, getting bylines and features and more money. He moved, pushed by ambition as well as talent, to a national. Recently he had made a further move, for considerably more money, to be one of the leading writers on a Sunday review. Rick Vincent talks to . . . Rick Vincent travels to meet . . .

His interviews were lively, they grabbed the reader by the wrist. He talked to statesmen and dubious politicians, businessmen and women, actors, beauties, and a man who had tried to strangle his dentist.

When he returned home at night, he listened to the ten or twenty messages on his answering machine, switching it on the moment he came into the flat.

Having fixed to see his sister for the weekend, Rick had to spend time unhooking appointments. He also had the curious task of giving away some opera tickets. Nobody wanted the expensive things; there was the usual cry, 'If only you'd let me know last week!'.

He spent the rest of the days before leaving for Dorset touching up his latest piece, an exposé on tax fiddles among the directors of Britain's ninth-largest company; going to meet an up-and-coming architect at the Garrick; and lunching out.

It was late on Friday when, the weekend settled, Rick sat down to a final burst of work. He shared a flat in the Temple, a fantastic bonus, with a barrister friend from Oxford days, away in South Africa for what appeared to be an endless case involving mining rights. He had to shuttle from Pretoria to Cape Town, while in London Rick reigned, content and solitary, in the peaceful seventeenth-century rooms.

The evening was quiet as the grave. The chill night outside in courts and gardens spread an icy cloak across earth, lawns, leafless trees. The goldfish in the pool in Fountain Court were under a roof of ice. It was a perfect time to work, and he was deep into it when the front door bell rang three times.

'Shit!'

He guessed who it was.

'Rick? It's Retta.'

'OK.' He pressed the outside bell and a moment later she was at his open door, broadly grinning.

'I know. I know. I'm disturbing you and you're working.'

He did not bother to deny it, but gave her a peck of a kiss and led her into the sitting room, where a fire glowed. The word processor shone its baleful greenish eye. The remains of some Marks and Spencer sandwiches and a half-drunk bottle of white wine said it all.

'I'm a pig,' said Retta, throwing off a black wrap and revealing yet more black, high-necked and clinging round her thin figure. He noticed with surprise that she was wearing high heels. They had come back when he wasn't looking.

'Vino?' he said, grudgingly.

She burst out laughing.

'What a selfish sod you are. Yes, please, white wine with some tap water. Don't raise your eyebrows, it's my new idea. The French do it. And – ah – Marks and Sparks gave you four and you've only eaten three.'

She poured herself a drink, went out to the kitchen as

narrow as the galley in a boat, filled the glass up, then returned to grab the remaining sandwich and plump herself down facing him. His annoyance, his lack of hospitality, his scowl, seemed to please her. He sat down gracelessly and joined her in a drink.

'Poor Rick, you could kill me, couldn't you?'

'Yes.'

'It's OK. I'm not staying. Now that's made the brown eyes gleam. But I'm here to tell you something, and it's not the stuff for a fax. Has to be in person. Know what I mean?'

At the news that the girl with whom until quite recently he'd been sleeping two or three times a week was not staying for long, he cheered up. He went into the kitchen and found some cashew nuts, gave the chair she was sitting on a shove closer to the fire and asked if she was comfortable. This amused Retta no end.

Self-invented Retta was as tall as he was, an impressive, exciting-looking young woman with dyed red hair. She was a successful journalist who took to writing sexy novels now and again. She was also a good broadcaster, often on TV. There did not appear to be a nervous bone in her body. She and Rick could never have been called partners. They had promised each other nothing. They had not been faithful to each other, yet the affair had lasted. Their sex was good and they admired each other's success. Retta was thirty-four, a year older than Rick; both earned considerable sums and were too busy to notice how the money poured in. Except that they never said no to themselves as far as things were concerned. First-class everywhere. Three-star restaurants. Cars or hire cars. What they did deny themselves as rigidly as ascetics and saints was time. Since they had left university neither had even tried the trick of leisure.

Polishing off the sandwich, Retta looked at him thought-fully. How well she knew that sharp-featured face, dark hair already thinning, the angle of the jaw, the brown eyes which gave his face a curiously fixed look. Shall I miss him? I've already given him up, really. Like sweets in Lent.

Rick had forgiven her for interrupting, since she had said she would not stay. She always did what she said. It was scarcely eight o'clock, and he calculated he had another six hours before he needed to sleep.

'You said you had something to tell me?' he said, refilling his own glass.

'Sure.'

'Am I expected to guess?'

She gave him a smile, showing big teeth which gave her face some of its schoolgirlish attraction.

'You could try.'

'Is it a toughie?'

'I think so.'

She recognised the gesture he made, rubbing his chin. His skin was rather olive and at night the beard showed. As she expected, he said he needed a shave.

'Let's see,' he said. 'You've got an assignment at the South Pole.'

'Christ! That's likely, isn't it? You know how I loathe the cold.'

'Not a bad idea, though. I can just see you striding across the snow.'

'With a television crew. Not on your nelly. Try again.'

'You've been promoted.'

'There isn't any promotion, my poor sap, that I want.'

'You're getting very uppity.'

And then something about her, some Cheshire-cat-like triumph which he had noticed in his women before, made him say suddenly:

'You're getting married.'

The grin broadened. She looked enquiring.

'Aren't you totally miserable?'

'Devastated.'

'You're an unflattering bastard, Rick Vincent. You don't give a monkey's. You might at least pretend.'

'Why? Getting married doesn't mean—'

'The conceit of the guy! No, I will not be available any more, as it happens. I realise a number of your women have been, or maybe are, married. Not me. This is our goodbye scene. In a way.'

She dug her long nails into the jar of cashew nuts.

'Am I asked to the wedding?'

He did feel a qualm just then.

'No. To be honest you're not, and nor is anybody else. Just a secret little rendezvous at the register office. Sweet, isn't it? We'll rustle up a couple of cleaners as witnesses . . . I suppose they do have cleaners on Saturdays? Ah well. Can't be bothered with that. My future spouse will have fixed it all. He's very competent.'

'Why the secret?' he said slowly. She was annoying him again. And he had the sensation he remembered from school when, during innumerable games of bridge in the common room, his opponents were clearly holding much the better cards.

'We just thought it best.'

An unexpected sexual jealousy blazed up. Unprepared for it, he said nastily:

'God damn it, Retta. What do you mean barging in here

without warning and sitting there like a Chinese idol waiting for me to lay out the burnt offerings? Why didn't you tell me sooner that you were getting married, and who to? It would, in common decency, have been fair. I thought,' he finished to his own surprise, 'I thought we were fond of each other.'

'We were. We are.'

'So?'

The rude voice, different from the unwelcoming one, satisfied rather than amused her. She came over, knelt beside him and took his hand. She felt extraordinarily fond of him.

'Oh, for God's sake get up. You look ridiculous.'

'I do, don't I?' She scrambled to her feet. 'OK, I'll stop teasing. It's your own fault, Rick, you're hideously easy to tease. The fact is, hold on to your hat, I've been seeing a lot of your dad.'

He couldn't believe his ears. She watched with interest. Sympathy even.

'*My father?*'

'That's the guy.'

'But you don't know him.'

'Oh, Rick.'

'Look, I don't understand a word of this.'

'Simple really, I met him at your birthday party, remember?'

'Five months ago.'

'Sure. And we've got to be quite friends.'

Flabbergasted, he sounded like a detective sorting evidence.

'You've been seeing him?'

'Now and then.'

18

'A lot?'

'Depends what you mean by— Do stop glaring! Yeah, well, a lot.'

'While you were seeing me?'

The question was a delicate one, and Retta had foreseen it. The truth was she had been sleeping with both men, occasionally on the same day. She hadn't planned it that way, and it had occurred to her with some interest that after sex with one of them – it was usually Rick first because they met at the Temple at lunchtime or around six in the evening – maybe she then had some extra sexual thing which excited the other. Like dogs. Oh dear, oh dear, that is not a pretty thought, Retta my girl, she told herself. She had given some reflection in advance to this interview and had made up her mind on what one of her girlfriends called the straightforward lie.

'Of course not. What do you take me for?'

'I don't take you at all, apparently,' he said viciously.

Where do we go from here, thought Retta. I've got to calm him down. Rick, opening another bottle, demanded like a betrayed husband:

'Why haven't you told me before?'

'I suppose I thought you'd be annoyed,' she said peaceably. She played with six rings on her right hand, pulling them off and rearranging them. All were made of silver, plain or plaited, and two were set with moonstones.

'You can be very nasty, you know. You'd only have been rude about Gerry.'

'Why the fuck should I be rude about my own father?'

'Don't kid yourself that it hasn't offended you, darling. Me taking up with your dad. I know you're fond of me in a way, though lately it's cooled off a mite, hasn't it? And

19

you don't see all that much of your father. You're angry now, I know. I might say you cooling off turned out to be rather a relief because of me seeing Gerry.'

'Sleeping with him, you mean?'

'To be honest, yes.'

'Charming.'

'You *are* taking this badly. Look,' said Retta, her vivid face the picture of reasonableness, 'your father and I have got fond of each other. We didn't expect it to happen, cross my heart. He's pretty crazy about me and I have to admit I do feel good about him now. And don't you dare say,' she raised her voice to stop him, 'That he's sixty: what's that got to do with it? Take it on board, Rick. It's no big deal. You were never in love with me, nor I with you. Which, one might say, was quite sad. But it suited us. Didn't it?'

He was not listening. He frowned and then said loudly:

'There's something not right about all this. Why in Christ's name are *you* here to tell me? Where's my father? Why hasn't he come to see me or rung me and told me? It's – it's disgusting.'

Retta had also been waiting for this, and it surprised her that Rick hadn't seen her errand and its hurtfulness sooner. The visit had been all her idea, and she was still convinced she was right. But . . .

She took his hands again. He tried somewhat ludicrously to pull them away, but she clung on. He said, still loudly:

'*Does he know about us?*'

'Of course he doesn't. Rick, do cool down. Please. It was my decision to be the one to tell you. Your dad's in a bit of a state about the whole family – and don't start shouting, he *is*. He feels guilty and sort of embarrassed, and I don't think at present he could take you being angry, or your

20

sister reacting in whatever way she does. I don't know her, but I gather she's a sensitive plant. Let alone your mother and her problems. You must see how difficult it is for him, and you know what a man he is for his dignity.' She spoke quite tenderly for Retta. 'So I talked him into letting me break the news to you. Of course he only thinks we've been mates, but he does know we've been friends for some time and he said he supposed I'd do it better than he would. He's going to ring your mother *after* we've done the deed. And we thought—' She paused. 'We thought maybe you'd break the news to Avril. OK?'

'When is all this?'

'Tomorrow, I'm afraid. Richmond register office. That's where I shall become,' she said, still in the unfamiliar and tender voice, 'your wicked stepmother.'

Chapter 2

After she'd talked to her brother and invited him for the weekend, Avril drove to work. Her job, which she described as silly secretarial, was waiting for her, as Hugh on his palm-fringed island was not, and she was glad to be driving to Bridport. It took scarcely half an hour from Fuchsia Cottage, if she wasn't unlucky and trapped behind a tractor. Today the crawling vehicles were absent, her car was not spattered with mud and straw, and she drove along the country roads in peace.

It was deep Dorset country, rolling hills and steep valleys which sometimes filled with mist like saucepans when milk was about to boil over. Avril knew the drive too well and scarcely noticed familiar farm cottages, haystacks muffled in black plastic or lonely spires sad against the blue sky. It was a crisp winter day.

She was in good time when she parked in the cobbled courtyard outside the Victorian house which was the office of Moffat and Tichbourne, solicitors, established 1947. They were now, as Keith liked to say, part of the scenery. But business was slow. Bread and butter kept the firm going. Wills and their redrafting, sometimes from revenge. The leases of shops. The suing, or vice versa, of landlords. Avril went through the heavy front door and the first person she met was Helen, the spirit of the place. Helen was carrying a tray of coffee and doughnuts and seeing Avril looked astonished.

'But you're in St Vincent.'

'I am, aren't I? Beastly trip was cancelled.'

'*Why?*'

Avril briefly explained what had happened.

Helen registered heartfelt sympathy. It was her strong suit. She was pretty in a soppy kind of way, and sympathy poured from her like paint out of a tube. A headache. A broken love affair. Pressures of work. A row at the supermarket. You could rely on Helen for exclaimings and support and rather too much 'Oh poor you!' There wasn't a soul in the firm who, dealing with Helen, didn't feel comforted while backing away.

'So you've come to work to take your mind off the disappointment. Your boss will be chuffed, Avril. You take the tray,' she unselfishly added. She enjoyed waiting on Keith. She opened his office and chanted, 'Look who's here!'

Keith was already at work on a long document which Avril guessed she was going to be landed with.

'I wasn't exactly expecting you,' he said, in the voice he'd used last night. His eye wandered to the tray.

'Doughnuts. Shall we?'

Avril's morning, which should have been spent flying across the blue Caribbean Sea, went by as if there was no such place. As if the ephemeral island of St Vincent had simply disappeared into the mist. She was a secretary in

23

Dorset, not a traveller towards romance.

Since she had worked for Keith the word 'secretary' had begun to be frowned on by a good many women, and Keith's word, assistant with a capital A, was getting popular. Avril liked working for him; he was good-natured and sometimes even grateful when she had to work hard. He made good jokes, too. But she had never had a real interest in his work or the law. She sometimes felt she was like a recorder, a scribe squatting in the courts of a palace in Ancient Egypt, carving hieroglyphics on blocks of stone.

She was busy typing when Keith, who had been on the telephone, finished his call and said:

'Since you shouldn't actually be here in the office at all, and I take it kindly that you are, what about a sandwich at the Plough?'

She enjoyed the unexpected treat. It was true that he spent the time talking about Sally again, but Avril had a delicious avocado salad and some sherry and was glad to listen. He was comforting. It was something to do with his hearty presence, and the shape of his mouth, which turned up at the corners. After last evening she stood on the edge of being attracted. She felt his warmth in the way she now felt the sun which came through the pub's latticed windows, shone on the red turkey carpet and reached her feet.

He went off to get them a slice of apple pie. When he returned through the crowd he sat down and said heartily:

'Don't think I'm turning into a pest, but what about supper tonight? Sally's flying on from Hanover to Heidelberg instead of coming home this week. I'm at a loose end again. Just as you are.'

'Have supper with me, Keith.'

'No, no. Of course not. I'd like to take you out. What about the Lodge? I hear there's a new chef there.'

It was the start of an unexpected friendship. Boss and secretary, solicitor and assistant. They had been friends in work for five years. This was new.

Keith took her out three times before the weekend. To meals at country hotels. To a movie in Bridport's run-down 1930s cinema. He came back for an omelette to Fuchsia Cottage one evening. And on Friday, the night before Rick was due to arrive, he took her back to his house after a meal locally. It was very late, a frosty midnight. And they made love.

Hugh's infidelities had nothing to do with what happened. He had not once been in Avril's thoughts when, slightly dizzy from champagne, she felt Keith put his arms round her and push her gently back on the sofa cushions. The room was dimly lit and winter pressed a thin white face against the window panes. As they embraced she let herself go. She returned his sexy kisses with a surge of pleasure.

Perhaps if Keith had said, 'Will you?' she would have refused. Conscience or self-preservation might have stopped the sex before it began. But he was so relaxed and soothing. His naturalness was wonderful. She let him undress her, watching him with languorous enjoyment, and when they came together it was so delicious she stopped thinking at all. Afterwards they lay on the floor in a knot of arms and legs and bare chest and her hair caught in the button of his open shirt.

'Ow, ow.'

'I'm cruel,' he said, untangling it, slipping out of her body and lying beside her. He lifted himself on one broad elbow and smiled at her; and in the look of his good-natured blue eyes there was not a speck of guilt.

He drove her back to the cottage at two in the morning. The frost was so thick that every blade of grass looked twice the size. Their breath came in clouds. He waited until she had unlocked the front door, patted her shoulder like an uncle, and crunched away into the frost.

Lovemaking worked like a sleeping pill. The sun woke Avril, pouring into her bedroom. She had forgotten to pull the curtains.

She shifted out of the glare and lay and thought about Keith. She had never meant to sleep with him. Of course she had been in situations like last night's before. When Hugh was away, friends sometimes called round; she recalled one evening when she had spent hours refusing a young officer, Peter, who was crazy about her.

'Go on, Avril. You know you want to.'

'Peter, you're a dear, but I don't. Do stop making me laugh.'

In a decade of sexual opportunity and precious few rules, Avril kept her marriage vow. But that had nothing to do with Hugh, it had seemed to Avril an honourable flag. Now it had been captured without even a fight.

Why am I taking this seriously? she thought. Hugh doesn't. Keith doesn't. People treat sex casually, even if we do all have to be careful. Keith was so cheerful last night. I will be.

Yet she was troubled. She had broken the one rule which had helped her in the messy marriage in which Hugh behaved like a pig and she did not. She wondered if some of their friends pitied her. Until now she had disdained that.

When she was dressed she sat down in front of the

dressing table mirror. Like a teenager she stared solemnly at her own face. It was worrying that she looked exactly the same.

A plan was necessary. She decided that when she went to work on Monday she would indicate that what had happened didn't mean the start of an affair. She'd return to being secretary and casual friend. To do that was going to be performing a back somersault, but it was the right decision. Yes, it was.

She cleaned the cottage, dusted books, did some washing, and now and then remembered the difficult mental trick ahead of her, the acrobatic back-flip. You had to spring up, throw yourself backwards, and somehow land on your feet.

She hoped Hugh wouldn't ring for a few days until this new problem was settled. Remembering a certain trait in her husband rarely seen, an unreasoning, fiendish jealousy, she gave an involuntary shudder.

She had only seen the demon twice and often tried to forget it. The first time had been after a party at which she'd innocently flirted with some man or other. When they got home he had yelled at her and hit her across the face. The blow was given by a man she did not recognise. A devil in the heart perhaps. It was then that Avril knew she had to accept him – or run. She had been deeply in love with him and pretended to believe him when he begged her forgiveness; he had spent a long night making love to her. The second time it happened, years later, again due to unprovoked jealousy, she recognised the dreadful changed face, rushed upstairs and locked herself in the bedroom.

But all that was long gone. There had been no sign of hoof or forked tail for three or four years. She never flirted again in front of him. Or even wanted to.

Now, thinking about Keith, she felt like a criminal wondering if she could be caught. The only danger might be from Isobel Sinclair, her neighbour next door and, like Avril, a Navy wife. Isobel, mother of two, clever and attractive, had the air of a manhunter despite her heavy programme of parenting. Her husband was stationed at the naval barracks where Hugh had been until six months ago when he had been posted temporarily to St Vincent.

Isobel was popular, hospitable, a snob, a friendly soul and unendingly curious. I must be careful with Isobel, thought Avril. Then, I'm being stupid. I'm not going to bed with Keith again, am I? And why in hell should Isobel have been in her kitchen at two in the morning when Keith brought me home?

While his sister polished the cottage and awaited his arrival, Rick Vincent clattered down the steps of the Temple building into the Saturday morning sunshine. Driving into a mess of traffic, he reflected on the sight of the empty Thames and the crammed roads. There was a time, a few years back, when he had actually taken a boat to Hammersmith, where there had been a public pier. The tide had been against both boat and himself; he had been hours late for a date at a riverside pub.

Traffic or no traffic, he was glad of the opportunity to think about what Retta had told him.

It was something of a farce. His ex-mistress – not that anybody used the word except for royals – was about to become his stepmother. A day had gone by since her bright arrival; he was no longer thrown by the news. It was strange how jealousy had struck when she had told him. Filial jealousy too. His affair with Retta had never been deep, although they had seen each other a great deal. He had known she did not love him and he had long been convinced that he himself would never fall in love. The tender passion was not for him. He was sexy, and he liked women's company, but he had never actually suffered over a girl in his life. When Rick was unhappy, it was always to do with work.

Driving steadily, stopping boringly, at last he saw the traffic thinning. And with the disappearance of driving problems as the road stretched towards the country, his own problems grew. Nothing to do with Retta and everything to do with his family.

His father had made what would seem a fair enough decision. Gerald Vincent was sixty and he and Susan had been divorced for over six years. Although not actually ancient, Gerald seemed to his son distinctly elderly. To have caught Retta was quite a coup, Rick saw that. He was sure she would never tell about her affair with him. Her line was a blunt frankness but she was not a fool. Unless, of course, Gerald had heard it from her when they first became friends – that was another angle. Retta was quite capable of telling Gerald about the affair when he was at that time merely a pleasant elderly man, father of her own friend. Rick made a grimace. The incestuous idea of sleeping with his son's woman might have added to Retta's allure. Maybe it gave his father a stab of triumph.

Shall I ask her again if he really knows? She did say he didn't, but . . . No, I think I'd rather not go into all that past history.

There remained two bigger problems: his sister and his mother. He considered Avril had not made a success of her life. The Services were an anachronism. And Avril was much changed from the lively girl who had been his adoring sister. She seemed subdued. Hugh was pleasant enough, there were few men who didn't like Hugh, but Rick was sure he did not suit his sister.

How was Avril going to take their father's second marriage? He had no idea. He came, then, to the worse problem of his mother. Susan was Rick's number one fan. Women liked and admired Rick, but his mother's fondness for him had always been excessive. He had seen her bore her friends when she went on about him, in front of him too. He made jokes to lighten the embarrassment but never scolded her afterwards. He had done that once and she had looked like a disappointed child.

'Mum, you really shouldn't,' he'd smilingly said. But he spoke like an addict who lives on golden syrup and hopes you will not close the tin.

Selfish, work-driven, successful and competitive, aware that success needed total concentration and the jockey's glance over the shoulder, Rick loved his family all the same. Gerald's second marriage would upset Susan deeply; he would have to cope with that. Avril wouldn't be the one to comfort her; Susan had never rated her daughter.

A low winter sun was shining on the hedges, the frozen grass lay flat like green hair on the verges of the road, sunlight had begun to melt the frost and everything looked sopping wet. The village where Avril lived was in deep muddy country. An ancient church, grudgingly opened for an hour and a half every Sunday, a settlement of new houses, a manor hiding behind high walls, and a line of ancient cottages resembling the flat-fronted little houses built in fishing towns facing the sea. Fuchsia Cottage was close to the new houses, with their smart cars and buggies a garden-distance away. When Rick drew up it was scarcely eleven o'clock in the morning; he had made good time. A thread of smoke like that in a child's painting of a chimney rose in the still air.

He gave a blast of the car horn.

The front door opened and Avril came pelting down the path, slithered on the icy stones, narrowly escaped tumbling over and arrived to pull at the wrought-iron gate. As usual it stuck.

He climbed out.

'Not fixed yet?'

He lifted the gate clear off its hinges and replaced it before kissing her.

'One of these days you'll get imprisoned for good.'

'I could climb over.'

'You'd be impaled.'

'I'm so glad to see you.'

She took his arm as they went back to the house.

Brother and sister were not unalike; both dark with olive skins, straight noses, brown eyes, slightly squared chins. What differed was manner. Rick's had an intensity, a slight swagger. Avril, friendly, still girlish, was a little shy. She never used to be.

Indoors she gave Rick the most comfortable chair (Hugh's), made coffee and produced a plate of ginger biscuits. He looked her over. She wore the usual appalling cardigan, one pocket bulging with a man's handkerchief (Hugh's). Her black leggings wrinkled at the knee, her hair was untidy, curls and tendrils wilder than usual. But she was remarkably lively.

'You look as if you've quite got over the disappointment.'

'Sorry for moaning on the other night.'

'I thought you were rather restrained. I'd have had a seizure.'

'You told me to calm down.'

'It seemed the only thing. If it had been me . . .'

'You'd have yelled at Hugh or whoever and insisted on taking the flight, even if you paid for it yourself.'

'Sounds like me,' he said, pleased.

'Rick, it would have been silly. What would be the good of plonking myself on a man who had to dance attendance on his senior officer?'

'I don't know. Hugh didn't have to pay for the cancellation, did he?'

'Oh no. The Navy did the cancelling. But as you know, when it actually happens, the trip's free.'

He considered for a moment.

'It's a sort of grace and favour, isn't it? Poor wives, dying of the separation.'

'I've been dying all right,' she said, offering the biscuits. She wondered if this was an invitation to confide. Why should he feel there was any reason? Odd, that.

Rick drank the coffee and asked for more. He liked Avril's cottage; it was poky and inconvenient, but it had its own character. It had been here a long time, the steamy refuge of farmworkers from one generation to the next. Babies had been born under its roof. Men and women had died. Did the great events of small lives remain somewhere in its bulging walls or under its floorboards, like mosaic from lost Roman villas ten feet down in a cornfield?

The cottage had been gentrified into a middle-class home for a naval officer. Rick wondered what the ghosts made of that. There still remained rusty iron rings and hooks here and there fixed into beams. What had hung on them? Bacon? Onions? Buckets? There was a well in the back garden where women must have bowed their backs under the weight of water. These were things which remained when you knocked down dividing walls and moved the cramped narrow stairs, replacing them with a trendier open ladder.

The sun outside came through a skylight at the top of that stair and tried to outshine Avril's log fire. She went into the kitchen to reheat the coffee. Rick shouted amicably:

'Hugh rung again?'

'Not yet. He will eventually when the VIP leaves, I suppose.'

Not so devoted? thought Rick, and held his tongue. He leaned forward and pulled out some paperbacks from a shelf under the coffee table.

'God, Av. What awful books. Where do you get such trash?'

'Isobel Sinclair. Next door.'

'You ought to know better, and so should she.'

As a teenager she would have flared. Now she smiled. Did her brother imagine she would read the seven-hundred-page self-serving autobiographies of politicians which toppled on the table by his bed in the Temple? Anyway, he *had* to read them, poor thing.

The winter day was short enough but Rick kept putting off telling her the news. When lunch was over and the rationed sun had started to sink in the clear sky to the west, he said:

'Shall we go for a walk?'

'You'll have to borrow Hugh's wellies. Everywhere's a sea of mud.'

Rick was given boots two sizes too big, which were going to make walking unpleasant; Avril then produced thick socks of her husband's which slightly improved things. Wrapped against the chill they left the cottage, crossed the lane and climbed a stile. They set off along the edge of an enormous meadow. Avril had been right about the mud.

A wood of hazels, forests of thin trunks and whippy branches, spread away from the meadow. Snowdrops, followed by primroses and later by the papery wood anemones, would flower there during the march of the seasons. Now there was nothing but lumpy stretches of mud and blackened leaves.

A great collapsed tree which had fallen in a gale years ago lay at the end of the path. Rick and Avril had halted there before. They sat on it, although its bark oozed. Avril was silent. Her brother gave her a nudge.

'I've got some news.'

'Good?'

'I don't think so, and I expect you won't either. Dad's getting married again. In fact he was married this morning.'

She gave a violent start. Her pale face under the white ski hat she wore went scarlet.

'But Dad's *sixty*!'

'So? Doesn't stop a guy from having another go.'

'How – how revolting.'

'Christ!'

'Don't sound so *holy*. I do think it's revolting. And anyway, how do you know? Why didn't he tell me as well?'

'It wasn't Dad who told me,' said Rick, taking it at a run. 'He's probably ringing the cottage right now. I heard last night from a work-mate of mine. We're on the same paper,

I expect you've heard of her. Retta Williams.'

'But how did *she* hear?' Avril was flabbergasted.

'Retta, Av, is the one he's marrying.'

She sat staring, her brown eyes large, almost circular. Her face was a picture of astonishment, of shock. She scrabbled in her memory for an image of the Williams woman on TV and vaguely came up with a redhead who made jokes.

'Why didn't Dad tell us himself? It's incredible.'

'I agree. I said so to Retta.'

'She must be a close friend of yours,' said Avril, suddenly suspicious. She wasn't usually so quick; she lived in a world of her own. Rick was accustomed to the lightning reactions of women and men who lived, as it were, by their wits. He decided on a version of the truth.

'Retta's been a pal for years. We've worked on stories together. We got into the habit,' he went on, it was something of an inspiration, 'of telling each other our problems. You know, sex and stuff. But I must say this time she's been very secretive. She met Dad at a party I gave. Can you imagine?'

'Why didn't she tell you before that he and she—'

'That's the point, isn't it, Av? She's been very quiet recently, I've scarcely seen her. Then last night she appeared at the flat with this bombshell.'

Avril took it in. Finally.

'He's so old.'

Rick snorted.

'And you sound very young. Haven't you noticed some women go for the older man?'

'Thirty years older!'

She sounded like their mother.

35

Rick was past the point where she would suspect anything about his own relations with Retta, and he relaxed.
He would never be able to tell his sister about that. Avril
was not hardy. And in any case he guessed that her husband
provided her with enough pain. It had always been a guess
– Avril had told him nothing – but he saw the sort of man
Hugh Brett was. And he didn't intend to land the poor girl
with his own complications.

Avril sat looking at the muddy grass and saying nothing.
Rick's London nose savoured the scent of the sharp country
air, leaf mould from the winter wood, something sharp,
bitter and, for a strange reason, almost tragic.

'The marriage was today,' he said at last. 'There's an
odd thought. At Richmond register office. While we were
having coffee this morning, they were signing on the dotted
line. The second Mrs Vincent. Stepmother.'

'What about Mother?' said Avril. Much too late.

'She is going to hate it.'

As they walked home along the path which skirted the
wood, the sun had begun to sink behind a tall group of
evergreens dark against the just-reddening sky. They
looked at each other and were silent again. Both brother
and sister were trying to imagine how their mother would
cope with the news. It was common enough, the older man
moving on to a young woman. Rick knew that his father
hadn't had a hope of escaping Retta once she had set her
mind on having him. Retta, with her insouciance, her shiny
red hair, her armed personality.

As Avril took the front door key from her pocket they
heard the telephone.

'Dad!' exclaimed Avril.

'Hugh!' said Rick. 'Quick!'

She ran indoors and snatched up the telephone, with
Rick standing behind her.

'Oh, hello, Mum. How did you know I'd still be here?'
The telephone quacked. Rick waited.

'I see. What a nuisance for you, trying to ring St Vincent.
Rick's here, would you . . .?'

She didn't bother to wait for the reply but passed the
telephone to him.

'Ma? Yeah. Here for the weekend.'

As the voice quacked again, he gave his sister an
expressive look, raising his eyebrows. 'Yes. I heard. No, I'll
explain later. Look, Ma . . .'

Avril sat down in the hall, tugged off her boots, then went
upstairs, ostensibly to get rid of her coat, but in actual fact
to avoid the conversation. A photograph of her father in
uniform was on the windowsill. She gave it an angry glance.
You were feeble not to tell us, but I'm being horribly
prejudiced, she thought. She wondered why the remarriage
was so hard to take. Children all over the country, all over
the world, heard such news all the time. She didn't
understand her own outrage.

She was combing her hair when Rick shouted up the
stairs.

'Ma's rung off. Come down, you coward. You weren't
much help, were you?'

She returned down the ladder staircase feeling uncomfortable, and said crossly:

'She'd much rather talk to you.'

'I know,' said Rick, who never denied he was favourite.
'But you didn't half get rid of the telephone, Avril, as if
it was red-hot. Anyway, she was busy keeping the stiff
upper lip, which means,' he added, sighing, 'she was

37

determined not to burst out crying.'

Avril went to make tea, and hadn't even filled the kettle when the telephone shrilled again. Rick put his head in at the door and repeated:

'Hugh?'

It was their mother again.

'Avril, I want to speak to Rick.'

During the second conversation, which Avril could not help hearing, Rick began to protest. He and Avril had just been for a walk, he said, there was a hard frost starting, he was sure it would be— No, Ma, the thaw earlier meant nothing, it wasn't a real thaw. He sounded like a man on *Gardeners' Question Time*. Then he said sharply:

'Do listen.'

Apparently to no avail.

He threw his eyes to the ceiling and then said, in an annoyed voice:

'Oh, very well, Ma. OK, OK. Yes. OK.'

He rang off and groaned.

'Wants to see us. Coming here.'

'When?'

'When do you think? Tonight. I hope to God she drives carefully.'

'She never drives fast.'

'And they're the worst.'

They went into the sitting room, where the fire was almost out. Rick fed it with half a dozen of Hugh's well-cut, near-symmetrical logs. Hugh had pulled down an old rose pergola months ago, and sawed it perfectly. The pile of logs in the garden was carefully covered with plastic, and a heap used for the house was stacked under the porch. All very organised.

Brother and sister had tea and sat in silence, busy with the same emotions just then. Concern and resentment. They recoiled against elderly misery. They had their own problems.

Their parents' divorce, the year after Avril married Hugh Brett and at a time when Rick's career was well into its starry progress, had been a difficult one. The Vincents were living in Hampshire. Gerald Vincent was serving the last few years of his career when he fell in love. The girl – her name was Polly – was on the clerical staff, young and pretty and about nineteen. Susan Vincent was stunned when Gerald asked for a divorce.

She saw the thing as a moral challenge to be bravely met. She tried everything to persuade her husband not to do what his middle-aged passion screamed at him to do. She was reasonable. He was adamant. Susan did not crack, although she wanted to. She lost weight, didn't sleep, and the tone of her voice was strange. Suffering, she sounded like iron.

Eventually she gave in and was forced to accept that she was never going to get Gerald back. A civilised divorce followed. But meantime, to Gerald's disbelief, the beautiful Polly fell for Gerald's junior officer and married him. The blow was a bad one to Gerald, still handsome in an elderly way. Still potent.

Poor Susan was full of happiness. 'There'll be a reconciliation,' she told her son.

Rick knew that wouldn't happen. His father was gone. He had not been happy for years, and even after losing the sweet comic girl he had lusted after, freedom felt good.

During the divorce brother and sister behaved, Rick declared, 'with perfection'. They stood by their mother, listened to her interminable complaints and regrets; she no longer kept a stiff upper lip, poor Susan. They also somehow managed to stay on affectionate terms with their father, a balancing act which children in a fractured marriage can find impossible.

All this was now in the past. Their mother, with money provided by an ex-husband rather too anxious to do the right thing, had settled in the Cotswolds, made some friends, and taken up the middle-aged obsession with gardening. She was out in her garden at all hours on her knees, hands earthy. Rick once saw her up to her waist in Madonna lilies.

'What's for supper?' asked Rick, breaking a silence which verged on the gloomy.

'Salmon. And frozen raspberries Hugh picked from our plants in August.'

'Ice cream?'

'You sound about twelve. Yes. Vanilla.'

'Let's eat before she comes. And drink as well. I'll tell you one thing, Av, when waiting for one's mother after she's heard her husband is marrying again, the great thing is to get drunk.'

During the long wait, both of them aware of the night which grew steadily colder and of the roads which grew icier, the telephone again rang. This time it was Gerald Vincent who sounded, Avril thought, revoltingly happy. He kept making jokes.

'Bit of a bad show not asking you and Rick, Avril. You must blame my girl, who stood very firm. She told me her own mother even weeps at weddings in *EastEnders*, and there'd be such sobs at ours we wouldn't be able to hear the registrar. So, as she wasn't invited . . . I do hope you and Rick understand.'

Very hearty and sailorlike.

'I was for telling you all after the deed was done, but Retta decided to tell your brother last night, naughty girl.' He chuckled. 'She said she wanted to see his face. We do hope you'll both come here for a celebration dinner soon. I gather – your brother told me – that your trip to St Vincent has only been postponed. But we all know what the Navy is, changing its mind and so on. We must keep our fingers crossed for you.'

Avril managed to sound natural, or nearly; in any case when people are happy they do not notice the tone of your voice. She passed the telephone to Rick, who did a much better job of it.

During the fish and raspberries, and later enjoying Hugh's brandy, Rick said drily:

'Wasn't so bad with Dad, now was it?'

She shrugged.

'You can't still be annoyed with him.'

'I can't be *annoyed* with my father for remarrying, Rick.'

'That's funny. I thought you were.'

She didn't answer. The truth was she didn't understand herself. Was it something to do with sex? Something to do with an image of her father? She felt for a second time the shock when she had been told he planned to marry the beautiful Polly, whom she'd once seen at a cocktail party.

As for Rick, he was following his own advice and getting slightly drunk.

Three hours after her telephone call, wrapped in an old-fashioned mink coat faded at the edges, their mother arrived.

Chapter 3

'I'm perished,' said Susan Vincent. 'I'm sure the car heater's gone wrong, Rick, you must see to it in the morning. Nice to see you both.' She allowed herself to be kissed, offered a scented, well-made-up cheek. They both hugged, although in fact Avril only tried to and Rick succeeded.

Susan was tenderly taken close to the fire and asked if she'd had anything to eat.

'I couldn't touch a thing,' she said, sitting down. Her children stood by her chair like attendants on a queen.

Susan had been pretty as a girl and admired by the young men in Surrey where she had grown up. Unlike her dark-haired children, she had been fair, and her hair was now tinted palely to a becoming colour called ash. Gerald was generous and Susan still dressed well. His conscience need not have been quite so lavish, since his ex-wife had inherited money from her family. Her clothes, like the wearer, managed to remain in the period of her youth. She looked as if she had stepped straight out of a 1950s movie in which the heroine wore a hat during a romantic embrace,

and drove her car in wrist-length gloves. Her father had
been a prince of finance in the City, and Susan retained the
air of being royal by birth. Even now she was suffering, her
father's wealth hung round her shoulders like an embroi-
dered cope.

'I disapprove of you driving so far on a freezing cold
night, Ma,' Rick said.

'I was perfectly all right, don't be silly.'

She accepted some warm milk from Avril, placed it
carefully on the local newspaper on the table so that it
didn't make a mark, and left it.

'Well?' she said brightly, daring them not to offer horror
and sympathy. 'What a surprise.'

'It was going to happen sooner or later,' said Rick, to
stop his mother giving a performance. 'After all, your
divorce was six years ago.'

'Five and three-quarters.'

'Oh, Ma.'

She looked at him for a moment with her solemn eyes, the
lids painted a faint mauve.

'Didn't you say on the phone that you know the woman?'

'Yes. Retta Williams.'

'What a ridiculous first name.'

'Apparently short for Henrietta.'

Rick then added that of course Retta was Welsh. Both he
and Avril waited for their mother to say that nobody
trusted the Welsh. Instead, like Cleopatra, she asked:

'What does the female look like?'

'Haven't you see her on TV?'

A tinny laugh.

'Goodness, you see so many people on television.'

'Red hair,' put in Avril.

43

'Dyed?' said Susan.

Both her children couldn't help laughing, and Susan looked pleased.

'She's a good journalist. Sharp and rather funny,' said Rick.

'And I'm not.'

Remarks like that, bridling, girlish, set Avril's teeth on edge. But Rick only said:

'Pooh. Everybody knows you're brill.'

'Now you're being silly again,' said his mother, less hard-voiced; she quite cheered up when Rick added that he was afraid his father had married a tough nut.

'Of course,' said Susan.

'Shall we have cornflakes?' suggested Avril suddenly. Her mother said no, thank you, darling, but Rick with the thin man's appetite said what a magnificent idea and coaxed his mother to join him. It was like a midnight feast at school.

The central heating had switched itself off; it was late and cold when Susan went up to bed. Avril came down the ladder stair with her arms full of blankets, to find her brother kicking at a final log which was expiring in the ash-filled grate.

'Ma OK?'

'She said my bed is comfortable. Do you think she'll manage to sleep?'

'Yes. The drive was long and she isn't used to doing more than pootling to Chipping Norton and back. Besides, we're here. She'll be OK.'

'She's very upset.'

'And determined not to show it.'

'Oh, gallant Piglet, Piglet ho, did Piglet tremble, did he

blinch?' said Avril, unfolding blankets. 'Don't you wish she'd let things rip.'

'Of course not. All that stuff about having a good cry and letting it all hang out. It's all balls for some people; they couldn't bear to. Ma's better armed and barred.'

Avril began to make him up a bed on the sofa, putting cushions into a pillowslip and bending seriously to her task. He said, kicking the log again:

'Do you know what's really bugging her?'

'Of course. Losing Dad for a second time. Having to give up forever the miserable little hope that one day she'd get him back.'

'You're wrong, Av. Ma realised quite soon that she would never get him back. She liked pretending to us that she still believed it. No, what throws her is that he's done the same thing as with that Polly character. Got somebody young. Retta's more than quarter of a century younger than him. Ma believes Dad is like Faust. Become young again.'

'Has he?'

'Don't be daft. Sixty, and from now on going to spend his time trying to be thirty.'

'Do old men always?'

'Oh yes, Av. They do.'

Avril was the first to wake. She had never slept in her own spare bedroom before. It had twin beds, dull furniture, a marble-topped chest of drawers too heavy to move and too low-slung to sweep underneath, and some engravings which Hugh had brought from his home. The Battle of La Hogue. Avril couldn't stand them. She pulled on her dressing gown and crept out, passing her own room from which the silence was total. She came barefoot down the ladder stair. There was a hump of blankets on the sofa, and a tuft of black hair sticking out like a feather. She patted the hump and Rick's face appeared. He yawned.

'What's the time?'

'Nearly ten.'

'Good grief, this sofa isn't as bad as I feared. Any coffee? God, Av,' sitting up, 'this olde worlde cottage isn't half cold.'

'I'll turn the heating up.'

'Doesn't it do it by itself?'

'Hugh fixed the clock,' said Avril, disappearing. There was a noise of switches. He called after her in a carefully low voice:

'Come out here before you make the coffee.'

When she opened the sitting room curtains, a winter sun of pure orange came in and lay on the floor. Rick stretched out his hand and pulled her to sit beside him among the tumbled blankets. She put her bare feet into the sun on the floor, but it was no warmer than the cold room.

'I came to a decision last night. I'm afraid I'll have to drive home with Ma this morning. And spend today and tomorrow with her.'

He sounded fractious. It annoyed him to do the right thing.

'So I shan't be around with you this weekend after all,' he unnecessarily added.

Not to be outdone in unselfishness, Avril said didn't he think maybe their mother might like to stay here for a couple of days?

'Alas no. You know how she likes her own home. What will suit her is for me to drive behind her – *that'll* be a speedy journey, I don't think – back to Sarsden. When we

get there she'll get me to talk about my work for a while, but
it will only be a blind. Then she'll pump me about Retta. I
shall try not to sound too enthusiastic.'

'Will you be rude about her?'

'Avril, you're the one who needs coffee. Shall we have it
now? You are not being very bright. Of course I won't bad-
mouth Retta; it would only feed Ma's jealousy or whatever.
I shan't go over the top about her either. I shall pick out
one or two of the girl's faults, but present a picture that is
partially true. I shall try,' he was irritable again, 'to make
the old girl accept the status quo.'

It was midday when Susan, in her high court heels, came
carefully down the ladder. Her appearance was perfect,
pretty ash hair curled, skirt creaseless, expensive Italian
silk scarf pinned with a jewel. Avril noticed that before
driving through the icy country for solace, her mother must
have packed an entire change of clothes, down to a second,
larger string of pearls.

'Are you sure you wouldn't like to stay here with me, and
Rick could stay too?'

Avril hadn't given up.

'You can't have her, I'm going to,' declared Rick. 'I'm
coming to dump myself with you at Sarsden, Ma, so don't
you drive too slowly or I'll bump you behind.'

Susan Vincent protested about breaking up the weekend
and did not mean a word of it. After more refusing of food
and leaving cups of tea, she was accompanied out of the
cottage. She turned, slightly awkward when there was the
danger of a kiss, to her daughter.

'We must all keep up our spirits, Ma,' Avril said.

'Of course, darling.'

She looked at Avril brightly, she smiled determinedly,

and Avril couldn't bear it. She gave her mother a sudden, impulsive embrace. But Susan moved her head and the kiss meant for her cheek landed on her ear.

Rick telephoned at the unearthly hour of seven on Monday morning; he had just driven to London from Sarsden, leaving at half past five to avoid the traffic. He'd left their mother, he said, in reasonably good spirits.

'Let's say when I drove off she was standing at attention by the flagpole, the red ensign raised, if somewhat lop-sided.'

With her father's marriage reluctantly accepted, Avril returned to her own problem. She was still convinced that the affair with Keith – though she could scarcely call it that – must be stopped in its tracks. If the trip to St Vincent hadn't been cancelled so suddenly, if she hadn't been so annoyed and disappointed, sex with Keith would never have happened. So she told herself. And now was the time to show that it had been, to be vulgar, just a one-night stand. She would be her usual secretary-friendly self, and Keith would catch her virtue like some holy infection.

Avril arrived at the office wearing the breastplate of goodness and called in to see her friend Helen. Now Helen, Avril often thought, *was* good. It was unfashionable to be so, but Helen did not know that. She was the most charitable girl Avril had met in her life. Her voice was soft, her smile radiant. How did she manage it?

Helen had already been out to the shops to buy the doughnuts.

'There you are,' she cried, always pleased to see Avril, who often felt she was not nice enough in return. She handed Avril the tray.

Keith, already at his desk, said a jovial good morning
without nuance. Avril sat down and they drank their coffee.
Both soon had sugar all over their lips from the doughnuts.
Keith told Avril who to ring, which meetings to fix and one
he wanted to cancel. He brushed off the sugar.
'How about dinner tonight? Sally's still away, blast it. I
need your company.' He licked his finger and chased the
sugar round his saucer.

Now was the moment. Somehow Avril hadn't the gall to
say no. It was so obvious that he had no serious feelings
about her, and when he glanced across at her, it was as if
they shared a larky secret. Weakly she accepted.

But she was nervous. The secrecy which adulterers call
discretion had begun to irk her. She had a horror-movie
fantasy that Isobel Sinclair would see Keith's car and draw
conclusions. When she left the office that evening he
suggested he should come and pick her up about eight.

'Is that OK? Sorry to be a bit late, but I've some calls to
make and anyway Sally's ringing at seven. That'll be OK,
won't it?'

'Of course,' said Avril, 'but—' She blushed slightly,
blurting out her worry about Isobel. She hoped he wouldn't
think her stupid but he knew what gossip in a small village
could be. Keith didn't laugh. He looked at her with the
same thoughtful expression he wore when studying legal
documents.

'Mm, I get the point,' he said after a moment. 'Look,
when I come round, why don't I park round the corner.
Didn't you tell me last summer Hugh had made a crazy-
paving path to a back gate or something?'

That he remembered surprised her.

'Then you can slip in and out of the cottage without my

car being particularly noticeable.' The larky look again. 'I remember that neighbour of yours. Service wives can be nosy. It's their dead boring life.'

Avril was packing up her desk when Helen appeared, to enquire tenderly if Avril's husband had telephoned yet. As usual, 'Oh poor you' was the burden of her saintly song. Her face beamed blessing on a bereft married woman. Avril was quite glad to get away.

Later in the cold night, she got into Keith's car and he drove her to Cheselbourne House, the rambling, dilapidated Tudor mansion which he and his wife had bought cheaply at an auction ten years ago and transformed into a treasure.

Not until he had closed the nail-studded door behind them did he draw her into his arms and give her a long kiss.

Avril had never had an affair before and did not realise how soon it would fall into a pattern. She and Keith met almost every evening after the hour when Sally rang. Hugh, due to a fortunate time difference of four hours, and his own ordered habits, only ever rang Avril at weekends. She had no need at night to remain nervously at home.

Keith, having finished long, jokey calls to his wife, would welcome Avril at Cheselbourne. He was always on the lookout, a tape playing something classy and classic and drinks at the ready. They made love as soon as she arrived.

'We'll do it before we go out for a meal,' he said. 'Then I can be more relaxed.'

After the sex, which Avril grew to enjoy more and more, Keith took her out to dine at expensive places. He knew a dozen of them all within a twenty- or thirty-mile radius. When the good dinner was over they returned to his house and sat on a sofa large enough for six. Avril liked him, fancied him, and was certain neither of them could be hurt. It became, almost at once, like a marriage.

He was a sanguine man, open-hearted; he was not a fool and he liked to laugh. His looks were Anglo-Saxon, fair-skinned. Both his fair hair and his personality reminded Avril of a boy she remembered at Rick's school. A prefect. She remembered the boy encouraging his team during the tug-of-war. Keith was like that. Setting a good example to the other boys, keen for the Honour of the School. Where was honour now? The goddess's shrine was crumbling, her statue weatherbeaten, and on the ledge where both Avril and Keith should be piling their votive offerings there wasn't a single daisy.

But there was never an undercurrent or a look from Keith to indicate that what they were doing was wrong.

One evening of bitter rain he decided to cook supper at home. The constantly absent Sally was in Copenhagen. Keith prepared some cutlets. Lovemaking as usual was the hors-d'oeuvre. Avril enjoyed it more than ever, much more than with Hugh, who rarely waited for her the way Keith always did.

With the meal over, they sat on the rug by the enormous sixteenth-century fireplace. Unlike Avril's small fire eating pieces of the old pergola, Keith's fire was rarely lit. The house's central heating was total; you floated through chains of Tudor rooms as in a warm bath. Tonight the fire had been lit specially for her and huge logs lay and smouldered. He picked up her hand and put her fingers in his mouth one by one, biting them gently. Then he stared at her, immune, it seemed, from guilt for what used to be number seven of the deadly sins.

Avril leaned back. Sally Waring, whom she'd seen occasionally but never spoken to, looked at her from a silver frame. A strong, plump woman in a white sweater. You couldn't tell that she was clever. You couldn't tell what she was like, except that her mouth was firm and her nostrils flared slightly. This was the woman who had created Cheselbourne; her fingerprint was everywhere. In the silky stone floor, in the nearly life-sized statue in carved wood by the entrance hall. Keith told Avril it was early Italian and was St Joseph; round his mild head the saint wore a tarnished golden halo.

Sally's Renaissance passion showed in the half-painted Italian furniture, beautiful, silvery, greenish, most of it too large for the rooms. Tiny dark paintings were on the walls, figures crossing snow-topped mountains, figures burdened and bowed. Art books too big for the bookcase were stacked here and there on the floor. Living among all these things, easy as a nursery rhyme, was Sally's husband.

'I like the shape of your nose,' he said, after a while.

'Too straight and serious.'

'Yes, but you aren't.' He stroked the nose as if she were a horse. 'Not about us anyway. We both know you'll be flying off any day now. What matters for us is now, isn't it?'

Avril believed every word. The banal, worn-out philosophy was perfect.

Delivered by Keith to the side lane at after three in the morning, shivering with cold, she crept to the cottage, unlocked the front door, and stood listening to his car driving softly away.

The next morning before leaving for work, she had an unlooked-for surprise. She recognised the writing at once.

Strong and old-fashioned. Slanting.

'My dear child,' wrote her father. 'It was nice to talk to you the other day. I am sure, my dear, you understood why Rick and you were not asked to the wedding. We would have loved to see you on the happy day, but it wasn't to be. Another thing I did not mention to you was that I felt, had you been there, that your mother might have been hurt. Naturally I have been in touch with her. She's being her usual doughty self.'

I'll bet, thought Avril.

The letter went on to say how much he and 'my girl' wanted to see Avril and Rick. He'd spoken to Rick and they had fixed a tentative day.

'We both know how busy the boy is; I do apologise for not giving *you* more notice. I have telephoned you once or twice in the evening. No luck unfortunately.'

The date was for tonight, and when she looked at the postmark, Avril saw with annoyance that it was four days ago.

Her father ended the letter as he'd ended his letters to her at school: 'Your affectionate Daddy.'

She stood looking at it. Somewhere under the commonplaces was a glitter of happiness, like the stuff children sprinkle on Christmas trees.

She dialled Rick's number at once. No answering machine, thank heaven.

'I've called you,' he began accusingly. 'So has Dad. I rang last night for *hours*. Where do you get to, or shouldn't I ask? All set for tonight then?'

'I've only just got a letter from Pa.'

'You don't need to bite the phone in half. Aren't you coming?'

She was thinking of Keith, not her father, and said grudgingly that she supposed she could.

'Get away early from work,' said Rick who would have objected loudly if she had said such a thing to him. 'Meet me at Richmond. You can stay the night there if you like.'

'I have no intention of staying the night with my father and her.'

'She is not "her", Avril, she is Retta, our new step-mother. You may even like her. Most people do, except rival journalists who are jealous. If you won't stay with them, stay with me. Okay? Tell that booming boss of yours you've got to leave really early.'

It was Rick who had fixed the evening. He dealt with life like a professional gambler in a Western; there was nothing he couldn't do with the cards. Slither them across a table. Throw them up into a perfect curve. Make them sit up and beg.

'Around eight, all right? I'll call up Retta and say we expect good food. Career women keep Marks and Sparks in business; she must make an effort tonight for her step-children. After all,' he added, laughing, '*we're* making one, aren't we?'

Keith was his generous self when she told him. He was so casual about their broken date that Avril was rather put out. Returning in the late afternoon to Fuchsia Cottage, she was sulky. There was nothing she wanted to do less than put on a dress and a smile for this unknown stepmother. She toiled up to her room and looked through her wardrobe. There was a black dress patterned with green leaves which Hugh had bought for her, paying too much, she'd thought. It had been for a naval cocktail party and was made of chiffon stuff with long sleeves. Would the Richmond house be warm? What would the new wife wear? Avril guessed trousers and a ski sweater.

Setting off for London in the dark, Avril tried for the umpteenth time to remember any impression that Retta Williams had left on her memory. That was the peculiar thing about people appearing on TV. They seemed memorable, fascinating, odd, brilliant. There were close-ups of their vivid faces. Yet, try as you would the next day, you couldn't remember a thing. All she recalled was the mop of short, over-red hair and a relaxed manner. Did she imagine beady eyes? Why do I think that? Because she married my dad. He isn't all that much of a catch.

The 1950s house where her father had settled after the divorce was neo-Georgian. Purists had shuddered when Vine Crescent was built on the edge of historic Richmond. Half a dozen houses rose in unrepentant red brick, with imitation Georgian doors, lavender bushes in front gardens and reproduction Adam brass doorknockers.

Susan Brett, who had better taste than her ex-husband, had shuddered. She told Rick the house was common. But Gerald settled comfortably with the sailor's touch of being domestic, and found a daily who adored him and polished the doorknocker twice a week. Avril noticed its brightness when she banged loudly, wishing she was with Keith in Dorset.

The door opened at once. A tall redhead.

'Avril. Hi. I'm Retta. I've been really looking forward to this.'

She did not shake hands or kiss or make a move towards Avril but stood, showing her large teeth in a grin. Avril was bustled down the passage to the sitting room. Chintz chairs and Le Carré paperbacks. Somebody on the old-fashioned record player was making a saxophone moan.

'Dear child.'

Her father strode over to give her the kiss Retta had not offered, holding her close and pressing her face against his tweed jacket. He released her and patted her back in the way you do when a baby has wind.

'So good to see you. Good of you to drive up from Dorset. Now, a drink. Sit by the fire. Yes, it's new. Retta's idea.'

An almost realistic gas fire pretended to be coal and roared in a grate which had previously sported a hideous electric contraption in which the lumps of coal had been made of plastic. While they drank champagne, Avril loyally batted social questions to bride and groom. How had the wedding gone? Had they had a celebration afterwards? What about a honeymoon? There was guilty smirking, but she ignored that.

The new stepmother was easy in the way that Keith was easy. She was totally herself. She wore her mild celebrity as carelessly as a silk scarf. When the front door bell rang she exclaimed loudly:

'Rick, always late. Do you think he's brought us a prezzie?' which made Avril inwardly curse. She'd never thought of one.

In fact Rick arrived with an outsized bunch of yellow roses – 'No smell but a nice colour' – and two bottles of Australian Chardonnay.

Avril did not talk much after her brother arrived, and did not need to. She noticed that her father, for the first time in his life, waited on them, trotting out to fetch things, refilling glasses and lending an avuncular presence.

After the meal, which was very good – Rick caught

Avril's eye over the pheasant and winked – they returned
to the sitting room for coffee and chocolates. Rick knew he
was monopolising Retta and showing off as well. But he
considered the thing was to make the evening go, and go it
did. His father laughed a good deal. So did Avril, for Retta
competed with Rick in stories of the great and wicked.

Avril, watching them, thought – that's my brother's life.
She'd never seen him on his own ground before. On the odd
occasion that she and Hugh visited him, he never invited
friends to meet them. They would go out to a meal and a
theatre as a trio. Avril wondered if he thought his sister and
husband dull dogs and kept them away from his smart-
aleck friends. Was Hugh boring? It was a new idea. Women
never thought so. Would Retta?

'You seem very settled in, Retta,' said Rick, helping
himself to chocolates. 'Are you going to make over the
house?'

'Make it over,' echoed Gerald, turning to Retta. 'What
does the boy mean?'

'He means change it to match me,' said Retta. 'I should
damned well think not. I don't intend,' she said, waving her
hands, 'to change one bleeding cushion.'

When his children said goodbye, their father hugged
them impartially. He and his redheaded bride stood at the
door, a carriage lamp shining down on them like a light
from heaven.

Rick and Avril went to their respective cars.

'Follow me. I know a reasonably traffic-free way,' Rick
said.

The Temple was a haven of quiet. Courtyard lamps shone
in pools, a few windows were lit, but most were dark. Rick
unlocked the outside door to let his sister in first, and up in

his rooms switched on the lights and yawned hugely.

'Jesus, I'm tired.'

'Me too.'

'You more than me, coming from the country.'

He threw himself into a chair and regarded her; he was pale from the late hour, but his mocking, dark eyes creased at the corners. 'Well?'

'She's all right.'

'Oh, very descriptive.'

'I said she's all right.'

'What you mean is that she showed off and she's exhausting and she's turned our dad into her poodle.'

'Not exactly.'

'Don't lie. Of course it's true. He's poodling because he's mad about her. Rather touching, wouldn't you say?'

'I don't know.' She felt tired and stupid.

'Take it from me, it is. I envy him,' said her brother unexpectedly. He gave another large yawn. 'Why am I still up? You've gone quite green, Av. Like the old sixties number, "A Whiter Shade of Pale". I'll tell you something you don't know and I bet you haven't thought of. One of these days we're going to see our stepmother triumphantly pregnant. She told me the other day when I popped in for a drink that that's what she'll be doing next.'

Avril did not reply. A pain so excruciating that it took her breath away went through her from breast to guts.

'If you ask me, it's why she married him.' Rick pulled off his shoes. 'The biological clock they go on about. Retta wants to settle. She's racketed long enough and Dad just suits her. I give her a year. Then she'll balloon about as if she's the first woman on earth to conceive. Dad'll be tickled pink. That will be boring too.'

'I thought she was a career woman.'

'Where have you been in your Dorset hideaway? What's to stop her having three kids, appearing on telly, and writing long pieces telling us all what to think about parenting? Blow by blow I shouldn't wonder. Starting off with classes for expectant fathers, poor sods.'

Avril was silent for a little pause, then, with a tremor in her voice which, loudly yawning again, he missed, asked:

'Did she tell you all that?'

'No, Av. It's just that I know her and she works everything out. Who's surprised? She's a planner. A fixer. She always gets what she wants.'

He said it with a smile. If it was forced, she did not see it. She was still struggling with the hideous pain and finally brought out:

'So it'll be misery for poor Mum again.'

'Yes, there'll be all that. Come on, Av, you look like death. The sooner you're in bed the better. Want a hot-water bottle to replace old Hugh?'

It was raining the next morning when she drove back to Dorset. Rick had been on the telephone when she left, and waved goodbye without stopping his conversation. She was glad to be leaving London. Her absorbed brother made her feel lonely, and so had her father springing up to make the coffee. Most of all she was glad to be at a distance from Retta, who had said, 'Come again!' Avril politely accepting, mentally refused.

She couldn't forget what Rick had told her about her stepmother's plan to have a baby. In her imagination Avril saw a little unborn creature in the womb, floating on its head, arms folded and all the future in its closed eyes. Before they were born, children were space creatures full of mystery. She longed to have one in her body. She was like a woman thinking of water while she dies of thirst.

Arriving at the office at last, Avril was given Helen's beaming welcome. 'You have made good time. I bet you left London before dawn.'

Avril, replying, tried to feel some of her friend's warmth. In Keith's office she found her boss busy but also approving. She concentrated on work, shoving aside as much as she could the consciousness of pain. It would wear off. Of course it would. It always did.

She had no date that night – Keith was Sally-ing – and when she was getting herself some supper the telephone rang. Surprisingly it was Hugh, sounding as if he was down the road.

'Avril! I'm glad I could get you. The exchange assured me they'd rung and could get no reply. How are you? Bearing up?'

She was glad to hear his voice. It was like returning to real life.

'No chance of getting you out here, I'm afraid. You've been so good, too. Most women would have gone spare. Any news at your end?'

Avril told him about her father. He was interested and amused, exclaimed and laughed. Briefly.

'You can tell me more when I see you,' he said. 'My visiting VIP, by the by, threatens to stay longer, God help us. I'll be in touch the moment I see him safely to the airport.'

'What's he like?'

'Amusing, as it happens. They both are.'

A wife as well, thought Avril. But he wouldn't dare, would he?

'Be seeing you soon, I'm sure,' finished Hugh breezily. 'The trouble is, with the Navy paying, I can't exactly make a fuss, can I? But cheer up. It'll happen. It'll happen.'

He was like an MP promising his constituents a new hospital wing. Avril in her turn sounded relaxed, and her husband on the other side of the world found he rather admired that. His wife was the right stuff after all.

When they had said goodbye, Avril sat and looked across the empty room. She felt almost indifferent to the promised visit to St Vincent, and her feelings rather jolted her. She knew very well why she had changed. It was all to do with Keith. She enjoyed being with him very much, and was still positively proud of a new-discovered ability to be in the middle of a love affair with love as the missing word.

On weekends or evenings when she could not meet Keith because Sally was around, Avril spent her time at the kitchen table, painting. During the week, after work and in the winter dark, she had to paint without daylight. It made the colours very harsh and the shadows turned purple. But in its way that was a challenge.

'What do you do when we can't meet up?' asked Keith one evening when they were together. The look he wore had a trace of conceit. *Poor Avril when I can't take her around, what can she do with her time?*

'I paint a bit.'

'So you do – awful of me to forget. You must show me your efforts some time.'

She smiled and said nothing. She would no more have shown her paintings to him than she had done – would do – to Hugh. When she was alone her canvases lined the windowsills and the shelves in the kitchen. They were in her bedroom too.

Once Keith arrived early for a drink and she had to rush into the kitchen, snatch a painting from the windowsill and push it – thank God it was dry – into the broom cupboard.

At present, painting was beginning to cure her of her despicable jealousy at the idea of a baby for her step-mother. And then somehow it was impossible for anybody to be depressed for long when Keith was around.

Christmas had begun to glitter on the calendar, and Keith told Avril one night after they had made love – Sally, of course, off on her travels again – that he wanted to buy her something special.

'Think what you would like. We'll go to Yeovil, shall we? There's a good second-hand jeweller I noticed the other day when I went to see that client, Mrs Dobson. Nice-looking shop. Shall we try them?'

Avril hid a smile. She wondered if there were other women here and there in Dorset with bracelets or rings bought by Keith from the good second-hand jeweller. One lunchtime he kept his promise and drove her to Yeovil, and they had fun choosing a ring for her forefinger. It was shaped like a daisy but set in different stones, tiny chips of ruby, emerald, garnet, amethyst, diamond. It spelled 'regard'. Avril was delighted with it and wore it every day, not missed by Helen.

'What a beautiful ring; I've never seen that before.'

'It was my grandmother's.'

A letter came from Gerald, affectionately saying how much he and Retta had enjoyed the visit.

'At present the girl is nest-building,' he soppily wrote. 'We must see you both again very soon.'

For a chill minute Avril looked at the phrase. Surely Retta wasn't pregnant yet? Avril knew her own thoughts were disgusting; jealousy, envy were humiliating vices and she loathed them. But the twin serpents had settled in her breast in a ghastly writhing coil.

On a weekend as grey and dull as any in the calendar, with Keith being a husband again, Avril pushed away an almost untouched cup of coffee. She needed to drive to Bridport for some canvases. She'd finished all hers and even some old over-painted ones. Her car was filthy from inescapable farm vehicles behind which she often had to drive. She left the car at the little garage to be hand-cleaned and walked back through the village to pass the time. As she rounded the corner by the church, the air suddenly filled with a sound as sharp and noisy as a flock of starlings. Crossing the road was a crocodile of children traipsing to the village hall. They were muffled like Greenlanders in anoraks and padded jackets, leggings, hoods, boots. Untrammelled by their thick clothes they hopped and shouted. At the end of the procession, gripping her two small sons, was Isobel Sinclair.

'Hi. The kids are off to rehearse the Christmas play. And we mums have been ordered to make the damned costumes. Lucky you, not having to sew your fingers raw.'

Isobel, whose hair resembled tortoiseshell fur, was herself like a cat, with a pretty pinched-in chin and a smile like a purr.

'Can't have slackers like you, Avril. High time you joined the mothers' union.'

She was tugged away by the boys.

Avril collected her car, thanked the garage owner, paid him almost nothing, and drove to Bridport. Saturday was crowded with cars and shoppers and she found a parking space with difficulty before walking down the street, jostled by shoppers with large bulging plastic bags. As usual she was fascinated that humans needed so many things. Food? Cleaning materials? She'd once stood behind a woman in a supermarket who had spent two hundred pounds without blinking.

Having bought her canvases, she wandered into Boots and went down the aisles in search of scented soap. When she landed up among the rails of baby clothes her instinct was to hurry away. But a self-lacerating curiosity kept her there. She looked at a row of miniature garments marked '0-3 months' and fingered a tiny primrose jacket. Was it possible for any being to be so small? The size was unbelievable. In all her life she had never held a baby in her arms.

'I'd be afraid to drop him,' she'd said to friends with their new-born.

'He won't break!' the mother would answer. But Avril laughed it off. Sometimes she crossed the road to avoid a buggy.

As she stood looking at the doll-sized jacket, a thought came into her mind. Surely what she was thinking couldn't be true.

During all her years of sterile marriage she had never had a reason to buy the womanlike packet she later took upstairs to her bathroom. Sitting on the bathroom stool, she read the instructions carefully. She scoffed at herself. Two and a half weeks late was nothing much, was it? It could happen to women, and of course she had taken the pill as usual. Keith had asked about that before the first time they'd had sex. He had also used a condom. But later they both decided this was not necessary.

'After all,' he said, embracing her, 'it isn't as if you or

I would ever go in for casual sex.'

Sex between them had been so simple. So what was she doing, trying the expensive pregnancy test whose result, to other women tremblingly using it, would resemble the Oracle's message in *The Winter's Tale*, words of destiny accompanied by thunder.

The leaflet said that, after following some simple instructions, she must wait ten minutes. She did. She sat staring at her wristwatch, at the second hand, at the crawling minutes. Catching sight of her face in the glass she thought – if Keith knew what I was doing!

At last the time was up. She looked at the little sample of urine in the glass test tube. She had combined it with some sort of chemical, and it had now turned purple.

I must have made a mistake, she thought, and nervously went through the whole rigmarole again. Very, very carefully.

The Oracle gave the same answer.

Avril was pregnant.

Her legs literally gave way, and she sank down on to the floor. How could this have happened? She scrabbled wildly in her memory and at last back came the thought that twice she might – she wasn't sure but it was impossibly possible – she just might have forgotten to take the pill. Had she checked? She had been happy and relaxed and it had been very cold that week, with a frost like breaking glass.

I did forget.

She was pregnant by Keith, whom she did not love. She had enjoyed him as he had enjoyed her – they'd made love because they were there. Not in quick, drunken couplings, but never with the grace of love either. Keith felt for her what she felt for him, pleasure and friendliness. There had been no reason for either of them to yearn or weep. No ecstasy, no sorrow.

And now she was pregnant by him.

She said aloud, 'I must use my head.' But her head would not oblige. As a child she used to dream she could fly. She would beat her hands downwards and up she soared over the astonished heads of her enemies. She'd flown to the top of cathedrals, casting herself in perfect confidence from the loftiest windows. She'd flown across the seas, turning somersaults from joy in the air. When an enemy arrived, as they often did, down she beat with her hands and up she soared into bliss and safety. This delight had left her with childhood. Tonight it came back. When she thought of the beginning of life inside her, she flew.

At last she made the effort to move from the markedly chill bathroom floor. This whole affair seemed connected with cold and heat, with the great fire Keith had built for her at Cheselbourne, with garden paths slippery with frosts. She went downstairs, poured herself a glass of water and turned up the central heating. She was too hyped up to cook herself anything to eat. She made some bread and milk and lit the fire, using four firelighters and watching it falsely blaze. She said again aloud:

'Avril. Use your head.'

She remembered reading somewhere in a newspaper that to conceive a child by a man without his knowledge was a crime against him. A secret theft. She had done that. Not deliberately, yet she had forgotten to take the pill. Perhaps something in her had been indifferent to risk, or worse had had a deep, unadmitted hope. What was going to happen? What would Keith say and do? And Hugh? Would he, as men did in last-century novels, nobly give the child a name? Probably not.

I really must stop feeling happy, she thought. Followed by, I really must be sensible.

Conscience finally nudged and she rang Keith, only to get his answering machine.

'Keith,' she said, 'it's me. You said you'd be back from Exeter early tomorrow, Sunday, after you'd seen Sally off. Could you manage supper? Only bacon and eggs. Don't bother to ring if it's OK. See you around seven thirty.'

Calm because there was nothing more to be done, Avril spent the rationed daylight painting a plate of green apples. Weekend painting was always by daylight and she enjoyed it more than by the electric light.

She slept like a log.

The peace of the following morning, Sunday, was broken by a call which she thought must be Keith saying he couldn't come this evening. It was Isobel.

'Sorry to get you so early, I'm just wondering if by some miracle you are free this afternoon?' cried Isobel, warmer than usual. 'It's Jack's party and far too many children are coming; I suppose you couldn't possibly lend me a hand?'

Avril had known about the party for a week and had been dreading the fact that Isobel might ask her to do just this. At such gatherings with mothers and their little children she usually felt self-conscious, and somehow the children knew that; only a few of them showed they were fond of her. But this afternoon in Isobel's cottage, Avril was the life and soul. She was the quickest grandmother in Grandmother's Footsteps, cleaned up jam from the carpet and saved a little girl from falling downstairs. She comforted a small sobbing boy who had lost (she found it) his teddy and took him with her to join in Musical Bumps. Isobel looked at her with curiosity once or twice.

'Well, now,' said Isobel, as muffled child after muffled child, each grasping a booty bag, vanished with parents into the foggy dark. 'You're the do-gooder if I ever met one.'

'I enjoyed it.'

'You're a marvel. We deserve a drink.'

'What I'd love,' said Avril, to her own surprise, 'is a fresh cup of tea.'

'Excellent,' said Isobel, deciding she could save her precious Meursault for her husband and herself. She busied herself in the kitchen, shouting, 'Don't you dare clear up after all your good work.'

Avril, refreshed with tea and village gossip, did not return to her own cottage until after half past seven. The moon was ringed with a nimbus of mauve and orange; the cold air crackled.

She heard a car horn toot impatiently and went through the garden and across the slippery paving to the parking place round the corner. A burly figure was getting out of the car.

'Avril, is that you? I can't see a blind thing.'

'Shall I get my torch? Look, let me give you a hand.'

There was a scuffling and a fumbling. She opened the small wicket gate.

'Why are you carrying a balloon?' he asked, laughing.

'Kid's party. I just got back. Well, hello,' said Avril hospitably.

He found the hand holding the balloon and they made their way to the back door, their night sight returning.

'I'm so glad I could make it,' he said, as they went into the house. 'Sally nearly didn't leave today after all, but eventually she decided there were things she had to do up at the University, so I drove home and – behold – got your nice message. Here I am, all set for the bacon and eggs.'

Avril took his big coat and draped it on the banister. He rubbed his hands.

'Blessed central heating. You left it on. The thing about you,' looking round, 'is that your home is so wonderfully cosy.'

'The only thing?'

The flirtatious reply was automatic, and she instantly regretted it.

'Let's get this right. The warm home is the main thing on a nasty night. The way you look is second. Bacon and eggs third and fourth.'

'Which would you like first?'

He chuckled and gave her a sexy you-know-what-I-want look. In a moment faster than light Avril had to choose. To make love? Or to tell him now? But sex seemed to have lost its power, and as well as that, she had a sense of fairness. A sort of pity because he did look happy.

'Let me get you a drink,' she said before he had time to come over and put both arms round her waist. She poured two drinks and put hers on the table, where she found it untouched hours later.

'Sit down and get warm.'

He smiled comfortably at the domestic tone; his broad face with its curling mouth resembled in its innocence one of the children at the party, waiting for his present. As she knelt down near him, the lamplight lit her profile. He took credit for her beauty.

'Keith, I have to tell you something.'

The cliché slipped out easily enough, but her heart was pounding like an engine.

'Damn. I can guess. Hugh's rung again and you're off in a day or two.'

'No. He hasn't. I'm not—'

He was going to interrupt but she stopped him, by putting her hand on his. The expectant look in all its ignorant hope returned to his face. She threw herself at the hideous task.

'I'm afraid I'm pregnant.'

Of course his expression altered. She had been expecting shock and tensed herself to be ready, but instead she saw her own pity landed in Keith's blue eyes. He said with great tenderness:

'My dear girl, what can I say? I suppose you are telling me you and I should never have made love in your condition. I've heard sex can be dangerous, it can bring on a miscarriage. Surely you knew that; you should have told me.'

She looked at him stupidly and gabbled:

'It isn't Hugh's.'

Then he did stare.

'You've made a mistake.'

'No mistake. I did the test twice.'

'But why do you say it isn't—'

'Hugh's. Because he's been away *five months*, Keith. It's only just happened. It is ours.'

Now he did look as she'd imagined.

Her heart swelled with the return of pity.

'You must make sure. You must go to a doctor at once.'

'Of course. Tomorrow. I'll see Dr Atkinson.'

'Christ, Avril, not a doctor we *know*.'

'Oh, all right. I'll drive into Yeovil. It should be possible somehow to find somebody there if I go as a private patient. But I know the test is right. It's no good pinning our hopes on the chance that I've made a mistake.'

Our hopes? How dared she say such a thing. He continued to stare, no longer at her but across the room. She said gently:

'Poor Keith. It's a shock for you.'

'A shock! It's appalling! How could it have happened?'

He sounded like a police officer about to grill a suspect. She managed lamely:

'I suppose I—' His accusing look did not change. 'I suppose I must have forgotten to take the pill.'

For the first time in the years since she had begun to work for him, she saw him really angry. His mouth was a thin line, his face twisted. He burst out:

'You *forgot*. Are you a mental defective? You forgot! You agreed it was OK for me not to use a condom. You had sex with me and you *forgot*.'

'I did take the pill!' she shouted back. 'I've been taking the filthy thing for years. Hugh always made me. But there was one night recently, I don't know exactly when' – she didn't dare say it could have been two nights, or more – 'when I thought I'd taken it and I suppose I hadn't and I suppose I didn't check – I don't know. It's the same with people who can't remember if they've taken their sleeping pills. It happens. People forget things sometimes. And it's too late for us to yell at each other. I realise you're upset.'

'*Upset!*'

'It is a shock for us both,' she said, and added, lying in her teeth, 'I'm as horrified as you are.'

He reached for the wine bottle and refilled his glass

without asking her. His normally ruddy colouring, the picture of good health, was blotchy. Part of his skin, perhaps part of him inside too, had gone white. Part was red. He drank.

'I just can't believe it.'

'I felt the same.'

'What do you propose to do about it?' he said in a bullying voice.

And then Avril saw what up until now she had been too misty to perceive. She had an intense feeling of danger. It was as if that minute call of new life, that being at present scarcely a tenth of an inch in length, that mystical piece of the future, was sending out warnings. Radio signals. Look out. Keep calm. Agree to anything and do nothing, said the being who had taken over her body because she had given it that briefest chance.

'Well? What are you going to do?' he demanded.

Poor man, she thought, you are so nice and you were so happy. Now you feel damaged and it is my fault.

The radio signals were louder. The invisible being was having none of that.

She said cautiously:

'I'm not sure.'

Unexpectedly his demeanour changed. He stood up and began to walk round the room as if he needed to move. He strode about, forced to bend at certain places where the great uneven beams were low. Then he returned to his chair and fell more than sat, stretching out his legs.

'Look, Avril,' it was a different voice, 'I've been behaving like a swine. Yes, it was a shock, but as you rightly say, a shock for both of us. Sorry I shouted. It was a disgusting thing to do. Men don't – don't behave too well in situations like this,' he oddly added, and Avril thought, This has happened to you before. How strange.

'The point is,' he went on in all his reasonableness, 'we must move quickly. The sooner we fix things up the better. We must find you a really first-class doctor and get things terminated straight away.'

He reached for her hand. Avril's small hand, stained with traces of green paint, was young and pale and decorated, apart from the paint, by his 'regard' ring and a narrow gold band. He picked at the paint stains. She left the hand meekly in his and he gave it a slight pressure.

'I'll make some enquiries, discreet, of course. Then I'll drive you to wherever you have to go. Don't feel you have to face this on your own.'

The radio signals were now so loud that Avril scarcely heard him. She only guessed what he said by his face.

'Forgive?' he finished, kissing her hand and putting it against his cheek. At night his beard was scratchy, and when they made love it often marked her face and neck. He closed his eyes as he pressed her hand close to the thorny cheek, and she thought wonderingly – will he or she look like you?

Although manfully behaving well, it was clear that the shock had not worn off. He asked if she would mind if he did not, after all, stay for a meal.

'I'm afraid I wouldn't be good company.'

'Of course. I do understand.'

'You always do.' He stood up as if she had given him permission to escape. 'Lunch tomorrow? I'll have found out various details by then.'

'Fine.'

'And don't worry.'

He was nearly back to his old self.

She went out into the hall to help him into the big coat. She patted the padded shoulders and he gave her something like a grin. She shut the door and stood listening to the sound of his car dying away in the country night.

She smiled. The radio signals told her with eerie approval that she had done well. They knew, as she knew, that she had no intention on earth of getting rid of the creature who had come to live for the best part of a year in her longing body.

Impossible at first to sleep. She saw again Keith's face, watched his angry alarm and reflected how, having thought of a route to liberty, he had hurried away. In one sentence she'd turned from a mistress to a threat.

The nimbus round the moon was right – it began to rain over Dorset. The soft, steady sound was like music. Avril's heart filled up with gratitude to Keith for giving her this marvellous gift. But it was not a gift, was it? It was something she had stolen from him. She couldn't worry about that just now; two great discoveries were enough for a single day. She had found that she was pregnant and she had decided to keep the baby. She refused to think about Hugh; for tonight she had had enough.

The rain fell all night long, drowning and drenching the hazel woods, turning gardens into mud, beating coldly down on tiny points of bulbs unwise enough to peer up too soon. It rained on the ancient roof of Keith's mansion, where he had many positive thoughts on how to help 'dear little Avril'. It rained on Isobel Sinclair's cottage, where she and her family slept, exhausted by the jollities of the party. No risk of Isobel in the middle of the night seeing a guilty car by Avril's gate.

And it rained on Avril's thatch, making a gentle sound. In new and mysterious company, she slept to its watery music.

Chapter 4

The telephone rang at scarcely seven o'clock, but she was awake. Lying, staring into the dark, hands behind her head. The telephone's interruption made her leap out of self-satisfaction and for the first few seconds she did not recognise the voice.

'Yes? No, it's OK ... Keith?' managed Avril, finally realising it was her child's father.

'Avril, I shan't be able to keep our date today. I'm so sorry!' How strained his voice was, almost hoarse. 'I'm at the airport. Sally's going to Munich again, you know that big do I told you about?'

Avril didn't and gave an understanding murmur.

'It looks as if the prize they've been talking about is going to happen. Something to do with international lectures, *vortrag*, can't remember the German. So of course ...'

'Of course you must go,' interrupted Avril, finishing the sentence. This simplified today.

'Avril.' He spoke her name in the hoarse voice. 'I just couldn't get out of it. And the trouble is I can't be back for three or four days. Look, would Friday do for us?'

'Don't worry, Keith. I'm fine.'

'But what we decided last night . . .'

'It can wait till Friday. *Please* don't worry.'

A pause.

'You're so good,' was the inevitable sigh. She could literally hear the strain beginning to loosen.

'So see you Friday? I'm certain to be back by then. I'll ring the office when I get to Munich and fix for everything to be moved on to the end of the week.'

'And I've lots to get on with,' said Avril, unaware of irony.

She thoughtfully put down the telephone.

It was still pitch dark. Dawn would not creep across the frozen fields for more than an hour. It was not too early to telephone Rick. Free of Keith for the time being, she needed to tell the human being who was closest to her. Her brother, after all, did love her.

'Av? What's wrong? Is Ma ill?'

Rick's voice was very sharp, and she wondered if it was concern or annoyance because he had already started work.

'No, Ma's not ill, I'm sure she's not, though I haven't talked to her for three or four days. It's just that . . . I was wondering if I could come to London and see you.'

'When?'

'What about today?'

There was a brief moment of silence which said a good deal. Then:

'Not sure,' cautiously.

'I needn't arrive until you get back from your paper. I suppose you've got all sorts of dates, including dinner tonight.'

'Hold on, I'm looking.'

Finally:

'Well, it's sort of all right. I can advance one or two things until tomorrow. What time would you be here?'

She quite liked the fact that he didn't ask why she wanted to come. He respected other people's selfishness.

'Sorry to ask another favour. I suppose I couldn't come this afternoon?'

'Aren't you at the office?'

An accusation.

'Not today.'

No further questions, m'lud.

'Want to stay the night?' Rick was not following up her lack of duty.

'I'd like to. Thanks, Rick. Tomorrow I'll leave at the crack and then I can be back at Bridport in time.'

'OK. See you.'

He was already returning to his work.

Avril dressed more carefully than usual that morning. Her brother often remarked upon her clothes, and rarely with compliments. He never missed anything. Not shoes, not sweaters, not hair; he was too noticing about the way women dressed. He was too smart about everything. She did like it, though, if he approved of the clothes she wore; she fished out a suit and took trouble with her make-up. She left Fuchsia Cottage in good time after a call to Helen, always punctual as the clock in the office.

Helen was already in possession of Keith's news.

'Did you know your boss has bunked off to Germany?'

Yes, said Avril; it was handy because as it happened Rick had been nagging her for weeks about coming up to see the family solicitor. This was the perfect chance; she'd cleared it with Keith, who approved.

'I'll be back in the morning,' said Avril. Helen, never fazed by anything, a trait much blessed by most of the staff but not by the directors, soothingly agreed that Avril's trip was a good idea.

The night rain had gone when Avril locked her front door, but black clouds were rolling up from the sea. Isobel, in hunter-trial padded coat, silk scarf knotted under her chin, and regulation green buckled wellies, shouted good morning. Avril had earned a pageful of Brownie points by helping at the party. But Isobel was still true to form.

'Where are you off to, all tarted up? Not to work surely?'

'Going to see my brother in London.'

'Really?' Laughter. 'I thought you might be keeping an away-day date with that sexy boss of yours. *He* didn't stay long last night.'

She had met Keith once at a local charity do and rather liked him. She also liked little digs.

'Isobel, don't tease,' was the cool reply. Isobel grinned brightly and hung about on the other side of the stone wall. They could have been miners' wives fifty years ago, hanging out the washing and shouting over the fence.

'Did you send him off with a flea in his ear?'

A gust of cold wind blew off the scarf; her tawny hair fell on her forehead. The tortoiseshell cat again.

'Keith only popped in to ask if I'd do some boring old overtime at the weekend,' said Avril, whose new capacity for lies quite staggered her. 'I told him he'd have to pay a top temp price.'

'I hope he agreed,' said Isobel, waving a disappointed goodbye.

There was no pressure for Avril to hurry on her long London drive. She dawdled, and stopped at Wylie to have something to eat in a tea shop. She knew the place well; she and Hugh often used it as their stop on London drives. Hugh liked it because it was attached to a snobby grocer's next door where he bought home-cured ham and what he called real cheese.

The café part of the place smelled of chocolate and peppermints; classy boxes were ranged on a table. It was pleasantly warm, and she went to a table by the window. There was nobody else around but a middle-aged couple who did not look up as she walked in, and did not look at each other either.

Avril ordered a sandwich and some tea. Now and again she took a covert glance at the couple seated in the corner. They didn't speak a word. The man, elderly, had a schoolmaster-ish face, prissy, thin, with ragged eyebrows that ought to be trimmed. His eyes were blue and faded, and from Avril's distance she thought they looked cold. The woman, on the contrary, was rosy and fattish, but seemed anxious. Poor thing, does she find him difficult to bear? thought Avril. Is that what happens to people who have been married for years? Do they become either anxious and put-upon or totally indifferent to their partners? I suppose it would have been like that with Hugh and me.

She was not aware that she used the conditional tense.

When she reached the suburbs of London the traffic was very thick, and once or twice she was stuck in jams. Bored, she turned on the car radio. A soupy woman's voice introduced a talk on the single-parent family.

'What we're going to ask our panel is how can women *cope*?'

Avril hastily changed the station to an organ recital, and then switched it off completely. Her own radio signals had started up again. It was difficult to concentrate on anything while they gave her, in their strange high notes, the promise of eternal bliss.

At last, with stops and starts and longer stops, she turned the car in under the arch and drove through the cobbled squares of the Temple. She parked in the place Rick had previously told Hugh was allowed, and walked to Rick's particular court and up the narrow stair. It complained at her every footstep with deafening creaks.

Outside Rick's door, painted black and looking as if it was made of solid iron, she knocked. It opened after a too-long pause, and there was Rick. He wore a thick Aran sweater; his hair was untidy and his face gaunt in the unflattering overhead light.

'Hi,' he said, bending to give her something which could not be called a kiss. 'Like some tea?'

It was obvious when she went into the sitting room that he must have been at work for hours, even days. She had never seen such a mess. Newspapers, magazines, books, pads of papers, cassettes, computer disks, notebooks and two empty wine bottles. The room badly needed a clean; she imagined his daily was forbidden to enter it on pain of death. Removing newspapers and their inevitable supplements from one of the chairs, she sat down. He went off to the kitchen. Avril, unlike her usual self, did not offer to help. She folded her hands and sat still, like a nun about to meditate. She had arrived with momentous news. The old Avril would have dashed out to the kitchen with a shouted 'Guess what?' In a way she wanted to. Somehow she remained quietly seated.

'I rang Ma. Just a quick call.' He reappeared with a tray on which no single thing matched. Mugs, plates, tea pot. The saucers were expensive flower-patterned porcelain and had nothing to do with coarse, hectic-coloured mugs. 'She sounds fine, and I'm going there next weekend.'

'Did she ask about me?'

'Sure. Wanted to know when you're off. I said nothing is happening at present.'

Oh isn't it? thought Avril. She was surprised to find how nervous she had become, much more than when she had told poor Keith. He had become 'poor' from the moment his thunderstruck face had gaped at her.

'Dad and Retta came to the Garrick for a meal,' added Rick, pouring out. 'She's certainly got him *there*.' He put down the tea pot and pressed his thumb on the table. '"What do *you* think, Retta?" "Should you have that second brandy, darling?"'

He mimicked his father's voice.

'Oh, Rick.'

He had spoken dourly. His reaction to the marriage was stronger than he had expected.

'You must have seen how he runs about after her when we were in Richmond the other night. "Can I get you another cushion?" He defers like a butler.'

'Do they defer?'

'I've never met one. Some of them do, I suppose.'

'Jeeves never did.'

He wasn't having jokes. He ignored that and went on, while Avril struggled with her own nerves. 'Don't think I don't like Retta; I always have. As you know, we've been great mates. But there's something pathetic in seeing Dad so knocked out by pulling a glamorous thirty-four-year-old.

And she's so tickled with him butlering. It'll be pregnant Retta soon enough, you bet. Most women, I'm told, get a big thing about kids after thirty has drifted past.'

'Yes, they do.'

Here was a perfect cue. She still delayed.

'Sorry, I'm not being very nice, am I? And I wasn't exactly my hospitable self when you rang,' he said grudgingly. 'The trouble is that I can't think of anything much right now but my fucking job.'

'But it's been going so well. That long piece the week before last, and you said there was a big interview with that new *enfant terrible* architect who's going to—'

'He's cancelled four times.'

'Isn't that par for the course?'

'No,' he said disagreeably. 'You can't bugger journalists around for ever. The thing goes off the boil. *I* go off the boil.'

'He must be very busy.'

'Oh, grow up.'

In her childhood when her brother used that particular voice, plain rude, Avril always shouted back. She'd been thin-skinned as a child and had not thickened her skin much as a girl. After her marriage she forced herself to be peaceable. Now she reflected that in the last twelve hours two men had shouted at her. She said calmly:

'Isn't the point, Rick, that *you* want something from him? So it's you who has to put up with it if he messes you around.'

This did nothing to appease him; she had not thought it would. She'd said it because it interested her. He poured himself more tea.

Avril decided to put her own joyful trouble aside for a

while. His bad temper was inconvenient, for after all she had driven to London for his advice, even for solace. Instead she began to talk about his work. It was a technique she used with Hugh; she had done the same thing with Rick many times. She had noticed with Rick that he wanted to talk about his work because he could test out his ideas, argue perhaps, discuss, inform, and possibly bore a willing listener. With Avril's interested eyes on him, his mood improved. He swore less, he looked quite human and when she advanced some carefully sophisticated theory about architecture he burst out laughing, but not ill-naturedly. At last he had the grace to apologise a second time for being difficult.

'I'm foul-tempered until my ideas are sorted.'

'Do your women friends object to that?'

Odd that she'd never met a single one of Rick's women. No trace in the flat here either. Not a whiff of scent, no lipstick on a collar, as the old song sang.

'I avoid them when I'm working. There used to be one,' he added – of course it had been Retta – 'who came here to cook lunch one Sunday. She got so mad at me she threw a half-cooked leg of lamb across the room and it cut me on the forehead. It poured.

'Two kinds of blood,' added Rick.

He had cheered up, and when Avril laughed he said he'd take her to dinner at the Garrick; she'd like that, wouldn't she?

The time was as right as it would ever be. Avril counted to ten.

'So when are you going to St V?' he asked. 'And why, disgusting of me not to have asked sooner, am I being visited today?'

'I've come with some news.'

He raised his eyebrows in a good-natured query. He looked brotherly.

'As a matter of fact, Rick, I'm pregnant.'

His reaction was uncanny. It was exactly like Keith's.

'*Hey!*' A smile spread right across his face. His brown eyes sparkled. He sprang up, came over and hugged her. Still holding her, now at arm's length, he laughed.

'That's great, that's really good news. Pregnant at last, and about time too. You and Hugh have waited long enough. He must be over the moon. When's the baby due?'

'Sorry. It isn't Hugh's.'

She looked straight at him.

She had never thought, stupid of her, that like Keith he would assume the baby was her husband's. How could it be, since Hugh had been away so long? Men didn't count months like women did, but all the same . . . She had also never told Rick that Hugh refused to let her have a child.

He stood there, arms dropped, as astounded as Keith. But rather angrier.

She said quickly:

'Don't give me the cliché about you don't believe what you're hearing. It's true. I am pregnant and the baby is not Hugh's.'

'So you just said.'

'For God's sake! Why are you so holy all of a sudden? I bet you're no canonised saint when it comes to sex.'

'I'm not married.'

'I wish you could hear yourself,' she said pityingly, while Rick remained in his statue's niche marked Righteousness.

'I presume you have told your husband.'

'Of course I haven't, do have some sense. Would I be

likely to telephone St Vincent and break the merry news like that? Anyway, I only discovered yesterday. Which is why I was stupid enough to come rushing up to see my brother.'

He made a prissy grimace.

'While you're sitting in judgement,' said Avril, returning to calmness – her indignation had been brief – 'you may as well be given the missing bit of the story. Hugh has always refused to let me have a baby.'

'Am I supposed to be sorry for you?'

'Rick,' she said with real wonder, 'are you listening to yourself? I am not asking you to be sorry for me, I am explaining.'

'You got yourself pregnant on purpose, is that it?'

Here was a teaser. Trust Rick to say it, ask it, see it. It was what she herself half-suspected, what she herself would not admit. She said brusquely:

'Oh, rubbish!'

But inside her she repeated – did I? Did I? It was not impossible. She remembered the crocodile of little children crossing the road on their way to rehearse the Christmas play. She remembered the ache in her soul which only painting could assuage. She thought of her nights of returning home to the cottage after sex with Keith. Did I?

She leaned back in her chair, keeping an impassive face against the sharp eyes of her too observant brother. She found just then that it was possible to be profound, to let herself sink into the depth and swim there. She lay back. She was paler than usual. Pregnancy made her face both wan and refined.

Rick went to his desk and switched on the answering machine, which began to drone messages. Quick and slow voices. Ring back. Ring soon. Ring now, OK?

How mysterious men are, she thought, looking at his thin back. Unfathomable. I almost never manage to guess what they are going to say or do unless it's blindingly obvious. I never get their finer points, their odder reactions. And then she swam back into the depths and stayed pleasurably on the sea bed where weeds swayed and fish glistened.

Switching off the machine, still with his back to her, Rick said:

'You knew how Hugh felt about kids before you married him.'

I see. More accusations, thought Avril, swimming up to the surface.

'I did not. I never asked. I was so crazy about him. I daresay,' she added, 'you don't remember any of that, but I was quite off my head over Hugh. So the subject never came up.'

He turned round at last with an angry shrug. He liked his brother-in-law and always had. He had little sympathy for the Services – he'd always scoffed at the straight-up-and-down attitudes – but Hugh was a man you couldn't help liking. He was amusing, hospitable, boyishly enthusiastic at times. Interested in Rick too. Rick respected and was even rather fond of him. This matter of having children, you could decide to have them or not, for crying out loud. Hugh had a perfect right—

'The subject never came up,' Avril repeated, watching his face. 'Odd, wasn't it? Later, when it did, I tried to persuade him hundreds of times. He just wouldn't listen. I expect Hugh never wanted a child because he can't bear competition.'

Rick sat down, still judge and jury.

'So you go off and get pregnant when he's abroad. I consider that a pretty filthy trick.'

'Of course I didn't go off and get pregnant, as you charmingly put it. I had a bit of an affair.'

'A bit.'

'Yes, that's right, nothing serious about it for me or the man. Until this happened, that is.'

'Who is the father?'

'You sound like a man in a Western. Who is the father so I can go and shoot him.'

He didn't smile, but nor did she. She hesitated, then said:

'Keith Waring.'

'Your boss.'

'Hackneyed, isn't it?'

She had put up a brave fight, and now she had to wait to see what would happen. She had spent time getting Rick into a good mood, and had failed. She had come here, she supposed, for love. Brotherly love. Rick had never been too profligate with that commodity; Avril had often thought in the past that he was fond of her in spite of himself. What an odd fish he was; they had so little in common. She'd accepted that success had stolen away her adored big brother, just as she had grown used to Hugh's humiliating sleeping around, and now her father's pathetic groping after his lost youth. The men in her life were a severe disappointment.

Rick, silent for what seemed to his sister a sign of deepening disapproval, had begun to see her point of view. Avril's affair was the kind of thing that happened. The people you went to bed with were the ones you saw every day, who shared part of your life, were linked to you usually by work. Avril and that Pickwickian guy in Dorset. Himself and Retta. She had sat on the other side of the crowded open-plan office where they worked and the affair had started with a lark when Rick discovered her e-mail address. It was 'Magical'. Typical Retta. One afternoon he'd sent a sexy message to her on her computer letter-box and watched her expression as she read it. They'd gone on from there.

He swerved away from the thought that he still occasionally lusted after his father's wife, and returned to Avril.

She mildly asked:

'So what do you think?'

'These days only a bloody stupid woman gets herself in the club by mistake,' he said crudely. 'How does that poor sod Waring feel?'

She noticed Keith was landed with the prefix again.

'Horrified.'

'Him and me both.'

Avril continued mild. In a movie, she thought, to indicate his seething mind Rick would light a cigarette and viciously pull at it, then stab it out after two puffs. I've watched too many old films. But all Rick actually did was stare into space. Then said:

'You don't mention what Hugh's reaction is going to be to all this.'

'Well ... I haven't quite got to Hugh. You came first,' said Avril, with what he considered outrageous coolness.

'You can scarcely expect him to—'

'Give the little bastard his name?' Avril was actually laughing.

'Christ almighty, Avril! You come here for advice but you don't need it. Your own common sense must have told you there's only one possible thing to do and it had better be done at once.'

'And what is that?'

'You must have an abortion.'

'Keith said the same.'

'See? We're both damn right. You must.'

She lay back, her head against a velvet cushion. The radio signals had started again. She'd been expecting them.

'No.'

Rick gave a loud groan.

'Use your head! You can't have this child. You've no right to. No right at all.'

'Really? I consider that's exactly what I have got.'

'Avril . . .'

'Rick?'

'You haven't faced up to how Hugh is going to feel.'

'That'll come soon enough. When I get to St Vincent.'

'A pretty prospect.'

'Yes. I shall have to be brave.'

He scarcely recognised the sister who had since her marriage so noticeably changed. And now apparently had changed again. She was eerily calm in the face of what lay ahead. The way she was now taking what must surely end in disaster for her marriage flummoxed Rick. He had a second or two of self-pity. Nothing but family problems. Their unhappy mother. Their father marrying Retta, of all women. He still minded intensely about Retta, and sometimes his own thoughts disgusted him. He told himself that their affair had been well over before she and Gerald were together. But he suspected this moral conclusion was probably not true. Retta was casual, sexy, enigmatic. Now he had to push aside his disturbed feelings about her to worry over Avril. He resented that.

Avril didn't feel hurt at his lack of sympathy; it would have been unrealistic to expect him to be warm or concerned. Her condition, as they used to call it in old novels, was a presence in the room just then. An angelic presence, she sentimentally thought, huge wings folded. So enormous that they might hinder the seraph from getting through the door.

Rick picked up the telephone and rang the Garrick to book a table. When he had done so, Avril said:

'I love that place. The room women are allowed into, I mean.'

He said briefly that he must clear up, and began to sort out his desk, shuffling through papers. Avril read some old newspapers, all of which carried huge stories of tragedy and misfortune and not one of which was meant to make her feel cheerful.

Rick finally finished his tasks, and Avril put on her jacket. Outside there was a drizzle so fine that it was more like water suspended in a jar than real rain. They left quiet cobbled squares and turned into the traffic-bright Strand.

'Shall we walk?' Rick said, looking up at the grey mist which hid the stars. The drizzle had stopped.

She took his arm, feeling rather happy as they swung in step along the shiny pavements. She'd told him. She'd done it. He would never truly understand, because the subject of children to her worldly, overworked brother was rather like the subject of religion. He and Avril had been brought up as Catholics, their mother's faith. Rick had gone to a Catholic public school; but Avril was well aware that he hadn't entered a church from the last day of the summer term when he'd left. She herself did go to mass sometimes.

Hugh quite approved. He was High Church Anglican and she believed he thought churchgoing classy. Nowadays Roman Catholics were no longer looked down on as they'd been in the past.

The Garrick was crowded; the portrait of Gladys Cooper, a goddess bathed in light, shone down on a roomful of people enjoying themselves. Rick was given a good table and took trouble to suggest the food he knew his sister enjoyed. If this is his way of showing he disapproves of me, she thought, it's an original one.

During the meal they talked about their mother, Rick himself, Gerald and Retta, about anything but a subject guarded by an invisible being sitting at the table too.

'No, I won't have a coffee, thank you.'

The waiter filled Rick's gold-rimmed cup, and then put a small dish of chocolates in front of them. Avril took one, Rick picked another. His mouth full of violet cream, he said:

'You seem rather confident, considering you are in such a serious mess.'

'I suppose I am.'

'Which?'

'Both. Confident. And in a mess.'

'Avril, I'm sorry but I have to say it again. You really must make the effort to see things from your husband's point of view.'

'Must I?'

'You know as well as I do that you've simply got to get rid of—'

'The baby.'

'It isn't that yet, so don't make things worse than they are.'

'I'm only calling it what it is. A baby. Will you, Avril, take this baby to have and to hold, from this day forward, in sickness and in health.'

Rick leaned over and squeezed her hand so painfully that she squeaked out loud.

'Do be quiet,' he muttered. A journalist at a nearby table – Rick knew him – was looking at her with curiosity.

'I don't know what's got into you, Avril.'

She couldn't help laughing.

'OK. OK. So what I said is very funny. I don't understand your reactions, by Christ I don't.'

How could he? she thought. There were no radio signals for Rick. He would never know or understand that from the moment she'd completed the test, the world for Avril had become transformed. She was charged with a mystical task, she was a priestess, she was blessed. Two men in two days had demanded that she must rid herself of her marvellous destiny. Trudge to a hospital and emerge the deflowered and tattered creature of *their* choosing. They were pathetic.

She regarded him gently and, no more pinches, he held her hand again and pressed it. When she returned the pressure he took it for surrender. He gave an encouraging smile.

'No, Rick,' she said.

And at once he let her hand drop.

Chapter 5

There was silence between them as they walked home to the Temple. When they went into the flat Rick made an effort, asked her if the bedroom was warm enough, and folded back the bedcover in the nun-like spare room. It was occasionally used by their mother or by Avril and Hugh on London visits. Rick's barrister friend also reserved it for his family.

'I'm going to leave in the morning before six,' Avril said. 'I promise not to disturb you.' She fished a small alarm clock from her zip bag. 'As I took today off, I really must be in time for work tomorrow.'

'I can't let you drive all that way without any breakfast.' He was annoyed with them both.

'Rick, I'm perfectly capable of making a cup of tea. I'll get some breakfast on my drive down. I shall enjoy that.'

When he saw that the idea of his rising early to do something for her distinctly got on her nerves he yielded. Oh, very well, if you insist.

'Goodnight Rick. Thanks for the delicious supper. What a treat.'

She dared him not to accept her matter-of-fact good humour.

But in his own room he did not sleep for a long time. He did not read either. He lay with his eyes open, looking at the pattern of light on the ceiling; it came from a lamp in the square outside and was shaped like one of those spiky tiaras the royals wore on big occasions. He felt disturbed. Avril's predicament worried him deeply – she had brought with her a new, worse interruption to his concentration. How could his sister be so stupid and so adamant? Not one for sentimental memories, Rick remembered how once, years ago when he had been at Oxford, he'd taken her for a walk through a wood. White anemones were growing thickly everywhere; he'd thought his sister was exactly like them: delicate, springy-stalked, bending the way the wind blew and not losing a petal. That was how she had been as she grew up, ready to lean or sway. 'OK, you've persuaded me,' had been her good-natured sisterly song. He supposed that was what she had done with Hugh Brett, bent the way *he* wanted. The result had taken away her liveliness and charm. Hugh looked the kind of man who always had his own way, and when Rick recalled what Avril had told him tonight about refusing her a child, he thought – still liking him despite it – 'selfish sod'.

Now Avril, whose pliant nature he had taken for granted, was unrecognisably changed. He was angry because he was worried. It was as if in the distance he heard the approaching wail of a police car or a fire engine; the noise meant danger and Avril was as deaf as a post.

It pleased Avril in the silent dark next morning that her brother didn't wake. When she listened at his door, all she heard was silence. She didn't know that he had been awake for hours and had not drifted off until after three. She went into the narrow galley of a kitchen, found some tea bags and stood drinking the hot tea hastily. She packed, gave a final check round the bare room, scribbled, 'Thanks, Rick, love, love, A' on the back of an envelope on his desk and crept out.

The breathless cold outside was a shock after Rick's central heating. The ancient buildings slept. Lamps dimly shone, looking like black-stalked tulips.

The hope of avoiding traffic out of London proved vain, and as she drove westwards she wondered who all these people could be, risen so early, many streaming into the capital and almost as many out of it. One person only in every car. At last, after tough driving, she arrived on the rolling loneliness of Salisbury Plain. The trees had vanished, there was only mile upon mile of dull green, rising, falling, stretching away as far as you could see in a winter mist. Relaxed, she drove easily, with time to reflect now upon the two men who knew her secret.

Rick had only been thinking of her last night when he urged her to get rid of the child. He was not like poor Keith, who naturally enough was thinking of himself and his wife. Nothing had been Keith's fault. She pitied him and wanted him to be happy. She felt charitable this morning. She forgave her brother too, for dropping her hand at the end of dinner.

But what could she do to satisfy them? Her quandary resembled one of those intricate games in a little glass-fronted box. You were supposed to shake each one of the tiny silver balls until they fell into the scoops of an allotted pattern. It was nearly impossible. Shake as you might, they always rolled out again. It was like that now. Whichever way Avril shook her puzzle, the balls in Rick's box rolled all over the place, and when she rattled Keith's the same thing happened. Am I supposed to ask their forgiveness for carrying my baby? she thought.

The day advancing was clouded and dull when she drew up in Wylie. She went into the same coffee shop, the window full of fresh home-made cakes. This morning she was the only customer, took the same table, and suddenly remembered Hugh sitting here with her one morning on their return from a Navy ball at Greenwich. He'd spent most of the evening with a sexy-looking girl, sister of a junior officer. Remembering Hugh strongly for the first time in over two days, she had an odd wave of being sorry for him. All these men I'm being sorry for, thought Avril, it is very unattractive of me.

She ordered China tea from the waitress, who recognised her and gave her a welcoming smile.

I've cheated Hugh, thought Avril, sipping pleasantly weak tea. Not in sex; I could scarcely cheat a man who never stopped cheating me. No, it is my pregnancy which is treason.

She looked idly out of the window. A few shoppers walked by, and across the road a vegetable shop, gaily lit, displayed a mountain of dazzling oranges, a great triangle of Spanish sunshine. Her own face was reflected in the window, with the distant oranges glistening behind her.

And for the first time, then, she knew that what had happened had not been an accident. How had she forgotten to take the pill? She had never done that with Hugh. When he slammed the door of hope in her face she had beaten against it until her knuckles were covered in blood. But she never thought to cheat him. She wouldn't dare. Her blows had weakened, and at last, accepting the cruelty, she had returned to her only solace, painting.

Stealing a baby from Keith is as bad as anything Hugh did to me, she thought. No, it is worse.

At once her radio signals began their imperious messages. They told her not to be a fool, to shut up, to get on with it. She agreed. But what about poor Keith? Was he like the male spider, and other creatures who die when they have mated? She thought of him kindly; the last thing she wanted was for Keith to be impaled on a thorn.

A fine rain began to spatter the café window. Looking through the silvery runnels as they made their hasty way down, Avril knew she did not want a single thing from Keith any more. She had enjoyed her time with him very much, his vitality and admiration, most of all the uncomplicated sex. But every time, after the sex, she forgot its pleasures so soon. She had said goodnight to him at the back gate, let herself into the empty cottage, climbed the ladder stair. She had gone contentedly to sleep. That pleasant time was past.

What I have to do now is calm him down, persuade him not to worry, she thought with perfect assurance. How she would manage that she had no idea. Over in Germany he would certainly be worrying about the abortion; the radio signals sharply ordered her to avoid the odious word. Let him down lightly, they said, he'll soon realise there is nothing for him to be upset about. Avril felt invincible.

Despite the before-dawn start, she was late after she had arrived home, had a hasty bath and changed her clothes. She telephoned the office.

'The traffic was a nightmare,' she lied.

'No prob,' said Helen, who watched Australian soaps. 'I'll alert everybody.'

Parking in the courtyard outside the office, Avril sat for a minute or two and collected her thoughts. She glanced at herself in the mirror attached to the inside flap of the car's sun shield. She looked tired. The winter light was harsh, her face drawn, her hair washed yesterday was already lank. Do I look like this because I am pregnant? she thought with wonder. She was a traveller in a new country and had no maps.

At the switchboard, Helen turned to put out a welcoming hand.

'How was the family solicitor? Did all go well? It's been so dull without you or Keith. He rang again. Oh, by the by, Peter Huskisson said would you pop in when you arrive.'

'What does *he* want?'

They exchanged looks.

'To use you as well as Wendy while Keith isn't around, I expect.'

Making a face, Avril went to the senior partner's door and briskly knocked.

Peter Huskisson was big and ruddy, stout and resembled the pigs he reared on his profitable home farm. He had a brutal efficiency, and nobody but Keith could stick him. Secretaries who worked for him left in droves. It astounded the rest of the staff that Wendy had already lasted a year. Fair and plain and nervous as a cat – boxes of Panadol in her desk drawer – Wendy never showed, either from nobility or a cowardly heart, the ghastliness of her boss. She was standing at his desk when in answer to his bellowed 'Come!' Avril entered the room.

Huskisson leaned dangerously back in his swivel chair and said loudly:

'Here at last, then.'

'Traffic, traffic,' said Avril.

The flip tone shocked Wendy.

'Yes, well.' Somehow Huskisson indicated that she'd had no right to take yesterday off. His attempt to put her out of countenance failed. She sat down.

'Wendy, get me a coffee, there's a love.' The endearment was disgusting the way he said it. Avril looked at him dispassionately, wondering how any human being could be so awful.

'Helen informs me,' he said, 'that my partner will not be back until Friday.'

'Yes. Sally's supposed to be getting an award—'

He held up a podgy hand.

'I'm aware of all that. There is something I have to go into with you, but I am waiting for my coffee.'

Go into what? thought Avril.

'OK, let's wait,' she said.

Huskisson scratched his heavy chin. He asked himself how Waring could be doing with this impertinent female. Huskisson had a lecher's eye; he was aware that she was not unattractive, but he couldn't stand women above themselves. God knows, they were everywhere now. You had to be on the lookout. Waring spoiled that woman rotten. Wendy reappeared with a tray set with real china cups, brown sugar lumps, expensive wheaten biscuits and a dish of plastic horrors containing cream.

'Open three, there's a love, you know how they spurt over my tie,' said Huskisson with a chuckle.

Avril thanked Wendy for the coffee, picked up the cup and found the smell, taste and even look of it made her feel distinctly sick. She tried again. It was not imagination; she put the cup down on a bookshelf as far away as possible.

Wendy went out, quietly closing the door. Huskinsson put four sugar lumps into his cup rather gingerly. His tie was by Gucci.

'Now,' he said, after drinking deeply. 'I sent for you to give you some news.'

'Yes?'

'About your boss. He and I had a chinwag before he left, long phone call and so on. Something I've had up my sleeve for some time. Keith was against it, but now I've talked him into changing his mind. I want the firm to open a branch in Plymouth. Got my eye on some premises. Keith will be heading up the new concern.'

He waited expectantly to see if he'd upset her. He knew Waring and Avril Brett liked each other, and what was more, he had recently caught sight of them leaving the office together at lunchtime. Something going on there? He enjoyed this chance to slap her down.

'Yes,' he continued between sips. 'Keith, to my mind, is too cautious. Bit of a slowcoach. He's been havering, but he's seen the light at last. Apparently Sally, nobody's fool, thinks she can find some academic fellow who'd buy Cheselbourne and give a good price. Beats me why anybody would want all that antiquary. Sally's quite keen. Good profit for the house and they can move to Devon with Keith up to his ears in a new project. So. Your boss will be your boss no longer in the not-too-distant. A lot of groundwork to do, of course, but our Plymouth contacts are first class. And young Dave Bexley's keen as mustard to sit in your boss's vacated chair.'

He eyed her, looking for damage. None appeared to show. He played another trump.

'Of course, Bexley is merely a junior partner. You'll

work for us both, with priority for me. More stuff will land on my desk. Over to Wendy. Then to you.' He grinned.

Avril was looking straight at him, but for a moment did not register the spiteful piggy face above the black and gold tie. She was deeply interested. So here was Keith's plan – escape. He'd be back to 'fix things up', as he had put it. He would try to be honourable and sympathetic, masking as far as he could his own alarm. He'd offer to pay over the odds for . . . the radio signals did not allow her to use the word in her thoughts. What Keith had decided was to get away. Clearly he couldn't bear the idea of having her around any more. And being Keith, he was incapable of doing what Peter Huskisson would do. Give her the sack. Besides, Sally must be pushing for all that money from Cheselbourne.

'So I'd better get on, Peter,' Avril said, standing up. 'Lots of Keith's stuff waiting for me.'

Balked from upsetting her, he swore when the telephone rang, did not answer it and pressed his buzzer, shouting:

'Wendy? How many times must I tell you not to put calls through direct to me, for God's sake.'

The telephone at once went silent. Avril turned to go. In the same loud tone he bellowed:

'Not so fast, if you please. With Keith away I want you to work with Wendy. There's more of *my* stuff to be done, so go and get it from her now. Off you go.'

Without answering, Avril left the room to speak to poor Wendy. Another 'poor'. I really must stop this habit, she thought. The girl, whiter than usual, was bent over a fileful of documents.

'Peter just told me to give you a hand. I'm really sorry, Wendy, but I think I'm coming down with flu. When I arrived at the office just now I thought I was imagining it. But I'm afraid I'm pretty sure now I've got a temperature.'

The girl looked horrified.

'You mustn't stay if there's any chance of infection, Avril. You know how Mr Huskisson feels about spreading it in the office. And he catches things so easily.'

She sounded desperate. In Wendy's mind was a picture of an infected pig, though mad bull was perhaps a better image. Avril gently agreed that perhaps she had better go home. Overworked Wendy was pathetically grateful. Helen, too, hearing of the threatened flu, was the soul of sympathy.

'Be *sure* to keep warm.'

Avril was sure of one thing. She was not going to work for Peter Huskisson even for an hour. She would stay home until Keith was back. There would then be a fraught interview with him face to face, but she was ready for that. Not, however, for three days as secretary to a barbarian.

Back at Fuchsia Cottage she changed into favourite jeans and settled down at the kitchen table. She had begun a study of some greenish-brown pears. Fortunately they had been hard as bullets when she bought them and still were – they would not begin to go soft and discolour for days, a never-absent problem for the still-life painter. She was content. Hours of daylight went by in blessed concentration.

She wandered dazed to the telephone late in the afternoon. She was scarcely surprised when it was Hugh.

'Avril? The VIP has gone at last! Nice chap, but I thought he'd never leave. I've talked to the travel people. Look, I'm sorry to give you such short notice, but it seems there's a seat on the plane tomorrow early. You can pick up your connection to Antigua at Heathrow, then . . .'

He had managed to arrange her ticket.

Excited and amused, Avril spent the evening talking to machines.

To Rick's. To her mother's – a new acquisition given to Susan by Rick. To her father's; Retta never moved without an answering machine. It was nearly midnight when, with a glass of hot milk in her hand, she finally dialled the office number. Helen's prettily pitched voice repeated the usual formula.

'Helen, it's Avril. You'll never guess – Hugh just rang. I'm off to St Vincent tomorrow very early. My temperature,' continued Avril, 'is only a tick over normal. I think I panicked this morning. I really do feel OK to travel. I know you'll understand that I can't miss this chance. Would you explain to Keith, tell him I'm so sorry to dash off like this. Tell Huskisson too, would you? And poor, I mean, and Wendy. Don't know when I'll be back. I'll send you a terrific postcard. Bye.'

Chapter 6

The hours went by between waking and sleep. In this tube for a limited time, Avril's ties were cut and her life – two lives now – belonged to her alone. She had left matters tidily enough. Poor Keith, knowing she was gone, would probably believe she had fixed the operation (which was so brief and so fatal). He would feel safe. Her family had been told she had left England. Rick knew he was powerless; he would see that she was beyond his help.

She sat for a while thinking, not about the drama ahead, but about the place where it was going to happen. Hugh was no letter-writer; his only description of the island on the telephone had been typically brief. 'Very humid ... work keeps me pretty busy ... done some sailing and scuba-diving.' Avril had loyally gone to Yeovil public library when he first left England, and read something about St Vincent, which was called 'a land of rainbows'. Looking at pictures of the island and other nearby islands even more romantic, in her thoughts Avril had seen Hugh walking on strange beaches, blue-green water washing at his feet. And the rainbows.

This island heaven was where the plane was taking her. She was on her way there to tell him something he would never, ever have thought possible. She had a pang. Do I blurt it out directly I arrive? Isn't that very cruel, when he will be pleased to see me? And after that, of course, very angry. And he will join, like Keith, like Rick, the male enemy.

He won't hit me, will he? I think I must tell him somewhere public, in a restaurant perhaps, when there is a table between us. What a pathetic plan, Avril. The only comfort was that he would have to behave in a reasonably civilised way most of the time. Thank God for the Navy, thought Avril.

She wondered if he would pack her straight back to England. Scarcely, since that would certainly raise eyebrows. Trying to sort out questions to which she had no answers, she could not help adding to herself – poor Hugh. At this charity she drifted into sleep.

'Mrs Brett?'

The stewardess was bending over her.

'May I get you some lunch?'

'What is the time?' said Avril to the girl, who, small and wondrously neat, smiled at her.

'Only eleven a.m. by Caribbean time, afternoon in Britain; they're four hours behind us.' She consulted a large and complicated watch which looked as if it was designed not only for telling the time across the world, but also the date, the temperature, and probably its owner's blood pressure for good measure.

'You were asleep when we served lunch a while ago. I hope you can manage a little,' said the girl as tenderly as if to an invalid. Avril said she could.

She glanced at her neighbour, a middle-aged man, asleep and snoring. Then sat marvelling at the sunshine pouring into the plane. Through the tiny window she saw great vistas, nothing but the clearest blue-green seas dotted with tiny dark shapes which must be islands. How beautiful it was. And how very strange. She leaned dreamily back.

But when a plastic tray of lunch arrived, Avril had to ask hastily if the stewardess would be kind enough to remove the coffee. At a whiff of it, she began to feel sick.

She ate her ham salad with appetite, finished a dish of tasteless trifle, and successfully pierced with the pin of her brooch a container of milk for her tea, remembering Huskisson. She enjoyed the meal until the stewardess passed by, carrying more coffee.

Refreshed by sleep, sunshine warming her, and all that big blue outside, Avril felt strong and interested. The big man snored on; with luck, she thought, he wouldn't wake until Antigua.

The flight lasted for eight and a half hours but to Avril it did not seem long. She slipped in and out of sleep. When she tried to read, she dropped her paperback. Her companion passenger finally woke, ordered a whole bottle of white wine, was blessedly taciturn and drank while reading some balance sheets.

At Antigua there was a boring two-hour wait, but Avril, still relaxed, let time drift. She watched the reunion of travellers, running towards each other to embrace and laugh. She felt at one with mothers and small children. Her second journey, via St Lucia, was much shorter. As the plane flew quite low, she could see a whole sickle of islands spread out, surrounded by deserted beaches. At last from her window she saw an island smaller than St Lucia, with a dramatic mountain which seemed enormous rearing up in its centre. The captain announced over the intercom:

'We are now landing at St Vincent.'

Avril looked out.

It was so extraordinary to think that in this unlikely place, this mountainous, far-off place where the sea creamed upon grey volcanic beaches, Hugh was waiting for her.

Quite suddenly she thought:

So here is the place where my marriage is going to end.

And was sorry.

The airport was small; every passenger seemed to have been here before. There were loud voices and incomprehensible announcements through an intercom. Among the surge of travellers jostling in the arrival lounge, with noise and movement all round her, she felt suddenly lost. She hadn't a link with anybody in the world.

A voice shouted above the hubbub.

'Avril!'

Over the heads of passengers, St Vincentians, Jamaicans, mostly appearing shorter than he was, she saw tall Hugh. He was in uniform. Shouldering his way to her he gave her a smacking kiss.

'I thought we'd never get you here.'

Smiling, blinking, moved, for a whole minute she forgot the fell message she was bringing him.

She had forgotten too that he was so handsome.

As he led her outside the air-conditioned arrival lounge, the heat was so intense that Avril almost gasped. Her English clothes weighed a ton. Hugh opened the door of a beat-up-looking taxi, a black driver stacked her luggage in the boot. The cab ground away through what looked like the shanty town in *Porgy and Bess*; Hugh moved closer to her, pressed her hand and smiled.

'How are you, darling? Did you sleep at all in that not-very-comfortable plane? You do look a wee bit pale.'

Avril assured him that it had been fine. She implied in her manner that everything had been – was – fine. She found herself wondering if there was the chance of a bath before she faced the destruction of her marriage. Then reminded herself that it would be wiser to take the horrible, inevitable step when she was safe behind a restaurant table.

The taxi had left the airport and was driving through Kingstown. Avril glimpsed pretty shaded Georgian arcades; some of the streets were cobbled. There was a pleasing, old-fashioned look about everything. Hugh pointed out the Cobblestone Inn, 'a lot of us use it for meeting up', and the over-gothic outline of a church.

In the distance, she saw a crowded marketplace, with stalls piled with brilliantly coloured fruit.

'The house I live in is up on that hill,' Hugh was saying. 'Quite a distance from Kingstown. Being high we have some brilliant sunsets.'

'It sounds fantastic,' she murmured.

A brief silence fell. She had not seen him for over five months, but it seemed five years. He asked her pleasantly if there was any news from home, and Avril strangely found nothing to say. As the road unwound and the taxi climbed and the vegetation on either side looked more and more like the beginnings of a jungle, she completely forgot to tell Hugh more about her father's remarriage.

The taxi finally stopped at a modern white house surrounded on all sides by trees, shrubs, flowers and rough grass. Built upon the side of a hill, the house had a curious effect, the roof steeply sloping and the whole place in an odd way appearing to be part of the hill itself. The driver carried Avril's luggage. Hugh did not offer to help, and when he had unlocked the front door he said in a voice reserved for the lower ranks:

'Put the bags over there.'

He paid the driver, who muttered something relaxed and sloped off down the path. Avril hoped Hugh had tipped him well, and doubted it.

Opening the door wide, Hugh said:

'Welcome.'

This was very much somebody else's home, temporarily inhabited by Hugh. There were a large number of rooms on the ground floor, all protected by Venetian blinds against the sun. Cane chairs stood about, with flower-patterned cushions which could have come from Dorset or the Cotswolds. Bottles of Scotch were ranged on a Habitat sideboard. The only gesture to the Caribbean was a silk wall hanging of a tree covered in flowers and fruit and loaded with heavy-looking bright-plumaged birds. There was a very English clock.

'Come and see our room. You'll be impressed with my view,' Hugh said, leading her to the steep stairs.

The first floor on the hill's side was much higher than in an ordinary house. In a pale-coloured bedroom with a large double bed and a floor of wooden planks polished like satin, he pulled up the blinds. And there was the Caribbean in all its emerald and sapphire loveliness, its expanses dotted here and there with dark humps, islands which the naked eye could not make out. A toy ship stayed motionless on the stretch of water. The horizon disappeared. Hugh came and stood behind her, naming various islands. 'Over there is Palm Island. And Union Island which has a devilishly dangerous barrier reef. Over there is Petit St Vincent.'

She sighed.

'How beautiful it all is.'

'You are what I call beautiful.'

He put both hands round her waist and turned her towards him.

There was a split second, it was no more, when she could have refused him, although she had never once said no to Hugh since they had first made love. Aware of his infidelities, bitter against him for refusing her a child, sex with him had still been good – at times much more than that. She pressed against him. They lay down on the huge pale bed with the seas below them washing as far as South America, and they made love with the familiarity of known and expected joy, looking at each other with heavy eyes. When it was over, they lay naked in the cool, air-conditioned afternoon. Hugh went to sleep.

Avril was awake. Listening to cryptic messages.

'See?' said her signals. 'Nothing to worry about, is there?' She thought, marvelling, no, there isn't.

He slept on beside her, the man who had possessed her body just now, looking in his nakedness like the painting of some sleeping warrior. You will be the father of my baby, after all.

She closed her eyes. And sleep, as with the shriven ancient mariner, slid into her soul.

Hugh woke and dressed and Avril, still lying against the pillows, noticed his proprietorial air. He always had that after making love. She had seen the same expression on his face sometimes when talking to other women.

'We don't mind, do we?' said her signals.

When Avril had talked to Isobel Sinclair, the best informed of the naval wives about life in places like St Vincent, Isobel had airily said, 'Social, social.' Once Hugh had sent her a photograph of himself at a dinner party, crowds of people at a table under the chiaroscuro of a bamboo canopy. All were laughing, the table was littered with bottles, glasses, piles of fruit. Part of Avril's indifference to her husband had been that she had lost the curiosity of a lover. What is it like, how do you spend your day, who are your friends, where do you work, eat? The details needed by the hungry heart. But Avril had had no room in her head to imagine Hugh here in St Vincent. When he was away during the first months she'd spent her spare time painting. Recently, it had been Keith. Now in the suddenness of a few hours, here she was.

And the awful secret with which she'd arrived, a terrorist carrying a bomb set to explode, was miraculously defused. A single act of lovemaking and she was safe.

When Hugh had first been sent here, he was told his posting to the island would be short. He had still been delighted with a change of scene. The prospect of another long Dorset autumn and winter had bored him. Hugh's CO explained that the lieutenant-commander in charge of the St Vincent station had twisted his leg slipping down a companionway. He would soon be back on duty. 'A short spell at St Thomas's. He has a brother there.'

But the lieutenant-commander's injury proved worse than had been thought; knees apparently were complicated things, Hugh was informed. He must stay put until the officer was fit again. And that pleased Hugh even more.

The Navy's job was mainly coast-guarding, not only the seas round St Vincent, but the islands of the Grenadines. The coral reefs were very dangerous and skippers needing help knew it was at hand on St Vincent. Working vessels, tankers, cruise ships, yachts, every kind of craft could – often did – get into difficulties. There was also the problem of guarding the ocean areas which were forbidden to fishermen. Fish and coral conservation was strict. And finally there were the sudden and dangerous drug patrols.

Hugh's job also included desk work, which he found tedious. But many of the twenty-four men under him were experienced seamen, and his bullet-headed chief petty officer knew the seas as if, like Venus, he had risen from them.

The island life suited Hugh. Happy, he was also hospitably glad to welcome his wife.

'We'll show you all the sights,' he told her. 'Kingstown, the market – the arcades have one or two passable shops. And the big thrill, our volcano. La Soufrière is terrific. The most energetic volcano in the Caribbean; people call it majestic and they're right. You can never be sure what La Soufrière is up to.'

He told her about his friends, the Lawrence-Scotts, who were longing to meet her, and so were other friends. 'We're quite a group.' But on her first evening even Hugh saw she was tired, not only from travel but from his energetic sex. Cold food had been prepared by his daily help, Florita.

'She's not a bad cook, but I fear she's not serious about the cleaning. My petty officer has had words with her.'

They went to bed early.

The next morning, Avril's first full day on the island, Hugh ordered a taxi.

113

'Hardly anyone has a car on the island. All you can do is drive up one side or the other. And taxis cost next to nothing.' They were invited to a luncheon party with the Lawrence-Scotts. Hugh rang the naval station early to know if there were problems. His chief petty officer said, 'Definitely not, sir.'

'Do you realise?' Hugh said, coming into the bathroom where Avril was enjoying a bath, and sitting on its rim. 'Do you realise, darling, I only have you for four weeks? We must pack in as much as we can. I know you're not much of a party-goer, but you'll like the folk here. And you've had such a rotten time, hanging about waiting for your flight. Miss me?'

He ruffled the damp hair at the nape of her neck.

'Very much.'

Avril noticed how thin he had grown. Was it the heat? It suited him. He was both angular and elegant; the attractive lines down his cheeks were deeper and so were the fans of laughter lines on either side of his eyes. You couldn't deny that Hugh was a beautiful man. A little pompous, but the self-confidence hung about him like scent.

'What are the restaurants like?' Avril asked, stepping from the bath. He wrapped her in an enormous white towel. 'Somebody in our office said Caribbean food is out of this world.'

'Somebody in your office is out of his mind. The food is dire. No restaurants worth speaking about. Three by the harbour are what they call bar restaurants. When you've been here a week you know the menus by heart; they never change. And most of St Vincent food' – he grimaced – 'is boiled! We rarely eat out. Do our entertaining in each other's houses.'

She had a stab of sheer alarm. Did he expect her to *cook*?

'You won't have to lift a finger,' he said, as he annoyingly read her thoughts. 'There's a good hotel opened lately by a mate of Iris Lawrence-Scott's. We can invite the odd bod there for a meal. And we'll give a big cocktail party to return hospitality. OK? And now,' he said, watching as she dressed, and wearing his critical face, 'we're due at the Lawrence-Scotts'.'

The taxi was under some tall palm trees at the gate, the driver the same young man who'd brought them here last night. He was even thinner than Hugh. He gave Avril a terrific smile.

On the journey Hugh talked about Bob and Iris Lawrence-Scott, who apparently figured large in his island life. Bob, ex-Navy, had lived here for years and his wife was the daughter of settlers from a previous generation. Hugh had a way of indicating that they were wealthy. He sold them rather hard. She despised herself for wishing she didn't have to meet them.

Their host came out to hail them before they had time to climb out of the taxi. Bob Lawrence-Scott, big and haggard and sixtyish, with a mop of grey hair and a loud voice, trumpeted his welcome, wringing Avril's hand in his own huge one, which he then placed heavily on her shoulder, moving her up the drive at a rate of knots. For once in her life Avril was ahead and her husband trailed behind.

'Iris!' shouted Bob. 'She's here. Rum punch, rum punch,' he added, as they went into the house.

It was spacious, rather similar to Hugh's, a mixture of English and Caribbean, with woven mats, lampshades in the shape of flowers, huge contemporary paintings and rough-cast walls. And the ubiquitous English chintz. Bob with fatherly concern, 'You *must* be tired after yesterday's flight,' settled Avril in a comfortable chair and placed a long drink in her hand. Hugh wandered out through French windows to a leafy garden, all light and shade, and a moment later returned with a fair woman dressed in white.

'Guest of honour,' said Bob. 'Haven't got a word out of her yet, have I, Mrs Brett?'

'He doesn't give you a chance, does he?' said Iris Lawrence-Scott.

Youthful at a distance, blonde and slender, she was well over forty but with a girlish air. Her fairness helped and so did her freckles and her boy's figure. There were lines under her eyes, which blazed blue. Her manner was jolly hockey sticks.

'Hugh has this plan to dump you on us because he works so hard,' she said gaily. 'Don't you believe him. In the Navy, as I know you know, work means drinks in the mess. But we are looking forward to showing you around, aren't we, Bob? Are you a dead keen sightseer?'

Avril said not usually but the island did look pretty amazing.

'What you mean is that Kingstown looked a mess. I bet you noticed our beaches are grey and not white. Visitors are so disappointed. They're looking for the *Desert Island Discs* stuff. But you won't be able to resist our volcano.'

'Biggest in the Caribbean and not to be trusted,' agreed Bob. Like Hugh, he talked of the volcano with relish.

More people had begun to arrive; the room soon filled up. Avril was greeted and asked the same questions. How was England, the weather, the flight, had she planned to see the volcano yet?

The whole atmosphere was exactly like the naval parties Hugh had taken her to in England – people behaved as if they were related. It was a chatty, noisy, closed society which seemed strangely locked into the past. She heard occasional patches of that Service slang which sounded as if it had come straight from *Bridge Over the River Kwai* or *Ice Cold in Alex*. There was no sign of the jealousies, disappointments and failures which must be here somewhere. Avril listened more than she talked.

Looking round, she noticed a long branch of white orchids in a vase on a nearby table and remembered, with a pang, the pink plastic satchel she had brought from Fuchsia Cottage. She'd had that satchel since she was fifteen. Scrawled on the inside flap were the names of the groups she had idolized then: Queen, the Jam. She used it now for her painting gear. Sketchbooks, paints, pencil cases, a small canvas or two were stuffed into the satchel before she travelled, and unpacked first thing when she arrived. She had brought it this time. But it was under her coat in the bedroom, still unpacked. The desire to paint seemed to have left her. Even orchids shaped like white butterflies.

But if her artistic perceptions were blunt, her eyes were sharp in other ways. She saw that Iris, although facetiously polite, disliked the short, pretty woman she was talking to. Avril guessed her hostess did not much like any woman who happened to be young. I suppose she doesn't like me, thought Avril with mild interest. Iris finally turned away from the small woman and loped over.

'We must make some plans,' she said, 'now I've been deputed to be your island guide. Music? Do you enjoy steel bands? And we'll take you diving.'

'I'm afraid I've never been able to swim underwater.'

'Of course you can! Anyone can snorkel. Hugh!' calling him. 'Here's your wife who says she can't dive. We'll have to teach her, won't we?'

Hugh and Iris began to talk about recent diving expeditions made from a small patrol boat belonging to the Navy. They spoke in the language of banter, casually, easily. As she stood beside them Avril thought their affair was still on. It was something in Iris's manner, a consciousness, a certain air, as if she were in front of the cameras. In Hugh it was unmissable. How well Avril knew his way with the women he was sleeping with. A respectful attention, as if the merest word they spoke was important. 'I am yours,' said his manner. 'I am your slave. I do everything you want. Because *you* do what I want.' Hugh's legendary technique still worked.

Avril put down her rum punch untouched and stood half smiling as they continued to chat and tease. Like a woman trying to recall the birth pangs long after her child is delivered and thriving, she tried almost idly to see if she could recall how she'd suffered over Hugh.

She couldn't remember a thing.

Chapter 7

Bob Lawrence-Scott was a party-giver and goer, an excellent seaman, a generous host; his good spirits appeared unflagging. He simply enjoyed life. He and Iris had two sons, both in the Navy, and a daughter, Dee, married to a handsome, cocky young politician in Washington DC.

Dee talked too much for my taste, Hugh told himself, after flirting and failing with Iris's beautiful daughter. He had been too old for her, something he'd suspected from Dee's manner. He pretended that this could not possibly be true.

The social life in the small community was limited; you relied for company upon your own kind. Some of the group were ex-pats, some had settled here when still young, others like Iris were the daughters, sons or grandchildren of British people who had settled years ago. It was peculiar, thought Avril, that they appeared to have no black friends. When she gingerly asked Hugh why, he said vaguely, 'They don't want to mix with us either. They're fond of their own company, have their own sense of humour, and they're all mad about that music of theirs, of course.'

It hummed and beat from loudspeakers attached to every lamppost in Kingstown.

Avril did find the social life that Isobel had foretold rather tiring. At least twice a day she remembered with relief that it was not going to last for long.

She felt surprisingly well and rather liked the heat. It was always in the mid-eighties, humid and sticky, and it sapped your energy – though not Bob Lawrence-Scott's. Avril more or less floated in it. The heat on her bare shoulders was like a heavy wrap. She found the island gorgeous and satisfying. The flowers whose names she was told and at once forgot were so brilliant. There was a tree on the beach whose sweet-smelling apples were a hectic golden-green; she imagined the fruit of the Hesperides. Hugh told her she must not even touch them; a drop of their milky sap was poisonous.

On a morning heavier than usual and presaging a storm, Hugh asked if she would mind waiting for him at one of the beach bars. They were due to lunch at the new hotel, but he had to go into the naval barracks first for one or two matters to be settled.

Avril was perfectly willing to hang about. She sat down in the bar under its roof of dried palm leaves, and dreamed. The motherly black owner came up.

'St Vincent coffee is very good.'

'I am sure,' said Avril, with polite untruth, 'it is delicious. But I'd really love some fruit juice.'

'Coconut the ticket.'

The woman bustled away to a trestle where coconuts were heaped like cannon balls, picked up a curved knife and split a coconut in half.

The milk was thin, bluish and thirst-quenching. Sipping it, Avril remembered the country fairs in Hampshire. Her father had always won a coconut; he had a straight eye and could knock them right off the shies. But her mother mysteriously refused to allow her or Rick to take the booty home. Avril had never tasted coconut milk until now.

She listened to the sea, and to the monotonous twittering of an emerald-green humming bird which had made its woven nest just out of sight, in a hanging basket attached to a bamboo screen. On the table in front of her the two coconut halves were arranged on fresh palm leaves.

Absently she pushed her hand into the straw shoulder bag Hugh had bought her and found a pencil. The only paper she had was an envelope given her by the bank in Yeovil. It contained her travel money.

She began to draw the hairy edges of the coconuts. She slightly falsified the curves, made the leaves smaller, tipped the coconuts towards the front of the sketch. She drew thickly, her chin on her left hand, absorbed.

'Hello.'

She gave a jump. The voice broke into her concentration as harshly as a shout from the audience to an actor deep in a performance. Myopically, she looked up.

Standing against the sun was the silhouette of a man. She made out broad shoulders, a head crowned with a straw hat pushed back.

'May I?' he said, indicating a seat facing her.

'Oh,' said Avril, mild but not polite. 'There's a lot of room at other tables.'

Indeed there was. She and the stranger were the only two people in the bar. She felt rather sick; it always happened when she was interrupted from drawing or painting.

'Sorry. I know I shouldn't have barged in, but the fact is,' he said, sitting down despite her, 'I've been looking for you. Now I've tracked you down. Friend of Iris and Bob. How do you do?'

He gestured to the bar's owner, who came swaying up in plump magnificence.

'Roseanne, one of your rum punches, please. And some bread. The bread you make is the best on the island.'

Pleased, she left them. The man gazed at Avril for a moment.

'My name's Michael Silver. I've been staying on St Lucia, just got here this morning. I'm what the Americans call a house guest with the Lawrence-Scotts. Iris told me about you. She always knows everything; you don't need to buy the local rag if you're around with Iris. She said your husband told her he was taking you shopping and then out to lunch. And that a hundred to one he'd have left you at the Oleander bar. I've come to ask if you'd like to ascend La Soufrière with me tomorrow. Would you? It'd be nice to have company.'

Avril, more politely, said she would very much like the expedition. Her husband had mentioned he'd already done the trip and enjoyed it.

'Three or four times is my guess,' said Michael Silver. 'My own score is twice; I somehow feel a third visit is expected of me. I'm so glad you'll come with me. Am I forgiven for breaking in on you so rudely? You were drawing.'

Her instinct was to stuff the envelope out of sight, but he stretched out his hand pleasantly enough and she couldn't scuffle it away. As she unwillingly passed him the envelope, well over a hundred pounds in dollar travellers' cheques fresh from the bank spilled over the table, exactly like a pack of cards. He did not exclaim or laugh, but rearranged the notes together tidily, replaced them in the envelope, said, 'May I?' and turned the envelope over. He studied the pencil sketch.

Saying, 'Mm,' he gave it back. She did not know whether to be pleased or offended.

Michael Silver was burly and bear-like, wearing a creased white tropical jacket, his straw hat tipped on the back of his large, well-shaped head. His face was heavy, with a fleshy nose and a chin with a deep dimple in its centre. His skin, more olive than her own, was slightly greasy. He looked as if he had never been burned by the sun in his life. The most remarkable feature of his face was the shape of his eyes, narrow, slightly slanting and very dark.

He was friendly. Not boyish and cheery like Keith, or deliberately charming like Hugh.

'I'm up to date with your biog, Mrs Brett,' he remarked, after Roseanne had swished over, squeezing between closely packed empty tables, with his drink and a plate of fresh bread. 'I've heard all about you.'

'I truly never know the answer to that.'

'I agree. It's a stupid thing to say, and I don't know why I did. What I meant was that Iris told me your husband is the naval CO at present, and is here for a time because Donald Matheson, poor chap, had that accident. I met Donald, nice fellow. Iris added that you're here on a visit and, good old Iris, said maybe I could persuade you to come with me and wade up through the lava beds.'

He drank his rum punch and crumbled a thick slice of bread.

'I'm a sort of relative of Iris's. Third or fourth cousin. No one knows how to work that out nowadays. I came to St Vincent because Iris asked me to stay. Work in London has been rather rough and I wanted to see a guy, a photographer I know, in St Lucia. The idea of also seeing Bob and Iris with their island thrown in was irresistible.'

He talked a little about the Lawrence-Scotts and their famous hospitality. Iris, thought Avril, was the sort of woman everybody called Quite a Girl. Isobel Sinclair was the same. It meant being good at organising, being strong, self-willed, keeping things, including your marriage, on an even keel. Just like me, I don't think.

Michael Silver said:

'She didn't happen to tell me you're an artist.'

Then he saw a rare sight in the modern world, a woman blushing. Her cheeks burned as she said shortly that she wasn't.

He looked rather entertained.

'Stepping on toes is my speciality. I do it sometimes at work and very popular it makes me. There isn't a thing anyone can do, you know, if like me you're born tactless. I'm sorry if you don't want to talk about being an artist. No, don't say "I'm not" again. I won't mention it any more, I promise. We're talking about my lack of tact,' he went on. 'Somebody should take me in hand.'

She bit back a cool 'What about Iris?'

'First I march up and land myself on you. Then I say something you obviously dislike,' he added with a faint smile, not at all apologetic.

Avril picked up a half of coconut and drank a little. Put it down again on the palm leaf and picked up, instead, the envelope bulging with unspent money. She examined the drawing.

'The leaves are not quite right,' she said.

'I like them.'

124

'The proportion is wrong, they should be smaller.'

Avril never talked to anybody about her work, and the fact that the leaves in reality spread halfway across the table and were far larger than the coconuts did not seem to come up.

He took the envelope, again with a 'May I?' and studied it in his turn.

'Going to paint it when you get home?'

'No.'

'You'll want to.'

'Sure. But.'

'I see,' he oddly said.

A pause.

'I like the roughness. The shapes are right too.'

'No good without colour. Not for me anyway.'

'Isn't that so with most of you lot?'

'Not if you go in for engraving. Etching. Glass. Crayon. Work like that.'

'I suppose the snag,' he said, carefully returning the envelope again, 'is that what you really need is to take the coconut and the palm leaves home. Then you could get on. Shall I ask Roseanne? She'd be only too pleased.'

'No, no. Thank you, but no.'

'Surely you need them if you're going to paint a still life?'

'I don't paint, I really don't,' she said almost desperately, and just then Hugh's voice called:

'Avril? Ah, there you are.'

He was edging his way through the empty tables. Avril's companion stood up.

'Commander Brett, I'm sure. Michael Silver, friend of Iris and Bob.'

125

The two men shook hands and exchanged banalities with Iris as the password. Avril collected her things together. Did she imagine that Michael Silver, glancing at her, muttered under his breath:

'It's OK.'

She said goodbye and was guided by her husband towards the main street and the shops.

Since her arrival nearly a week ago Hugh had taken her shopping almost every day. He liked her, he said in his dated way, to be 'dolled up'. Hugh was not generous with money. In Dorset he often questioned the housekeeping bills, and when she mentioned birthday presents for her family or his aunts, he groaned. She often paid for them herself – he never noticed. But on the matter of her clothes he was lavish. Another kind of woman would not have believed her luck, married to a man interested in her clothes, recognising style from yards away, choosing the most expensive as well as the prettiest things and paying big bills without the flicker of an eyelash. If Avril hesitated between this outfit or that, he invariably said, 'We will have both.'

But St Vincent was not the avenue Montaigne. When Iris heard they were going shopping again, she mentioned Singapore.

'Hugh, you would simply love it! Orgies of shopping. Mall after mall. Italian, French, all the big names – most of them fakes but totally splendid. Poor old St V does its best, but it's mostly swimsuits and sandals.' Iris's own style was good. 'Old things, most of them from Singapore,' she said, but whatever she wore she looked wonderful. Avril was impressed and knew that, next to her hostess, she managed to look more mouselike than usual.

That riled Hugh. He found little in the shops for Avril that pleased him, and all *she* did was tag along. This morning she was thinking about Michael Silver. Had he actually muttered, 'It's OK,' and if so, what had he meant?

Hugh finally settled on a plain white dress of thin cotton, hand-embroidered with butterflies. It was a miraculous fit, and when she peeled it off and the young black girl, all smiles, took it away to pack it, Avril had the astonished thought that it was not going to fit for long.

'You'll be able to wear it at your party,' Hugh said as they left the arcade.

'What party?'

'God, Avril, you look like a scared rabbit. They will give a goodbye party for you when you leave, everybody has one. It's an island tradition. Lucky that you aren't some official on the island; they get given enormous open-air parties and a goat is killed to celebrate. You're lucky, you'll be given salads and champagne. You must save this,' lifting the smart carrier bag, 'to knock them in the eye on your last appearance.'

They walked along in the heavy noontide, skirting the market noisy with shouts and the loud reggae music.

'That man you were having a drink with. Did he say something about taking you up La Soufrière?'

'Yes. Iris asked him to.'

'Good, good. I don't think I could do the day trip again just yet,' he said. 'Iris is a great one for delegating. She told me Silver is some kind of banker.'

'He doesn't look like one.'

Hugh was in scoffing mood. Did she imagine you could tell a person's job by their appearance? Apart from the obvious one of uniform, naturally.

'I suppose you think a man can't be a banker if he is not in an Armani suit.'

'I didn't mean clothes, Hugh. Clothes don't matter.'

Immediately conscious of the expensive carrier and the huge price he'd paid for the featherlight dress, she blushed crimson for the second time that morning.

'Sorry. Sorry, I didn't mean that.'

If her sharp reply surprised him, her apology did more. He looked at her with an unfamiliar moment of curiosity. His wife was slightly, very slightly changed. The mild, co-operative young woman, the wife who suited him, except for her pathetic lack of clothes sense, rarely contradicted him. He did not bully her or lay down the law. He didn't have to. Avril was adaptable and reasonable. She saw your point of view and changed her own. There was something amorphous about her. Other women today were aware of a growing power and threw their weight about. At dinner parties, except of course among Service people, women actually dominated. Many women in civilian life had pretty high-up jobs and wanted you to know it; they spoke with an authority that older women were astonished to hear. Hugh never looked at beautiful women except with the eye of the predator, and he found the young Valkyries, the Spartan warriors with naked legs against which their sharp swords swung, a challenge. Paying lip service to women's power, he had no such trouble with his wife. He had always believed in the principle, 'Start as you mean to go on'. Twice in their marriage Avril had made a bid to do – to have – something he did not approve of. He'd laughed her out of any serious belief that she could paint. A messy and time-consuming hobby which irritated him. He knew perfectly well she'd turn into a closet painter. That was fine. That was not out of order. Though the dazed look she wore when he came home from work sometimes was tiresome.

More important had been the matter of not having a child. She had, of course, capitulated there as well. But he had needed to be blunt. She had taken his decision badly and there had been scenes. He considered he had behaved in an exemplary fashion. Fair but firm. She'd accepted his decision eventually. Peace had returned.

In his way he loved his wife. He liked to give her treats, to hear her laugh; he enjoyed their sex together and he needed her admiration. But it was other women, pursued and conquered, who gave flavour and the sexual *frisson* of the unknown to his inner life. Sated with them, he was unaware that his wife's love had grown thin. Like very old and worn fabric when you held it up to the light, its fragility showed. There were places where it had begun to tear.

The new, more definite manner which Avril used now and then since her arrival struck Hugh as odd. He put it down to their separation. He must not let things get out of hand.

Very early next morning – the expedition was to take all day – Avril was delivered in a taxi to the Lawrence-Scotts'. She walked up the paved path, admiring the trees whose orange flowers like furled flags peered between gigantic shiny leaves.

Iris came out, wearing a straw hat with long blue ribbons.

'Hi! Feeling strong and hearty?'

'Oh, sure.'

'What did Hugh buy you yesterday?'

'He said I'm to keep it as a surprise until the end of my holiday,' said Avril, smiling.

'Sounds as if he picked a winner,' said Iris, not bothering to pretend she thought Avril chose her own clothes.

She took Avril into the great spacious sitting room. The Venetian blinds were down; the room was tiger-striped with the first strong sun of the morning, and full of heavily scented flowers. Iris had flowers everywhere.

Stretched out in what was still called a planter's chair was the bulky figure of Michael Silver. He stood up, with a pleasant smile.

'Michael has been put in charge of you for today,' said Iris. 'It's his job to take you up the volcano to enjoy the excitement, and bring you safely down again. I do hope you don't mind that it isn't me? I'm afraid I've done the climb four times, and I'm beginning to think that's my lot. Michael says it'll be fun to take somebody who's never been up La Soufrière before. While you're with him, Avril, get him to tell you the horror stories. About the eruption in 1979. *And* what happened in 1902.'

'Don't scare the girl out of her wits,' said Michael.

'Why not? That's the whole point of the volcano. Do you know, Avril, ash from the crater turned everywhere *pitch dark* right as far as Barbados!' Iris gestured dramatically. 'Isn't that amazing? Anyway, while you're both toiling up, I shall be doing the garden. I've got a new boy who is very keen, and we're going to plant a tree.'

Michael and Avril left the house. Iris had lent them the Lawrence-Scotts' Land Rover for the day – Bob was away. She stood on the veranda, putting up both thumbs.

'That means she'd rather it was us than her,' said Michael, leaning out to wave.

They drove away into lush green country along a dirt road. Coconut groves were thick on either side of them; the trees glistened.

'I've never even seen a volcano at a distance until I came here,' Avril said.

'Not in Italy?'

'Hugh and I haven't been there. France a bit. No volcanos in Portsmouth or Bridport.'

He glanced at her sideways.

'Interested in volcanos, then?'

'Respectful.'

She meant more than that. The enormous volcano which they were driving towards, over four thousand feet high, was too alive for her taste. She knew nobody visited St Vincent without being expected to climb its famous slopes, paying homage to the dangerous mountain. Hugh had done the ascent in his first week and had told Avril how much he enjoyed it. 'Great stuff, great stuff.' He'd added that Avril must climb La Soufrière, but hadn't offered to accompany her. All he had said was that she would find it exciting and she'd better borrow his rain coat.

'Thick fog around the crater.'

Michael Silver continued to talk about the volcano as they drove between the beautiful groves of grey-trunked trees. La Soufrière, he said, had roared and exploded during every century. Destruction in the past had been impressive. But during the last eruption thousands of the islanders had been safely evacuated. 'Not a single person even grazed their elbow.' The volcano hadn't shown any recent signs of wanting to give a repeat performance.

Not just yet.

The air was filled with unfamiliar odours, sweet and

sickly like the combined scents in a perfume shop. They lay everywhere like an eiderdown. She was enjoying the adventure as she sat back in her seat watching the branches and leaves. Then the road ahead simply petered out.

Michael drew the car to a halt.

They were facing the stony bed of a great river. On either side was rain forest, high, thick, inextricable masses of bamboo, of creepers, of thin fallen trunks covered with matted grasses, of climbing trumpet-like white flowers blooming and dying. And all round them, save for the river bed like a road to eternity, the impenetrable green.

He sat in silence, looking at the river bed. Avril began to feel frightened.

He said suddenly:

'Are you quite sure those shoes are up to this? I see you're wearing trainers. But the soles look pretty thin to me.'

He was gazing at her feet.

'The lava bed is like a glacier. And the boulders, damn great excrescences the volcano pitched out centuries ago, are so sharp they can cut rubber soles into ribbons. Mind if I take a look?'

He climbed from the car, came round to her side and put out his hand for one of Avril's feet, like a man about to give her a pedicure. She stretched out her leg with the solemnity of a child.

He studied the sole of her shoe. He returned her foot to her.

'Mind if I call you Avril?'

'Of course not.'

'Fine. Well, Avril, those shoes of yours, if you will excuse me saying so, are fairly useless. Didn't Commander Brett'

– Hugh, it seemed, still retained formality – 'break the news to you that we have a trek of six miles ahead of us to the summit, and every yard is rough and tough?'

Avril had a kind of knife-wound of alarm. She cursed herself for being a fool. Hugh liked expeditions like this. He enjoyed physical challenges, measuring himself against nature. He was a reckless rider. By the sea she'd known him swim out dangerously far. If he had served in a war he would have been wounded and covered with medals. He prided himself on twenty-five-mile walks, on sailing in the worst weather. If you could say such a thing, his courage was his vanity. When she had first been in love with him she had seen him as intrepid, and literally longed to walk as far and climb as high so that she would earn his admiration. Whenever she tried any kind of physical trial she always hated it.

But when the infidelity began, she simply stopped her trials of strength and stayed at home. His scoffing at her lack of courage never lasted, whereas a long walk or an exhausting climb might continue a whole day. Later she found a way to avoid the jeers. Compliments. You are stronger, fitter, bigger, braver – and so he was. He could scarcely despise her feebleness when she set it outrageously against his power.

Now she wondered if Hugh had sent her on this expedition as a test, comparing her perhaps with Iris, so that he could be proud of her.

The radio signals had begun. There was no time to consider such questions.

'Michael,' she said, taking a breath.

'Why are you looking at me,' he said, 'in that charming way?'

'I was hoping you wouldn't think me a wimp. Yes, do think me one because I am. The fact is, I couldn't possibly climb six miles up – up there.'

She was staring at the stony road to eternity.

'I'm so sorry. But it does sound steep,' she lamely finished.

He roared with laughter. She would have been offended if she had not clearly heard that the laugh was not unkind. He stood beside the car against the extraordinary background of things writhing and growing, with the strong scent of vegetation sweet and rotten and the buzz of flies, and laughed.

'You don't even like climbing, do you? Yes, the six miles ahead are a real pull. Pretty hellish, and the last mile is the worst. If you do make it to the crater – lots don't, although of course Iris did – the gradient is precipitous, nothing but loose sliding pumice and slippery boulders. There's a wind so strong you can't stand upright, you have to crawl on all fours. And if you want to be really tough and look into the crater, it's not unlike seeing hell.'

He looked at her.

'Sounds bloody awful, doesn't it?'

'It does, rather.'

He climbed back into the car beside her.

'Why did they talk you into it?'

'I don't know.'

'I don't either. But I can guess why you agreed to come. Ignorance and pride shaken not stirred.'

He, too, had fixed his eyes on the dry river bed which stretched away ahead of them as rough and uneven as virtue, vanishing into a greenish fog.

'The trouble with dear Iris,' he said, 'is that the girl has no imagination. When she told me yesterday that your husband was keen for you to spend a day going up La Soufrière and would I like to take you, I did say twice that I wasn't sure she'd got that quite right.'

'Why did you ask her that?'

'Guess,' he said humorously. 'I was correct, wasn't I? Now we're here you hate the idea.'

'I'm sorry. I'm so sorry.'

'Don't be daft,' he said. 'Why in hell should anybody do something like this – or other things like diving from the highest boards, surfing in rough seas, that sort of stuff – unless he or she actually *wants* to? And if the guy or girl pulls it off, you don't think that makes them any more admirable, do you?'

'People worship physical courage.'

'Don't sound so doleful. Anyway, you are not being quite honest, Avril. You don't admire physical courage as much as all that.'

'I envy it.'

'Ah, that's different. Most of us, contrary beasts, envy the thing that we haven't got. The trait that is foreign to our nature. Now I think I'm going to take you for a long drive, another kind of sightseeing; we've got the whole day to decide on our story.'

He turned the car away from the symbolic mountain.

He drove westward into a lush fertile land of plantations, banana groves, coconut groves. At one point the road skirted a forest and on either side were gigantic ferns as large as trees, the sun shining through them in long spears.

'What a wonderful place.'

'The earthly paradise.'

He stopped the car by a shallow river which was

sparkling and pouring and rushing over white rocks. Three girls were washing their clothes. They slapped them on the rocks in whipping movements, shouting at each other over the steady sound of the water, and now and again almost collapsing with laughter. They were knee-deep and the river swirled round their shining, ebony-coloured legs.

'And there are the inhabitants,' Michael said.

He climbed out and stretched a hand for Avril. They wandered across to the river and sat down on a large flat boulder at a distance from the trio of girls. How they laugh, thought Avril. I used to laugh exactly like that. I remember real stomach-ache with laughter at school and having to stuff a handkerchief in my mouth. And at home with Rick. He made me quite helpless. My legs gave.

Michael Silver leaned back on his hands.

'So. What are we going to tell 'em? Iris is a nosy parker. She told me once she had it on her school report: "Iris is something of a nosy parker". Thought of a good story for us?'

'We could try the truth.'

'Now that really is a terrible idea. They would all think it a simple case of you losing your nerve, exactly like what happens when one is riding. Get up on the horse's back immediately and start again. Up La Soufrière you must go, Mrs Brett, and smartish.'

It was what Hugh would say. Yet this man did not know Hugh or herself. Are we as transparent as all that? she thought.

'The truth is powerful stuff; it should be doled out in small measures. It's a sort of moral plutonium, ought to have a government health warning. 'Telling the truth is bad for your health.' I've got a suggestion. We could tell them

136

the track up the volcano is temporarily closed.'

He looked at her with satisfaction.

'Good, isn't it? And perfectly possible; it happens quite a bit. There's been a rock fall which has blocked our way to the summit. We started our climb, and lo and behold, to our intense disappointment, the path was completely blocked. What do you think?'

'That you're brilliant.'

'I can't deny it. By the time any of Iris's friends sets off for yet another climb, doubtless it will be all cleared away, won't it? In any case, Avril, climbing La Soufrière is definitely the sport of visitors, not local inhabitants. So. Since we are not expected for hours I'll take you to lunch on the other side of the island. Then I think you might like to see some flowers. Frangipanis? How about the triple hibiscus?'

The hours she spent with Michael Silver gave Avril her real impression of the island. This little place had been a British colony for over two hundred years and independent for less than twenty. Michael Silver knew St Vincent well – apart from Iris and Bob Lawrence-Scott, he had other distant family connections. His grandparents had once lived here, he said. The island people were the proudest his grandfather had ever met.

'The Indian name for St Vincent is Youroumei, meaning human. That's them. Sweet-natured and loving music. But poor.'

In the past, he said, the Grenadine islands were rich, the trade was sugar. But because of the history of slaves, brought over to work in the sugar plantations and factories, nobody would touch that trade now. There were ruins of eighteenth-century sugar-making factories rotting away in the rain forests. The only trades now were fishing, coconuts, bananas, breadfruit . . .

'And what with volcanos, hurricanes, and the odd tropical storm, all those can be ruined in a few nights,' he said. 'Not such an earthly paradise after all.'

She liked the man who drove her down the green roads and through the green forests. And she was grateful indeed, thinking over what she had escaped. Pregnant as she was, how could she have attempted to do such a climb, risking accident or exhaustion? Suppose by bad luck Iris or Hugh himself had come with her. She would have been teased and persuaded, talked at and bullied.

'Come on, Avril, you'll be glad when we get to the top.'

'Look, let's start. It isn't half as difficult as people say.'

Thanks to Michael Silver she had escaped not only the mountain but Hugh.

They lunched right on the other side of the island – 'safely out of Iris's range,' said Michael – in a small, open-air kind of café not unlike Roseanne's. They had chicken, rice and avocado which had been picked that morning and tasted exquisite. During the afternoon that lazily followed, Michael drove her around to show her fascinating things, such as the sealing-wax tree. It was a species of palm in which red sap poured down the trunk, making it seem as if the poor tree was bleeding. She saw the starry white flowers of the clove, and the tangled, twiggy cannonball tree. Legend said the flowers opened with the noise of a gun exploding.

'All nonsense, isn't it a pity?'

He drove her up steep, steep roads, two thousand feet up, overlooking emerald valleys, nutmeg groves and in the distance the sapphire and green sea set about with islands.

They rose in humps and bumps like the dark shapes of whales.

'The skies are good,' he said as they sat on downland grass overlooking the enormous panorama. 'Something happening all the time. Look over there, that high white stuff. Then it's black as ink. We may get rain.'

'Heavy, I suppose?'

'Oh yes. Raindrops as big as fifty-pence pieces,' he said, laughing.

'You really like it here, don't you? Have you ever thought of making it your home?'

'I'd never live here, Avril. Not in a million years. I don't think I could stay in St V for more than a month, preferably less. Otherwise I'd catch the disease Iris calls "islanditis". Same people, same jokes, same food. The old Brit colonies must have suffered from it a lot. I always try to get a flight before the start of an attack. Now I come to think about it, *you* must do the same.'

'Maybe I shouldn't catch it,' she said, her eyes fixed on the sea, 'if I stayed.'

'Then stay,' he said merely.

'The Navy paid for me to stay a month. A sort of grace-and-favour gesture they make sometimes to naval wives with their husbands abroad,' she said. 'Didn't Iris tell you?'

He was too kind to say that Iris hadn't spoken of her at all except to persuade him to go on this expedition, referring to her as 'Hugh's tongue-tied little wife'.

'We don't know much about each other, do we?' he said, as if in a slight challenge.

'I'd like to know more about you,' replied Avril with what he considered a disarming simplicity. 'There is nothing to know about me. Naval wife full stop.'

'Children?' he asked, and she felt a certain particular interest in him. 'Surely not. Women can't help talking about their kids. And you haven't uttered.'

'No. No children.'

She said it so peacefully and gave him so candid a smile that it was as if she'd said, 'And that is how we like it.' She then asked him about his work, the old, old technique she used on Hugh, on Rick, and upon which she naively relied. This time she did not get far. Oh, he said, he worked in the City, and that wasn't too riveting or even comprehensible unless you were in it. It was a gambler's world.

'Where do you live, Michael?'

'In a flat which used to be a warehouse beyond Tower Bridge. Great views of the river, and handy. I can walk to work.'

There was for an instance a silence that, with Michael looking at her quizzically, made her suddenly come out with:

'You used to be married.'

It was not a question. A man in his late thirties, as she judged him, was never single nowadays, unless he was gay. Another judgement made her think that he was not that.

'Yes. A few years ago. It seems an age. I used to have a son, Toby. He was quite little when we married; my wife already had him and separated from his father. While she and I were together, he did become mine in a way.'

She met his eyes and saw that they were graver than his voice.

'When we parted she went to the States, and of course Toby went too. Don't be afraid I'm going to treat you to confidences of the kind men go into when they get drunk at parties. It's all history now, and besides, I'm not the interesting one. I'd like to talk about you.'

'Please not.'

'Don't fend me off again, Avril. It's only one question. I know you're a naval wife and you and your husband live in the West Country. I'd just like to know about your drawing.'

She said nothing for a moment. Then:

'I'd really rather not talk about it. In any case, I'm no good.'

She looked at him with an appeal he could scarcely refuse.

'If that's how you feel. Sorry.'

The panorama which stretched round them had in it all the colours of deep enamels used in the setting of ancient jewels, or in the background of medieval paintings of the Très Riches Heures. The clouds changed, melted, rose, clustered and flattened. The air grew heavier.

'I'm afraid you intrigue me, Avril,' he said, looking not at the skies but at his own large feet in battered walking boots. 'Mysteries do. You warn me off. I am not allowed to say that you are a painter. Just now I accepted your caveat but I think I shall change my mind. That envelope the other morning bulging with cash . . .'

She did smile at that.

'I've always liked painters,' he continued. 'I've known a few. They get hold of things. Don't be afraid I questioned the Lawrence-Scotts about you, or anybody else for that matter. I go on my hunches. The coconut halves the other morning. And the way you looked at the sealing-wax tree.'

He met her enquiring face with a plain:

'You wanted to paint that all right, didn't you?'

141

'Do you always grill people when they try to escape you?' she asked with commendable good humour. 'Here's my answer. Please.'

Whatever he saw in the thin, flushed face worked.

When the day was ending they drove home; the late afternoon had grown dark from the gathering clouds and by the time they arrived at Hugh's house, Michael had to put on the headlights. There were lights shining in the house through the trees.

'Come in and have a drink. I'm sure Hugh's back—'

'Thanks, but no. Iris will be expecting me.' They sat for a moment in the car. 'There's just one thing I want to say while I've got the chance – I don't expect I'll have you to myself again.'

He had switched off the engine, and in what should have been the quiet, dark evening, they heard the pitiless sound of Jamaican reggae beating away in the distance.

'I'd like to see you again, Avril. But I'm not going to do anything about it when we are both back in England. I have this rule. Since my divorce, actually. If a lady is uninvolved I ring her. If she is married or partnered, then she has to call me. Do you think that's fair?'

'Very.'

'I have liked today,' he added. One large hand covered hers for no more than a moment.

He drove away, and Avril went up the path between the flowering shrubs. A great drop of rain, a fifty-pence piece, fell on her head.

The house was empty when she let herself in. Florita must have left the lights on deliberately; they shone down the vertiginous stair to the front hall. She shut the door and the beating music faded a little. No sign of Hugh; she was sure he was at the Lawrence-Scotts'. Or with Iris some-where?

As she went upstairs in the silent house, she heard the first heavy rain. In the bedroom Florita had folded back the bright Caribbean cover, and the bed, cool, inviting, could not be resisted. Listening to the now thunderous rain, she lay down.

She thought about Michael Silver and recalled the tone of his voice when he said 'I've liked today.' It seemed to reach her heart somehow. That was the way a man spoke to you when he thought you attractive. Despite the sweet knowl-edge of pregnancy, she had felt the same about him. Has poor Keith started me on the primrose path? she thought. Does one affair since I married mean it is going to turn into a habit? And then she remembered – how could she forget for five minutes? – the child-to-come.

Somebody once told her that having a baby was another kind of love affair. That settled it.

Chapter 8

In the few weeks allowed to Avril on St Vincent, the long afternoon of the failed expedition to the volcano was the single time when she was not in crowded company.

The twenty or so friends, mostly English, with a scattering of French and a few Americans who worked for the Peace Corps, were in the habit of seeing each other all the time. It appeared to Avril that this seemed to be their only way to bear the earthly paradise. As Hugh had told her, they never dined in the bar restaurants where, Iris said, 'The menus are written on stone.' There were drinks parties, barbecues, yachting expeditions, and the diving which Avril, firm this time, avoided. The group also visited a newly opened hotel owned by two close friends of the Lawrence-Scotts.

Iris, possibly from conscience, having not done much looking after the visitor, took Avril round Kingstown, where they met friends at the Cobblestone Inn, a gathering place for Vincentians with a strong colonial atmosphere and a garden of feathery palms.

Life was exactly that of the naval stations in the past,

when officers and their wives, the men and *their* wives, formed a close-locked community which turned inwards for company. It was as if the far-off world where they had landed up, where foreign faces and lilting foreign voices filled the unfamiliar days, where the people worshipped strange gods and the very scents were troubling, made a kind of composite enemy. Admiring their island, enjoying its beauties, they remained barricaded.

Everybody, including Hugh, accepted without question Michael's story about the road to La Soufrière being closed by a rockfall.

'Of all the bad luck!' they cried when hearing of Avril's failure to reach apotheosis. To make up for her loss they described their own adventures, how they crawled, every man jack of them, on their stomachs, throats choked with pumice dust. They described their terror when at the crater's rim they discovered that it curved inwards. They lived again the emotion of seeing down into the volcano's heart where Dante's Inferno existed, bubbling 'like a soup in Hades,' said Bob Lawrence-Scott, describing the heaving lava. They told her about the 1972 eruption when a mysterious island appeared in the middle of the crater lake . . . Legend said the inside of the volcano was bottomless.

'The first time I took Iris up La Soufrière,' said Bob at drinks one evening, 'she hadn't grasped the fact of the inward curve. She's so keen to do things and she looked right over the crater's edge. By God, for a moment I thought I'd lost her.'

'He *was* disappointed,' said Iris, 'when I popped up again.'

Avril had adapted to the total idleness of her island life. Florita's cooking, highly seasoned and peppery, did not upset her stomach, and in any case she and Hugh almost never ate at home. St Vincent food was certainly not varied, but Avril enjoyed the papayas, the pineapples, and became accustomed to the pretty inescapable chilli pepper sauce. It was curious that nothing was fried and everything boiled, even the breadfruit.

The heat suited her still; she liked to drift and move slowly. Never lazy, she became so. Apart from the moment, so accurately diagnosed by Michael Silver, when she had looked at the sealing-wax tree, she did not want to paint. Not the ferns bowing down after the rain, not the golden-green apples of the machineel tree so poisonous that when after the rain she'd stood beneath the branches, Hugh had dragged her to safety.

The music was too loud and ever present, but Avril did not resent it. She wished she knew some of the people: all she got when she talked to Florita were broad smiles and agreements.

'Oh yes,' said Florita, clearly not listening, and after a while – how could you be friends with someone so uninterested? – Avril gave up. Hugh took her for drinks on one or another of the rich yachts lying at anchor in the harbour. She was treated with hearty bonhomie and hospitality; nobody called her by her name. She was known as Hugh's wife.

'Where's Hugh's wife?' was a familiar question at pre-lunch or pre-barbecues, at expeditions to other islands where the friends sat around under thatched shelters on the never-ending beaches. Avril discovered she was quite popular. She supposed it was her novelty. Or more likely she was the satellite who shone by the light of Hugh's success. It was the same old story. With men as well as women he almost never had a failure.

As far as his sexual forays were concerned, the only woman Avril was sure about was Iris. Was the affair still on? Was she 'poor girl, Hugh's wife I mean. Rotten for her, really'? It was impossible to know.

Hugh's way of treating Avril could not be faulted. The irritability and occasional downright rudeness of Dorset was gone. He spoiled her, bought her presents, talked to her affectionately, and most of all, he made love – night after hot night he took her in his arms. Avril quite enjoyed his sex, now so familiar, but she hadn't a trace of emotion or bliss as she lay with him in the hot, humid night. Yet without at first being aware of it, that back-flip, that somersault where she threw herself backwards to land effortlessly with the acrobat's skill, made her begin to believe a wonderful thing. The child in her womb was actually Hugh's. The idea, like the baby, grew inside her. Pregnancy did unexpected things to the imagination. When she had painted some object and found it a failure, it could be painted out, made to vanish under thick white brush-strokes. She had done this with poor Keith. In the painting of her present life, he had been replaced by her heroic and flawed husband. It was comfortable, it was glorious, to think Hugh was father to the baby treasured inside her. And an inexpressible relief to realise she need not tell him so until she was safely thousands of miles away back in England.

Michael Silver was still around, staying with his cousin, but he and Avril rarely spoke two words together. He was Iris's equerry; she appeared to enjoy the big, relaxed man beside her; or possibly it was to tease her husband or Hugh or both. Hugh did not seem to like Silver much. He was cool with him, and Avril had the impression that he laughed against his will when Michael made a good joke.

Avril watched the small dramas with indifference. Hugh's affair, her own lack of social aplomb – she knew very well that in company she was dull – her loss of the desire to paint, nothing bothered her. In their place had come a lazy good nature and a sometimes radiant smile. Dull she might be, but people liked her.

It was on a second boat trip to one of the islands, Petit St Vincent, the most southern of the Grenadines and a private resort, that Michael wandered across the deck to where Avril was lying under a canopy in the shade. The yacht had tied up in a small protected harbour, well inside the coral reef. Most of the party, including Hugh, Iris, Bob and the Americans, were diving from an open boat. Avril had refused to join them, and Hugh, in his proprietorial after-sex mood, chaffingly told the company that his wife never wanted to swim underwater since she had seen an old video of *Jaws*.

As she moved one foot out of the sunshine, Michael lounged over. He sat on the deck beside her.

He wore brief trunks, and his body, fattish and powerful, was glistening wet. So was his hair, which was plastered back to show the well-shaped skull above his slanting eyes.

'Did I tell you? I'm off tonight.'

Avril sat up rather suddenly.

'Nobody said.'

'They don't know. I got a fax this morning from a woman at work. Can't do without me apparently. Well, that's not fair, she does very well, but she says something's coming up and I ought to be around. She's right, it's time I went back. I've had one or two symptoms of islanditis already.'

He looked down, smiling.

'The last time I examined your feet, Avril,' he said, brushing one foot with his finger, 'I was measuring the thickness of your soles. Picture me tomorrow in the square mile.'

'Hugh said you're a banker. I never exactly know what that means. You said that afternoon that it's a kind of gambling.'

'So it is. Money instead of chips. Ever played roulette?'

'At home. My parents enjoyed it. I quite did, but my brother was the brilliant one. He took huge risks. I never won and I never lost.'

He gave his slow smile again.

'Your brother sounds as if he ought to be with us. You, I'm afraid, would be a flop in my business.'

A pause.

'Well?'

She had shaded her eyes; he was against the light, and she repeated with his own intonation:

'Well?'

He translated.

'Well, Avril, have you done any more drawing?'

'Oh no.'

'Not the sealing-wax tree?'

'I haven't seen another since we were in those gardens.'

'Excuses, excuses.'

He looked down.

'I like your feet. They are like a little girl's. I'm glad I stopped them being cut to bits. Coming!' he called out as Iris, her blonde head streaming with water, appeared over the side of the deck. 'Don't forget that rule of mine, will you?'

Avril waited a moment, just to see if he would hurry off to Iris. He did not.

'I don't somehow think I shall be ringing you, I'm afraid.'

'Ah. But you remembered.'

Avril was given a farewell party at the Lawrence-Scotts' although, as Iris told her, 'We are sparing you the boiled goat.' Everybody, which meant the usual twenty or so, had been asked, and Iris hired a steel band. For once the music, instead of coming falsified by cheap microphones from the tops of lampposts, filled the big airy house with twangs and tinglings and voices as sweet and lovely as Nat King Cole's.

The party went on until very late, and when Avril thought about it afterwards, she could scarcely sort out who she had danced with and which of the three Americans, all tall, rangy and sexy-looking, had made a pass at her. And when exactly had Hugh swept her out of the drawing room, said goodbye to a somewhat drunken Bob Lawrence-Scott – who had kissed Avril and hugged her breathless – and driven her home?

Goodbyes meant lovemaking, and tonight, with the thought that it was the last time for how long, Hugh was at his most passionate. Afterwards he fell deeply asleep, snoring rather.

The next morning the rain came back, heavier than ever; the house, the day outside was dark. Avril said goodbye to Florita, who looked as if her going were a special kind of joke. When Avril gave her too large a tip, Florita laughed more.

Hugh was proprietorial again. He guided her at the airport to the check-in desk as if she were incapable of finding her way. Harking back to some old tradition from his aunts' days, he bought her an armful of magazines and a box of chocolates. It gave her a funny little pain, almost of love. He then insisted that she should recheck her tickets.

'Have you really looked at them, Avril? Now let me.'

When they walked to the barrier, he turned round and took her in his arms. He gave her a hard kiss.

'God bless.'

'You too.'

She heartily returned the embrace.

'Take care, darling.'

Avril said to herself, So I will, I am carrying your child.

'It was brilliant being able to show you St Vincent. You were such a success,' he tenderly said. A moment later she was through the barrier; he was still waving.

Then she was gone.

It had been the strangest four weeks of her life, and the brightest in colour. In the plane, as it rose and flew, she looked down on the jewelled islands and thought of Iris's boyish head, wet from swimming, and Bob Lawrence-Scott's hearty welcome every time she came to their house. Of the rocky road up the volcano, and the coconut stall where in a familiar movement a woman would split the nut in half. 'It's St Vincent's answer to Coca Cola,' Hugh said when she drank the milky stuff.

Avril leaned back. The hum of the engines was lulling as she remembered the days just ended. It was like shaking the fragments of coloured paper in a kaleidoscope. Each new shake, another pattern.

She settled down to read the magazines and to daydream. And then she remembered something she'd forgotten. Last night at the end of the party Iris had given her a small packet wrapped, in the American way, in gold gift paper with a fancy nylon bow.

'Don't thank me, it's not from me,' Iris gaily said. 'Michael Silver asked me to give it to you before you left. He said I wasn't to forget. Apparently it's some kind of delicious candy which you can eat in the plane. He said not to open it until you were on your way. I daresay it's good for airsickness.'

She had given Avril a mocking look, as if she knew her secrets.

Avril thanked her and absently put the package with her handbag until, when she was leaving, she picked it up without curiosity.

Now she remembered it and pulled it out of her shoulder bag, fiddling with the ridiculous bow. A beautiful Jamaican air hostess went by, giving her a smile Avril found hard to return. The girl was carrying a trayful of sickening coffee.

Perhaps the candy will do me good.

She tore open the paper.

Wrapped inside more paper was a bamboo box painted with thin green leaves. Inside it, an army of paint brushes. Some of them were so fine that their camel hairs were almost invisible.

PART TWO

Chapter 9

The final months of Avril's pregnancy were in high hot summer. She was very large, often remarked by Isobel from one garden to the other. The heat exhausted her and she spent much of the morning under the dappled shade of an apple tree Hugh had planted five years ago. Objects that she wanted to draw were arranged on a garden seat in front of her. Her sketchbook was on her lap.

As the heat steadily rose towards afternoon, she retreated to the kitchen and worked at the table, hampered by the bump of her belly which, like the unborn St John the Baptist, often leaped for joy.

She painted simple things. The June cherries bought in a bag from the village shop. An old silver cream jug and a roll of caraway-seed-scattered bread. At night she was too uncomfortable to sleep well. She gave herself the old treat, taking her current painting into her bedroom, propping it on the easel and turning the easel with its back to the bed. If she woke in the night she could make out a friendly, ghostly shape. In the morning she would climb out of bed with a real thrill of excitement to turn the easel round and see what she had done yesterday. Disappointment always followed. And expectation always came back later. She'd do better today.

In contrast to the fecund womb swelling under her thin, loose dress, her face had become haggard. She had a wan, spiritual look very far from the glowing image of pregnancy; with her stout, ungainly figure, she looked fragile.

The drama of breaking the news to Hugh was long gone. It had been less fraught than Avril expected, because she had written first, well before speaking to him on the telephone. With every line of the careful letter she thought how glad she was not to be telling him to his face. When he read it he would of course suggest ... She banished that from her mind.

The letter – many rough drafts – struck right notes: 'I can't think how ... I was sure I'd remembered ... I realise, Hugh, it's a bit shock ... To be positive, I do feel pretty well, and Helen at the office has been really kind. She's managed to get me some part-time work ...'

Hugh must have rung the moment her letter was delivered by the St Vincent postman.

He was angry and incredulous. Avril's radio signals soothed her while she sat listening to the unpleasant voice. The signals said the line was probably faulty.

'What is this you are telling me?'

Of all stupid questions, said her signals, that took the biscuit. She played it calmly, which wasn't difficult: she felt calm. The strange serenity which had wrapped her round on the island still enveloped her. By God protected, thought Avril, who had become rather pious now she had got her own way.

Hugh, given the opposite of what *he'd* wanted, was

bullying, but that must surely be the faulty line. Faced by his distant wife's stodgy tranquillity, he did not suggest the unsuggestable. She'd covered that in her letter, saying that it was too late to do such a thing. After a good many useless questions and some obvious outrage he finally accepted the situation, and said loudly:

'I must get compassionate leave. I ought to be there for the birth.'

Dear me, thought Avril, am I supposed to be grateful?

Her reply was meek. He was still rather angry when he rang off.

When she first came back from St Vincent, impregnated, so to speak, by her husband, she found a letter postmarked two days after her departure five weeks before. Keith's handwriting.

Inside, with a scrawled 'Sorry we couldn't meet up' was a cheque for five hundred pounds.

Avril picked up the cheque and looked at it thoughtfully. What an orgy of shopping for the baby it would fund. Or what fun to return it. But that would have been unkind and even threatening. A female gesture unintelligible to a man of Keith's nature. Besides, it would not be exactly safe to send it either to the office or to Cheselbourne, which he had probably left by now.

She tore the cheque into small pieces and sprinkled them in the dustbin.

There was news of Keith from Helen who, exuding delight at the news of Avril's pregnancy, drove out to Fuchsia Cottage now and then at weekends.

They had tea in the garden.

Keith, said Helen, had been 'so disappointed' when Avril had been whipped off to St Vincent. 'He looked shattered

157

when I told him, Avril.' During her absence and before he finally left the office he'd asked for news of her. 'I don't know why my assistant didn't send me one,' he had said when Helen showed him a gaudy postcard of some hummingbirds. Now, with the new Plymouth office planned and soon to open, Helen had not seen him for a while.

'I do miss him. Such a dear.'

If Helen was overjoyed at Avril's news, her own family did not give her the same exaggerated attention. Rick, of course, knew only too well and did not mention what was in his mind when he telephoned. She wondered if he violently disapproved of what he guessed she must have done, and was not going to ask her. Susan Vincent was pleased, but not enough for Avril, who would have enjoyed old-fashioned motherly gush. Her father was facetious. Retta was the best. She laughed delightedly.

'I can't work out what your baby is as far as I'm concerned. Stepgrandson or granddaughter? How are you feeling?'

'Rather well. But everybody in the village keeps telling me their own horror stories, usually about backache. I feel apologetic because mine doesn't.'

'Are you still working? My pregnant friends say it's vital,' said Retta, who couldn't imagine anybody not having a job if they could possibly find or keep one.

Rick, away a lot, telephoned at last.

'Can I come this weekend?'

He was back from one of his Hollywood-Washington style trips.

'I'd like to hear about St Vincent. Look out any photographs if you've got them. Ready to be interviewed?'

It was clear that he had asked himself to stay because

somehow, talking to her about the island was connected with his work.

She looked forward to seeing him and hoped he wouldn't dare mention poor Keith, and the tricky subject of Hugh as father.

It was Saturday morning and she was in the garden, sketching, when she heard his car. He gave a merry toot-toot before climbing out. She came down the path slowly, leaning backwards.

'You're as big as a house.'

He gave her a kiss, dodging the bulge.

'That's what I call really gallant.'

'You don't want all that Victorian stuff. Glad to see me?'

'What do you think?' she said, frankly laughing.

She had brought out another chair, put it under the apple tree and placed a bottle of white wine in Hugh's ice bucket. The ice was already melting. Rick gave a grunt of approval and sat down beside her, accepting a drink. He looked up at the canopy of leaves.

'Why don't I live in the country?'

He leaned back luxuriously, his face as thin as hers, but not wan, filled with confident energy. He reminded Avril of a highly bred dog. Greyhound? Whippet? Too aggressive for either.

'You'd hate to live in the country, Rick. You need to be in the thick.'

She always forgot when she did not see him for a while the pleasure of being with her own flesh and blood. Not with her parents; they were too old and she did not feel she resembled either of them very much. With her brother there was a bond. They led lives as different as could be, but their past linked them as closely as the Vikings who cut

159

their wrists and bound them together, mingling the blood. A thousand things did not need to be said.

'Now you're here, Rick, tell me everything that's going on. And don't accuse me of not reading your pieces; I practically know them by heart. If I miss one, Ma rings that morning and tells me to go to the shop and get it. I want to hear all the stuff you have to leave out.'

She waited to be entertained. He enjoyed describing his journeys, the famous and the unknown people, the legendary Hollywood star as mean as muck and the statesman's admired wife with her dubious City dealings. He accepted sisterly attention, sisterly fascination.

It was after one o'clock when she stood up, saying she must mix the salad.

'Come and talk in the kitchen.'

'In a minute. Let me finish my drink.'

The cottage, like many ancient buildings in summertime, was thankfully cool. In the kitchen she found a cabbage white butterfly helplessly trying to fly through the closed window.

'You are a fool,' she said aloud.

She put a large tumbler over the terrified thing, which beat its wings against the rounded walls of its new prison. Then she slid paper beneath tumbler and butterfly, opened the kitchen window and thew it into the air.

Incredulously, unbearably free, off it went on its crooked flight. She was still watching when Rick lounged in, bringing the wine bottle. He refilled his glass.

'I know you don't drink at present. All this mother-to-be virtue,' he said, and patted the top of her head.

He was aware, late in the day, that he'd neglected her since she had returned from St Vincent. The horrible problem she had brought with her to the Temple that night had been in his thoughts too much. Soon after her return from the island she had blithely said to him on the telephone:

'Hugh's finally got over the shock, poor old thing. He'll soon be quite reconciled about being a dad.'

The huge question mark remained like an exclamation mark over a figure in a cartoon. Black as ink. But Rick that time had heard a warning-off in her voice and obeyed it.

Now, standing by her in the kitchen, he said:

'Stop messing about with the olive oil and tell me how you're feeling.'

'You said it in the garden. Like a house.'

'When's the great day?'

'Eight weeks. No, seven and a half. If it's on time.'

'Will Hugh get compassionate leave?'

Avril heard the question and ignored what was hidden in it.

'I wish he could, but his job is nearly over in St Vincent. They'd never let him come back when he's only got three or four weeks more duty to do. He will probably be home about a month or slightly less after the baby arrives.'

Silence followed. Avril, her movements measured, finished mixing the salad and carried the round wooden bowl which she often used in her paintings into the sitting room. She knew its shape as well as that of her own face. Cold lunch was ready, and she had picked some roses and put them in a pewter tankard. The loveliest, pink but almost white, had begun to drop.

They sat down and she served him.

Rick, almost without meaning it, said:

'Tell me how Hugh took the news when you broke it to him.'

'I thought I did tell you. Annoyed at first,' she said, laughing slightly. 'Apparently lots of men are. Isobel says men divide into two categories. The born fathers who are crazy with joy when they hear, and the cross ones who never wanted it to happen. Hugh, of course, is the second. I wrote to him after I got back. He was *not* pleased. But he is quite reconciled now, and when he actually sees his baby with luck it'll all be great.'

A vision of the happy father hung about a bit.

Rick smiled dimly.

He did not know why somehow he felt he could no longer go on with this scene. He said what they were both thinking. Said it without emotion and with curiosity:

'You never told him, did you?'

Avril, peaceful, lazy Avril, great heavy, pregnant Avril, was ready. Apart from poor Keith, who was now as unreal as Achilles, there was not a living soul but Rick who knew the – to Avril – unbelievable truth. She had not been alone with her brother since the night at the Garrick. When she'd seen him this morning she had known he wouldn't be able to resist spelling things out. He was like that.

She picked at her salad.

'No. I never did. When I got to Kingstown I was all hyped up to do it, but when I met him he was so welcoming, and when I thought of what I was going to say I was really sorry for him. I wasn't nervous at first but then I began to be. My heart absolutely thumped. But I'd made up my mind it was only fair and I thought – best get it over at once. No, don't interrupt,' she added when he made an inarticulate sound. 'You'll only waste your breath if you start ranting on and putting me in the wrong.' She looked at the roses and picked up a fallen petal, virginal pink, browning slightly at the edge. 'You see . . .' She brooded for a moment, deep in her thoughts, then pulled herself together. 'We had rather a lot of sex when I was there. You know how it is when one's been apart. I mean, we had sex very soon, right away in fact,' she confessed. 'So there it was. I just left things as they were. Well, as he thought they were.'

She knew he would never grant her absolution. It was interesting to Avril to see her brother struggling with the fact she had just given him. Such a fact. It bumped against the table just then as if it needed exercise. It made a perfect somersault.

'You think me very dishonourable, don't you?'

'Yes.'

'Cowardly?'

'Very.'

Men, thought Avril with pity. Poor things. There is such a lot of life they simply don't get. Like my radio signals. They had stopped the day the baby quickened but they had been in control of her for all those weeks. What would Rick make of them?

'And shall you forgive me?' she humorously asked.

Only at that moment did Rick notice – he had periods of blindness about his sister – how worn was the olive face round which her hair rioted, thick and curled as a poodle's. He had an involuntary pang of disapproving love.

'And you think,' he said, the question blunter than his voice, 'you are going to get away with it?'

'Rick. I don't think about it at all. We made love. A lot. The baby's his. That's what I believe, and so must you.'

It didn't prove as difficult to press the button marked 'Cancel' as Rick had imagined. Dorset was so beautiful and

Avril so peaceful, dignified and clumsy-moving. The sun was hot and steady. Sweet peas twined round a palisade of poles on the far side of the garden. They put out new flowers every morning.

'You have to pick them every day,' Avril said next morning after breakfast, when he found her hands full of mauve and white, salmon, pink and crimson, in the garden. She buried her face in the flowers.

'I'll put them in your room.'

But in spite of the green rolling hills, the nearness to the sea, the smell of sweet peas and the spell of the country to a Londoner, Rick did not waste time. When Avril declared it was too hot for her to go out on Sunday afternoon he said, 'OK, I'll interview you indoors.'

The experience was unfamiliar to Avril. She had never been much of a talker; painting was a quiet job. Her local friends, mostly wives, were voluble and glad of a listener.

'Want a cushion, Av? No fidgeting. You have to be relaxed.'

'Oh, I am.'

'Good,' said Rick, who rarely was. 'Now start at the beginning.'

She obligingly did. His patience, persistence and quickness in work were new to her. Avril realised that this surprised her because her brother had never spent time asking *her* questions; it had always been the other way round. Now it was tiring to talk, to answer, to think, to be exact. During the session she lost count of the times when she paused and he said:

'OK. Go on.'

'You don't want more stuff about La Soufrière when you are actually writing about Jamaica.'

'I want it all. Go on.'

At last it was finished. He shut his notebook which was covered in scrawls. He had suggested using a tape but Avril had been self-conscious at the idea and he'd relented.

He flipped through the pages.

'You notice more than you realise you do. Like the knife for cutting the coconuts. And those poisonous apples being poison green. Have I tired you?'

Avril dutifully said no, but added that she really ought to sleep for a while. She always did in the afternoon.

'I'll go back into the garden,' he said.

She climbed the ladder stair, hanging on the banister, and when she was in her room, the bed had never looked more inviting. She pulled her curtains and fell on to the bed.

Rick sat in a deckchair under the apple tree. He tried to follow his pregnant sister's lead and sleep. It was impossible. His mind teemed with plans, hopes, frustrations, ideas. His friend, the owner of the Temple flat, would be home soon, which meant the end of his undisputed sway over the four rooms. He'd need to withdraw and make do with two. There was the little, not so little, matter of his women friends. He had two at present and – a man who kept his own counsel while coaxing people to forget theirs – didn't fancy his flatmate either commenting on or even making a play for either of the two. Quite suddenly he thought of Retta.

He had not seen her for many weeks, although now and again he talked to her on the telephone. He liked her familiar voice. He refused to admit that there were times when he needed her.

He must ask her about the girls and the difficulties.

'I'll sort you out,' was Retta's favourite phrase.

Chapter 10

Everything was ready for the baby's arrival. There was one particular point on which Avril was immovable. When Isobel next door, the concerned and sympathetic Helen at the office, Hugh from the island wanted to know whether it was going to be a boy or a girl, Avril flatly refused to ask the doctor. Instead she instructed him that she did *not* want to hear. Isobel and Hugh were incredulous.

'But this day and age, when you can be told! It's ridiculous!' cried Isobel.

'Surely, Avril, we may as well hear if it's a boy,' from Hugh.

Avril was polite, and stubborn as a mule.

Hugh, as he had guessed, would not be returning to Dorset in time for the birth. Leave so soon before his actual posting back to Dorset was out of the question; Avril would have to go through her drama alone.

She was secretly delighted. The idea of Hugh in the labour room got on her nerves. He would, to use an old phrase of her mother's, 'make his presence felt'. She didn't want to be forced to think of Hugh at that time. She would have other, wonderful, frightening, tremendous things to think about.

Her suitcase was packed, she made calm plans. She waited.

'If it starts in the middle of the night, you've only to ring our bell,' said Isobel. 'We'll drive you in. Poor you,' a favourite phrase, 'I really don't know what I would have done without David around. I mean, he was such a support. He's so strong. And Hugh would have been wonderful too,' purred Isobel.

Knowing the opposite, Avril agreed. When, rarely, she had been ill, Hugh always managed, if making her tea and fetching aspirins, to be the martyr.

The baby arrived on a hot day at the end of August. Her luck was in: she happened to be in the hospital for a final check-up when the pains started. Everything, said the doctor and midwife, bustling in and out of a small white room to examine, listen to her stomach, time the coming and going of the spasms, everything was going well. Excellent. Ah, here comes another.

Like every other first mother since Eve, Avril had had no idea of the intensity of birth pangs. Excellent, was it? She would have used the worst language if she hadn't been too busy.

Eight hours after the first pains, muzzy with gas and oxygen and at a distance from the people helping her, she heard the uplifted voice of the midwife.

'It's a lovely boy, Mrs Brett!'

And in the same far distance an angry, coughing cry.

As soon as Avril was comfortable and back in her own bed, after she'd had a first look at the red-faced scrap wrapped in a blanket, the nurse trotted in and plugged in the telephone. She put in a call to St Vincent.

Two hours' delay.

'What a disappointment for the new daddy,' said the nurse, a big-bosomed girl who talked like that.

Later Avril rang her mother. Gerald, Retta and Rick were all away. Avril had never in her life heard her mother truly excited. The heightened laughing voice kept repeating, 'How gorgeous, oh, how gorgeous.' She asked if she could come at once.

'Will they allow you to come home soon? I'll look after you both.'

Avril liked that 'both'.

'I'm sure they'll let me,' said Avril, knowing the hospital would be only too glad to see the back of any mother and baby who could be landed on somebody else. 'If you really could, Mum.'

'I'd love to.'

Feeling very strange, her arms cradling a little person muffled in an unnecessary shawl, accompanied by her mother in pearls and silk, Avril was driven back to Fuchsia Cottage.

The moment the taxi drew up at the gate, out rushed Isobel. There was a stream of congratulations, jokes, 'Do let me look at him!' and oohs and ahs. Susan was gracious. She approved of Isobel, whom she considered classy. As for Avril, she stood there with the baby in her arms, feeling so weak she could have burst into tears.

It was actually Isobel weeks ago who had warned Avril she would have 'the usual boring reaction'.

What did that mean? asked pregnant, peaceful Avril.

'Oh,' said Isobel, widening her eyes. 'First there's the day of *total* happiness. Somebody called it the Day of Bliss.

You think it'll last for ever. Bang afterwards there's the day of feeling sorry for yourself. I was in floods.'

'Why?'

'Search me. Weakness and reaction, the doctor said. I just kept thinking, poor me.'

On her first evening at home, her mother had told her to rest and had taken over the kitchen and the supper. Avril went to her room and lay down. Could annoying Isobel be right? She leaned against the bed back, tying her handkerchief into knots. What am I snuffling about? I've got him, haven't I? The one I always wanted. Why am I sorry for myself? As Ma says, he is magnificent.

Indeed, the new character occupying a Moses basket in the corner certainly was. He was large, just nine pounds, his podgy hands had bracelets of fat round the wrists, and there was very little hair on the well-shaped head. When he opened his eyes, they were dark. Genuinely forgetting who had fathered the noble fellow squinting at her, she thought: 'He looks just like Hugh.'

And then, why not a kind of holy miracle? Why not indeed.

The health visitor was pretty, dyed blonde and energetic. Around forty. Susan was gracious when she discovered that Fiona Leveaux, like Isobel next door, was somewhat upper-crust.

'Isn't he magnificent?'

It was Susan's word of the week as she joined Fiona staring down into the basket cot.

'He sure is. What is his name?' turning to Avril. 'Have you decided yet?'

'Edward. But I shall call him Teddy.'

Fiona said brilliant, and did Avril know that the trendiest name right now was Oscar, and wasn't it sweet?

To Avril's relief during the new few days while she herself was much at sea, Fiona and her mother got on like a house on fire. They had common interests; not so common. Polo at Windsor Great Park, for instance. A royal garden party. Feeding the baby, Avril listened to the snobby chat downstairs, and later, up came Fiona to ask cheerily if Avril had remembered her pelvic floor exercises.

By the time Susan was due to return home to the Cotswolds, Avril had settled into a routine. She was becoming used to the broken nights, but was grateful that her mother, in a dressing gown, hearing cries, always joined her in the small hours.

'What is it, precious?' Susan would say, looking admiringly at the angry baby. 'He's hungry. That's because he's so big and strong. Give him some more.'

Avril was busy, it seemed to her, every hour of the day and often at night. She still looked wan, and when she saw her mother off and stood waving goodbye and the car turned the corner, her eyes brimmed.

She went back to the cottage.

It was late afternoon, and upstairs the baby, thank heaven, was asleep. She recalled with dull wonder the peace of the summer gone by. All during her pregnancy she had been untroubled, befriended by a certain angel visitor who had shaded her with his giant wings. He resembled a being painted by Rossetti and had stood beside her, whispering lies. About future ease and simplicity and the perfect happiness after the baby had come. Now she badly needed her angel, but the unearthly creature was hanging about near the front door.

'Where are you going?' she asked suspiciously.

His Rossetti smile curved the full-lipped mouth.

'I am leaving you, dear child.'

'No, no! Please don't go.'

He shook his golden head. Admittedly his wings were on the bulky side, but he could have flown off through the open window. He didn't bother. He simply went through the door without opening it.

And Avril began to sob in earnest.

By the time Fiona Leveaux's visits were less frequent, the crying jags had stopped. But Avril was still nervous. Suppose the baby broke. She picked him up as if he were thinnest porcelain. Fiona chuckled.

'He's tougher than you think. Let's see you give him his bath again. Your mother helped, didn't she? Now you must get expert at doing it on your own.'

With a towel on her lap, Avril tremblingly soaped the baby, slippery as a fish and purple-faced with rage. But when he was lowered into the warm water, the yells stopped. And across the gnomic face came a thoughtful look. He began to kick like a frog.

One evening the bell rang and to her amazement, when she answered the door, she saw the bulky figure of Peter Huskisson. He was bluff, hearty, office-smart and wore a jovial smile.

'I know, I know, too bad just turning up like this. I should've rung first. But I happened to be driving through your village and took a chance. How are you?'

He followed her, booming away, into the sitting room and caught sight of the cot. 'Is this the sprog? May I take a look. I say, that's a fine fellow, he'll be a prize-fighter one of these days.'

His laugh was loud and boisterous, palely echoed by

Avril. Mystified by her visitor, she offered him a drink.

'Well, now, wish I could stay,' he boomed to her relief. 'The fact is, I've come to bend your husband's ear. Is he about, by any chance?'

Avril, even more surprised, said Hugh was not yet returned to England.

Huskisson looked disappointed. It was clear he now considered his visit a total waste of time. He asked when Hugh was expected, made a note in a diary from his pocket and said that next time he would telephone in advance.

'Mustn't drop in like this or I might wear out my welcome! Don't bother to tell him what I want him for.' He got to his feet. 'Just a do-gooding idea I've had in my head lately. Nice to see you. And the sprog. Bye now.'

He bustled off.

I should have asked him about his pigs, thought Avril. Didn't Helen tell me he's having trouble with them?

It never occurred to her to ask about Keith.

She couldn't resist ringing Helen the next day. Her friend giggled.

'Poor Avril, what a shock. Yes, I know what he came for. Wendy's been having a terrible time with him making her do the donkey work. It's for a Promises auction. Peter's been roped in to run it for his local youth club. So *he's* decided to rope in your Hugh as well. Do they actually know each other?'

'Only slightly.'

'That's enough for Peter. Any news of when Hugh is back?'

By coincidence, that very afternoon when she was feeding the baby, staring down at him, fascinated, the telephone rang.

'Avril? It's Hugh. Hold on to your hat. I'll be with you tomorrow evening.'

When he rang off, Avril crooned to the baby, too busy sucking to listen:

'He's going to see you. His son. He's going to see how wonderful you are.'

Hugh arrived in the middle of the night, after she and Teddy had spent a dramatic evening, the baby at his crossest and Avril at her most nervous. Both were exhaustedly asleep when Avril woke, as if she had been shaken by the shoulder, to hear the sound of a creak on the ladder stair.

She reached for the light and switched it on, looking at once towards the cot.

Mercifully not a sound.

The door quietly opened.

And there, tall, handsome, uniformed, a stranger again, carrying a bag and looking at her as if he was not quite sure how to behave, was Hugh.

She put out her arms, filled with love and triumph.

'Darling, darling.' It sounded as if he were going to cry. 'May I look?'

Avril, motherhood itself, pointed at the cot.

He crept over and stood there for a long time. He bent to look in silence. She watched him with deep fondness, proud and happy. He came over to her at last.

'Do you know, darling, he looks exactly like my grandfather, the Admiral.'

Hugh was an exemplary father and quite adept with the little boy. He doted too.

'Men are soppy old things, aren't they?' said Isobel,

having seen Hugh with the baby in the garden. 'David was just the same.'

Hugh was indeed rather soppy, walking about the cottage with the baby in his arms, rocking him and sometimes kissing the rounded cheek, his own eyes closed in pleasure. He was always asking questions to which Avril didn't know the answers. Why did Edward go so red? Why did he need gripe water and what did it consist of? Was it safe for him to sleep without a pillow? He never said Teddy. It was always Edward.

Fascination and concern did not extend to his wife, and he rarely noticed that Avril tired easily and that silly things upset her. He took 'all that' for granted. He did once mutter something which distinctly sounded like 'There, there' when she began to cry. But his interest was all in Edward ('I dislike pet names'). He took innumerable photographs without – or with – Avril.

He was back at the Dorset base but not, it seemed, permanently. There was a chance of promotion and another posting, though this was still in the air; he and Avril might be moved to Portsmouth. The idea of leaving her home, of being uprooted just as she was settled, made her inwardly quake. But she was glad Hugh was jovial nowadays. She often heard him laughing with Isobel in the garden. He flirted slightly with her. And with Fiona, who called now and then to check the baby's progress. Both women flirted back.

Although Hugh was intrigued by his role as father, Fuchsia Cottage oppressed him. The rooms had always been too cramped for him; when not in a ship he needed space. He'd grown up in large houses, had been educated in the great halls of Dartmouth. At sea you had to adapt to cramped quarters, it was part of naval life, but on land it was different.

Truth to tell, he had never liked the cottage. With the baby's arrival the place became even smaller. Teddy's possessions seemed to seep (Hugh's word) into every room. Hugh was glad to escape from parenting whenever he could.

A handy reason to be absent was provided by Peter Huskisson, who turned up far too soon to 'rope you in, Brett!' for the planned auction. Avril had never known her husband so obliging. The auction was to be a local event to raise funds to buy a snooker table – and a table tennis table for good measure – badly needed by the local youth club. Promises were to be coaxed from anybody and everybody, and on the day would be offered for sale to the highest bidder.

Huskisson was cast as auctioneer.

'I'm slow with the hammer, I'm telling you.'

Both Huskisson and Hugh seemed to get a great deal of fun from thinking up likely promises and persuading likely givers. There were promises for permission to use a computer for three hours, to provide fresh flowers for two weeks; there were free tickets to the local cinema. One generous patron offered to walk somebody's dog for a month. There was a handsome set of encyclopaedias, any number of home-made cakes, and Huskisson's own promise – a cartload of manure delivered to the gardener's door.

'Mind if I drag him off?' he would shout heartily, before driving Hugh away at weekends or in the evenings.

As if Avril would object. She had never done so when Hugh's own excuse had meant other women. Now she merely looked up and smiled.

Late autumn was turning into Indian summer, a string of ravishing days which smelled of bonfires. Isobel called in one evening to invite Avril and Hugh out for a drink. She and David were going to the Trout, a popular pub some miles away, with a garden, by the side of a small river. It was a favourite haunt of theirs.

'I decided to dump the boys on their grandparents,' said Isobel. 'You must come, both of you. Now, Avril, I'm sure you can lay on a baby-sitter.'

She knew, and so did Avril, that that was impossible at such short notice. Avril thanked her and refused. There was a good deal of the expected 'What a pity!' Isobel then said, rather in the Huskisson way, could they steal Hugh for a quick Buck's Fizz?

'It's by way of being David's birthday.'

Hugh accepted with alacrity and was in good spirits as he drove behind the Sinclairs on the usual journey through the narrow Dorset lanes. He was not a particular friend of David Sinclair's; he thought him a know-all. But Isobel's obvious admiration of himself was not without its charm, and she was certainly attractive. As it happened, David Sinclair also had reservations about his fellow officer. He thought Hugh a shocking snob. But each settled for the other's faults. Anybody seeing them together would have imagined them close friends.

The Trout, in the last golden sunshine, was crowded. The flag-floored bars were full, and more people, sitting at tables and on the dry autumn grass, drank and talked; the noise of voices was as jolly as that at a large wedding.

'This is all very festive,' Hugh remarked, as they found a recently vacated table near the river.

'Perfect for birthday champagne,' agreed Isobel. She

was done up to the nines this evening in pink silk pants and a white top cut low to show her full breasts. She used with Hugh a slightly actressy manner. She emoted. David had gone to get the drinks.

'But I should be doing that,' said Hugh, half rising, to be told gaily by Isobel, 'You'll be buying the next round.'

Alone with Hugh, she began to talk about the baby.

'What a pet.'

Then about Avril.

'Radiant, radiant. Well, we all say that about new mothers.'

She was being what Hugh thought of as too womanish, and if she had not been seductive-looking he would have made his escape on the excuse of helping David carry three glasses and a bottle of champagne. He was glad when David and the drinks did arrive.

They talked naval shop, at which Isobel was also quite skilful. They laughed and gossiped. After the second round they became more animated, and the jokes grew distinctly weaker. David told a story, encouraged by his wife, and looked pleased at Hugh's genuine roar of laughter. Again it was David's turn to go to the bar.

'Same again?'

'Ooh, please,' from Isobel.

Her husband made his way across the garden.

'Well,' said Isobel, turning to Hugh and rounding her eyes, a familiar habit of hers, 'you're feeling very chipper, I bet.'

'Something like that.'

'So you should. Your boy is a treat to behold. And I must say, Hugh, David and I were glad to see Avril had really settled down again.'

'After her weeks in St Vincent, you mean? Yes, she did have a good time.'

'No, not that. I gather it was a big success, she was very enthusiastic. I mean at the end of last year when she was a grass widow, poor love.'

There was a fraction of a pause.

'David and I,' said Isobel, never averse to the catty remark, particularly about other naval wives, 'thought she was rather taken with that boss of hers. You know, the one who could lose some weight.'

'Peter Huskisson?' said Hugh in disbelief.

'No, the other one.'

'Oh, Keith Waring.' Hugh laughed. 'You can't be serious. He booms around like a sports master. Anyway, Avril never falls for anyone.'

'Unlike someone not a hundred miles from Bridport.'

'How people exaggerate.'

He liked his successes talked about in moderation.

'I don't expect they do, dear Hugh, but I shall pretend to believe you. Anyway, we aren't talking about you, the Don Giovanni of Dorset, but about Avril. David didn't agree, but I'm afraid I was rather glad to see you getting a little comeuppance. I mean Avril flirting with Keith Waring for a while. He did seem rather devoted. Hung about non-stop. Avril looked quite pleased with herself, I remember.'

'What nonsense you talk, Isobel.'

'Do I? But you weren't there, Hugh. I was.'

Just then David Sinclair came back with the glasses, carrying them carefully, and with a small plastic packet of cashew nuts under his arm. He put them down on the table, glanced not at his wife but at his friend, and said at once:

'Anything wrong?'

Isobel frankly laughed.

'Sorry, sorry. I've only been teasing him, I can never resist it. I told him what a *succès fou* Avril was months ago with that boss of hers. Didn't he vanish to Plymouth when Avril flew to St Vincent? Must have been a broken heart.' She was enjoying herself.

David Sinclair's freckled face grew slightly red, but if Isobel noticed, she ignored it.

'Hugh will have to keep a beady eye on his wife or she might turn into as much of a flirt as he is,' said Isobel.

'Women do talk rot,' said David loudly. 'My wife, for all those declarations of her feminist principles, is nothing but a village gossip. Avril never flirts.'

He spoke with conviction. Isobel, indeed, had told him during the winter her imagined theory about Avril and Keith Waring. He had thought it rubbish. The idea of the dark young woman next door actually having an affair was totally absurd. A quiet little thing.

'I hope I haven't upset you,' said Isobel, burying her nose in her champagne. 'You ought to be pleased to hear your wife is in demand when you're away. Why shouldn't she enjoy herself when she's on her ownsome? Most of us' – looking at Hugh with the rounded eyes again – 'do.'

Hugh laughed, and David, recovering from his unease, joined in. The talk moved back to Navy shop and Isobel was content to listen. She had enjoyed the chance to tweak Hugh's tail. Life was flat and the complacency of Service husbands in that closed world of theirs – oh sure, there were women in the Services, but Isobel knew nothing about them – galled her. She didn't see why Hugh Brett should be allowed to dog around and Avril not be permitted a tiny fling.

When Hugh left them, the sun had gone behind a group of tall trees. It was the end of a bright day. The Dorset evening was breathlessly calm, the colour of straw. He drove up the steep hills; on either side of the road the land dropped away in female curves.

Something in him stirred and half woke. Something which in another man could have been the start of pain, a nagging consciousness, a warning. But in Hugh it was small and black, a serpent, a krait, swift as lightning and mortal to its enemies.

He began to think in a new, cold way about Avril's pregnancy. He had never done this before. When exactly had she written to him from England? Yes, it had been a few weeks after her return, but supposing . . . His thoughts, for a moment, appalled him. The krait's poisoned teeth bit into him. From the very start he'd told Avril he did not wish for a child. After some scenes – she had been quite hysterical at one point – she had accepted that. And then, seven years after their marriage, that thunderstriking letter and his own telephone call. He felt again the surge of fury. 'How? Why? *It is your fault.*' She had not been apologetic, not the woman he had moulded her to be, the one who suited him and who, in his own way, he loved. When he had demanded that the pregnancy should be terminated, she'd been cool as a cucumber.

'I know, I know,' had been the astonishing reply. 'Poor Hugh, I know how you feel, but as I said in my letter, the doctor says it's too late.'

He had been too unnerved, confused even, to question that.

Now that alibi forced dreadful questions. Had the possible termination been too late because she had been pregnant before she came to the island? He felt degraded. As he drove through the exquisite evening he literally forgot the leading actor in the drama, the little boy. Not once through the suspicion growing in him, the Othello-like obsession, did he think of 'his' son. Only of the woman he was now convinced had betrayed him. A slut. And that bitch Isobel Sinclair knew it.

It was deep dusk now. The cottage stood in its gardenful of roses and lavender; the apple leaves were beginning to turn scarlet. The scene was as sentimental as an old-fashioned watercolour. He parked his car, and as he walked up the path he saw a figure in a pale dress which glimmered through the twilight. Sitting in a deckchair was Fiona Leveaux.

'Hi!' she called out. 'I shouldn't be here at all, it's darker every minute, but it's so lovely out of doors and I've finished my rounds for today. Avril begged me to stay a little longer. She's just coming out for a chat when she's finished feeding His Majesty. Don't disturb them or you'll give your child a bad case of hiccups.'

'Let me get you a drink.'

'You're so polite, Hugh. Another drink would be more accurate.'

She proffered her empty glass and he went into the cottage. He returned a moment later, sat down and stretched long legs. Sexy, thought Fiona. A womaniser, I shouldn't wonder.

'My professional visits here are just about over,' she remarked. 'Young Teddy is doing so well, putting on weight like a wrestler. One has to admire those impressive legs. I do like big babies. Of course he started off, bless him, at over nine pounds.'

He said casually:

'That's quite big, isn't it, considering he was slightly premature?'

Fiona smiled.

'You are funny, Hugh. Fathers never cease to amaze me. Of course they are usually present at the birth, which is very important. I know you had to miss that; you must have been so disappointed. But there are a lot of other things fathers still don't grasp.'

She looked at him and spoke gently.

'I hope you don't mind if I explain? Your baby couldn't possibly have been premature with that impressive weight. He was quite a bit late, ten days, maybe even more. There was talk of having to induce your wife. It isn't good for the baby to go much beyond full term. Doctors don't like it.'

Hugh sipped a drink. He drawled slightly.

'Must've got it wrong. At Dartmouth we used to say, 'Not my subject.' By the by, talking about something that *is*, I meant to ask you about the Wincanton races. Have you been studying form? There's a horse I heard about last year . . .'

They slipped into talk of racing until in the falling light she looked at her watch.

'Golly! It's late, I really must rush. Say goodbye to your wife, would you? I'll ring tomorrow, I want to talk about changing Teddy's routine a bit.'

She picked up her shoulder bag, called, 'Bye-ee,' and tripped off down the path. The sound of her car died away.

Avril tucked in the baby, gave her hair a hasty comb – Hugh said rather often that she looked a mess – and came down the ladder stair. The silence in the dusk outside was broken by the shrill call of excited swallows swooping to and fro. They'll be gone any day, she thought.

Hugh was sitting in the dark under the apple tree.

'Where's Fiona? Has she gone?'

'Yes.'

'She never said goodbye.'

'She's going to ring tomorrow.'

'Good. Is there a drink for me?'

She had walked across the grass and was standing beside him. At first it was too dark to see, but now her night sight had come back. She saw him lift up his head and stare straight at her.

'Hugh, what is it? Do you feel ill?'

'Yes.'

'My poor dear. Are you in pain? shall I ring to make an appointment with the doctor?'

She was full of alarm looking at the strange, fixed face. She saw he had not heard a word she said.

'That kid's not mine, is it?'

She froze like an animal smelling imminent danger. No longer enveloped in a cloak wrapped round her by the angel, alone, undefended, she managed an incredulous smile.

'What *are* you talking about?'

'Don't give me that crap. I spoke to Fiona just now. She said that kid was overdue. Not premature at all.'

The only thing she noticed was the repeated 'that kid'. It froze her blood.

'I don't know what you're saying.'

She was still standing, and he also stood up. He took a threatening step forward and she instinctively backed away.

'What I am saying,' he said slowly, 'is that you were very

clever. You worked out the months to make me think you conceived in St Vincent. A lot of lies. That employer of yours, Keith what's-his-name, fucked you and when you came to St Vincent you were carrying *his* kid. Quite a neat job you thought you'd pulled off. Well, it's over.'

She stood looking at him in the gloom. The expression on his face was twisted, as if he had had some kind of paralysing stroke.

She said carefully:

'You will only go on and on if I don't tell you, and you could find out more details from Fiona, of course. So she told you the baby was overdue, and you did some pathetic arithmetic. Well done.'

'Don't you dare talk to me like that,' he spat out. 'Don't you jeer at me or I'll—'

'Yes?'

He paused. Then said viciously:

'If you want to know, you cow, your friend Fiona did say something, but the person who told me the charming truth that you've been fucking around was Isobel Sinclair.'

Avril looked aghast.

How could Isobel have done anything so filthy? Avril was too shattered to realise that what he told her was a kind of travesty. She went to the garden table, picked up Fiona's empty glass and twisted it in her hand.

'What's the use of calling me names?' she said in a level voice. 'It's too late.'

'The child isn't mine. I want nothing to do with it.'

'It? It?'

'Nothing to do with it,' he repeated in a hoarse, hideous voice. 'Or with you either. You must go.'

'Go?' Avril repeated stupidly.

And then, like a dam cracked long ago, which suddenly bursts with a terrifying sound of thundering water, she shouted,

'So Teddy and I have to go, do we? Because I had the bad taste to sleep with somebody while you were away? What a mortal sin. How terrible of me. If that is the rule, why didn't *you* go years ago, six months after you married me? Why didn't you bugger off then?'

'What are you—'

'Talking about? My turn to answer that. I am talking about your endless sleeping around, Hugh Brett, which started six months after we got married. Did you really think I was such an idiot as not to know? You can't keep your hands off other women, and I've known about dozens of them. Sally. Nicole. The two in London and that female you met at Terry's party. The Wren, Hilly something . . . You've had more women than – than hot dinners,' she vulgarly finished. Before he could speak she went on recklessly, 'You're just a man who fucks all the time. You can't stop, can you? Is it that you must have new women, or are you just proving over and over again what a great big man you are? There's a name for what you've got. The doctors call it satyriasis.'

He'd already taken a threatening step towards her, and when Avril, filled with the humiliation and misery of the past, shouted that out, he took a long stride, lifted his hand and hit her with all his force across the face.

The blow was so violent that he felled her like a boxer knocks out his opponent in the ring. For a moment she lay gasping, and he bent as if about to kick her where she lay. Rolling away and cringing, she cried out:

'No, no!'

Muttering something obscene, he rushed from the garden, and she heard the car roar as it went loudly down the lane and round the corner.

She got to her feet, feeling violently sick and shaking so much that her teeth chattered in her head. Automatically, pitifully, she felt her breasts, fearing for her milk. But the fall had been on her side; her breasts were unhurt. What pained agonizingly was her jaw; she could scarcely open her mouth. When she touched her face it had already started to swell.

She stood for a moment trying to stop shaking. She was frightened. She had twice before seen the demon in Hugh and it had terrified her. He had hit her once, but not so violently, and later, horrified at himself, had been penitent like a sinner begging absolution. In the lovemaking that followed he had tried to show his remorse and she had tried to accept it. She'd told herself that she must forget the act of violence.

Now she saw the demon again. But this time Hugh had been like those souls possessed with devils in the New Testament, a loathsome stranger. Another being had glared out of his eyes. He despised her because she had been unfaithful, because she had lied, because she had made a fool of him and palmed off another man's child on him. To Hugh, with his fornicating history stretching round him, his wife was a whore. Any affection he'd had, a mild emotion spiced with desire, lay stone dead.

Maybe it would pass. Probably not. But what made Avril shake were the two most terrible words he'd spoken: 'that kid'.

He hated Teddy as well.

It made insane rubbish of all his previous fatherly

feelings, and for a few moments she could scarcely grasp it. How could a man, whatever he discovered about his woman and her child, change from love to hatred for a little baby he had adored five minutes ago?

The spasms of shivering wouldn't stop as she went into the cottage. She slowly climbed the stair.

The baby was deeply asleep. He always went pale when he slept; he was the colour of a camellia, his eyes closed and his dark lashes like tiny fans. The immobile little face was full of mystery. He resembled a baby painted by Mantegna, asleep in his mother's arms five hundred years ago. He looked eastern. He looked a godling. The minute face was calm, but then in sleep he wrinkled his button of a nose.

She felt such an ache in her heart, the ache of love. And remembered the devil which had glared out of Hugh's eyes.

'We must get away, Teddy,' she said aloud. 'We can't stay here. it is not safe.'

Chapter 11

Rick Vincent was dissatisfied with himself that autumn. There had been successes such as his recent piece on Jamaica. Rick would say, 'Of course' at the mention of success, but there was no of course about it. He worked hard for the Sunday magazine which had given him a contract and paid him very well indeed. His plus, to the management, was that he was young and wrote of youthful things. When things were new, Rick was in and with them. Fresh music, intriguing architecture, acting, drama, the most original movie talent, even money. He was in advance of established taste, he was clever, quick, he scented the air for new style. But the fact was that this did not get easier. Rather the reverse. A long piece of his the previous month – it had taken him weeks of research – had been trumped days before its publication by a rival paper and a marginally cleverer article by a younger writer. After all, Rick was thirty-four now.

So he was grumpy. His sex life was not going too well either. A new girl in his life, Natasha, scarcely twenty-one and startlingly beautiful, was fending him off. She liked him and nothing more. To make things worse, his room-mate in the Temple, the rightful owner of the flat, having returned for a month or two, had then gone away again on a case taking weeks in the north, but would soon be back once more, getting in Rick's way.

He went for a walk, crossing the river at the Embankment, passing the National Theatre and walking all the way to Southwark Cathedral and back. The evening was sultry and when he returned through the Temple gate he felt no better.

He turned into his own court. And came to a dead stop.

Huddled on the steps of the building with a child in her arms, resembling some Victorian painting-telling-a-story – *Homeless* would be appropriate – was his sister.

Seeing him she made an attempt to smile.

'I did ring. I kept getting your tinned voice.'

'What in God's name . . .'

'Can I tell you when we're indoors?'

She spoke in a low voice, glancing in the direction of a man going by, briefcase in hand, totally wrapped up in his own thoughts. Girl and baby might have been invisible.

In silence Rick picked up her suitcase and unlocked the door. He scarcely glanced at the child as he accompanied his sister up into his rooms.

'Well?' he demanded, shutting the door and turning round. It was obvious that she'd brought trouble.

Avril muttered, 'Wait a moment,' and went into the spare bedroom, where he heard mysterious noises. When he followed her he found her busy pulling out an empty drawer. She began to make a kind of bed in it.

'Avril, the child can't sleep *there*!'

'Of course he can.'

189

She continued to tuck and fold, then picked up the child and carefully laid him in his temporary cot. She looked at him for a moment, then followed Rick into the dark-panelled sitting room. They sat down.

It was not until she was seated that he saw the great purple-green bruise which ran from cheek to jaw.

'Christ! Have you been in an accident?'

'Hugh hit me.'

'*What?*'

'He knocked me down.' She felt her jaw with her fingers and said, 'Ow.'

'Let me look. But that's awful. Is anything broken? Can you open your mouth properly? Have you been to hospital?'

'No I haven't, and I'm sure nothing's broken.'

She again brushed her face slightly with her fingers, opened and closed her mouth. Her lips were swollen.

'Why haven't you seen a doctor?'

He was accusing.

'Rick, I can't. I absolutely refuse to be a battered wife.'

'Even if that's what you are?'

'Even if.'

'What happened?'

He was still thunderstruck. He had a disgust amounting to horror of men who hit women. When he saw it on TV it made him want to vomit.

Avril leaned her poor bruised head against the chair and managed a lopsided smile.

'Isn't it obvious? He found out about the baby. And went mad. It's funny, when you think about it. He has slept around ever since we married, fucking everybody in sight – sorry, I dislike bad language, but that's how he makes me feel. I never talked about it to you, it's so sordid, but of course I knew. Then by accident, I suppose, the woman who lives next door, Isobel Sinclair, must have caught on about poor Keith Waring and me. She's the village voice. I don't know what she actually said to Hugh, I suppose it was nudge-nudge, wink-wink. She is a bit of a cat. And then my health visitor innocently told him about Teddy not being premature, my alibi of course; even Hugh, who isn't into anything about having children, can add up. So he bashed me.'

Rick listened in sickened silence. Finally:

'But I thought when we talked recently you told me he adored the baby.'

'So he did. Till he found out.'

'That doesn't make sense.'

'It doesn't, does it? But the fact is he now loathes us both. It was really strange. He yelled at me and knocked me down, but before that he talked about the baby as if Teddy were a Victorian foundling picked up in the gutter. He was horrible. Scary. So here I am for the moment. I promise not to stay long,' she added.

She took up what he hadn't said.

'You're thinking, why didn't I go to Ma? Simple. Because she'd try to patch things up between Hugh and me.'

For the second time in their lives Avril was the dominant one. He was in a weak position because, despite real shock and concern, the last thing he wanted was this invasion. She knew it. And if he suggested any form of reconciliation Avril would be sure to think he was considering only himself. Well, wouldn't he be? He didn't know what to say.

Avril continued to stroke the blue-green bruise in a gesture like a caress.

'I shall never go back to him, Rick. Don't think that I will. I'm not suffering from shock. Of course it *was* a shock: I never realised he was capable of being so awful. No, that isn't true. He did do it before, not so violently, ages ago. But the worst thing, the really dreadful thing, is nothing to do with Hugh's rage at me for being unfaithful. It's about Teddy. I can't stay in the same room with a man who's turned against his own son.'

'His own?'

'Oh, how literal,' she said with a scornful laugh. 'Of course I began to think Teddy was his, and why not? We had so much sex in St Vincent. We made love every night and I thought if I put my mind to it, remembering *he's* my husband, then the baby will be his. Is his. And when he came back last month after Teddy was born, he was so pleased and loving and fatherly, and he said . . .'

She had begun to cry.

Rick didn't move. He didn't offer her the masculine clean handkerchief.

'He said?'

'That Teddy looked just like his grandfather the Admiral. He said the baby had the Brett nose.'

She was crying and laughing.

'Av, you are getting hysterical. What you need is a drink.'

'No I don't. It might affect my milk. Where's my shoulder bag?'

She scrabbled in an outsized school satchel, blew her nose, and lifted the battered face which still shocked him.

'I suppose Teddy and I couldn't stay for a day or two?'

'Don't be stupid. Of course you can.'

He thought of Natasha. Of his work.

'Married sisters with bundles in shawls won't half cramp your style,' she said, sniffing. She was at his mercy and refused to give an inch. He repeated that she was being stupid and added that there was not a female of his around at the moment. Then suddenly:

'Can babies really sleep in a chest of drawers?'

What, thought Avril, carrying the baby out into a clouded morning and finding a handy seat in the Temple just near the little pond, what did people in family dramas do before the invention of the telephone? She vaguely recalled French novels where people sent each other urgent messages by things called blues. Blue pieces of paper delivered by hand. There also used to be those outdated things, telegrams. The telephone was now, it was inescapable, and as she had foreseen, the first thing that happened this morning was that Hugh rang Rick.

'Say I'm not here,' she said before he answered it. She was having a scrappy breakfast broken by a fractious child.

'It may not be him.'

'It will be. So say I am not here.'

'Think about it. That isn't very clever.'

'For Christ's sake, do as I tell you.'

Rick could scarcely refuse. He was a logical man and there wasn't a whiff of logic either in his sister or in the mess she'd found herself – put herself – in. He left on his answering machine and both he and Avril – at present apparently gifted with second sight – listened to her husband's voice. Hugh rang twice.

'Rick? It's Hugh. My crazy wife seems to have upped and left. I expect it's the aftermath of childbirth or something.

She's dotty.' A laugh. 'You don't happen to have heard from her, do you? Please ring when you hear this.'

The second call an hour later was more tense.

'Rick, Hugh again. I have telephoned both your parents, who are quite worried since I told them she's gone. They haven't a clue where she is.'

'You see? He doesn't mention Teddy,' said Avril, listening.

'If you have seen or heard from her, please ring me at once. I am naturally very concerned. I'll be at the barracks all day. The number is . . .'

Rick switched off the machine.

'Well?'

'He can stew.'

'He sounds worried.'

'Good.'

As she sat in the Temple, and lawyers and clerks and tourists went by, and one friendly American woman stopped and said, 'May I?' and peered down at the shawl-wrapped baby with a universal look of love to murmur satisfactory things, Avril knew only too well that she could not stay with her brother. Poor Rick. He had turned into a bachelor. He had that singleness of state and purpose, that selfishness, that polite detachment however hard he tried, of somebody who had once said, 'I am twenty-eight and unmarried. Why should I do anything I don't want to do?'

Avril dispassionately viewed her limited family. It looked as if, *faute de mieux*, she was going to land up in the Cotswolds. Susan Vincent was not only mad about Hugh – she was a pushover for handsome men – she would be determined to be mediator and peacemaker. She would also be shocked to the depths of her fifty-seven-year-old soul at Avril having borne another man's child and lied to make Hugh believe it was his. So it will be Ma. What a prospect. She looked down at the baby and a sentimental melting emotion came over her. She felt as if her whole being was so full of love that her heart might split. I've got you. You. I shall never be lonely again.

While his sister sat doing nothing in the dull London noonday, Rick took a taxi to the office. The offices of his paper were modern but not brutally so. Taking the express lift, he made his way across the huge open-plan rooms. Silence gave a thrall to the place. Computers were so quiet; they had banished forever the old merry clatter he remembered when he first started work in the provinces.

He sat down at his littered desk and stared at the square of greenish glass.

Finally, as unaware of the thirty or more people in the office as they were of him, all busy in their softly clicking way, all screen-staring, he picked up the telephone.

Answering machine, he thought. It's sure to be.

He was in luck. A lively, hard voice said:

'Who is this?'

'An old mate of yours.'

'My stepson as I live and breathe. And on the scrounge. I do ask myself for what.'

'I suppose you wouldn't be free if I could get to Richmond this morning?'

'Jeez, Rick. Can you make it up the Amazon? All the way from the office. The crisis must be really serious.'

'How do you know I don't just want a little talk with my stepmother?'

'Poor fool. Sure, come this morning, I'm working at

home, but for such a rare visitor I can stop, I suppose. Take the Underground. Half an hour to here; if you take a cab it'll be two hours.'

'OK . . .'

Public transport was not Rick's thing.

'Shall I give you lunch?' inquired Retta, laughing. 'Cheese and apples.'

When they had gone to the Temple for a little sex in the lunch hour, she had often brought those in a plastic bag.

Rick did as she suggested and had to admit that the journey by Underground was reasonably quick and pain-less. He read a newspaper and in forty minutes was walking down the road towards the cul-de-sac where his father and Retta lived. He saw the river in the distance. Greenish, flattish, a few ripples and reflections. A man in a rowing boat went by. Then an old-fashioned river boat, loaded with end-of-season tourists. A loud voice shouted a com-mentary. Rick thought, the juiciest of the guide's facts will be invented. After all, who checked?

Rick, now accustomed to the sixteenth century, thought the neo-Georgian house hideous. But Retta wasn't. Her sweatshirt had a foxglove on the bosom, her hair shone like new money. She kissed him warmly, exchanging the glance that one-time lovers use, then took him through the house to the back garden. There were garden chairs and un-needed parasols.

'I know, I know, they're silly now summer's gone, but I can't bear to bung them away in the garage yet. *What* do you want, Rick? I'm eaten up with curiosity.'

It was a treat to be with her, and to be himself. With Natasha he had to play-act. She seemed to prefer it. With his unfortunate sister he had to watch his tongue. But whatever he said would not make Retta think less of him, and he told the story without frills.

Retta was pop-eyed.

'Your kid sister! What a thing. I always thought she was the quiet one; she *seems* so quiet. Rather good, really. Quite rare that, isn't it, actual goodness. I remember you once told me you suspected her husband slept around. Nice to think he got his deserts.'

'Not nice to be smashed in the face.'

'Don't sound self-righteous, Rick, it is very unattractive. You never used to be like that. I was enjoying the earlier part of the story, not the bit when he clouted her, that's disgusting. And now you're here to ask me what in hell she and you do next.'

His face was always thin, but it looked pinched. She noticed that. She noticed everything about Rick. His self-absorption. His humour and talent. His enjoyment when he argued. At present she could read every word in his head. She twisted her finger into one of her red curls.

'Dump her on me.'

He gave a start. The garden was quiet, the morning still.

'I never meant . . .'

'Never meant! You came here meaning nothing else, and it just shows your common sense. Ask her if she'd like to come and live here with us until she's sorted herself out. There's lots of room. Something I can't get used to, all those spare bedrooms. So? Break it to her, anyway *ask* her, OK? Give me a buzz.'

Rick was both overcome at the success of his selfish plan and determined that this was the answer for Avril, the baby and himself.

Retta put out a thin hand weighed down with international rings. Mexican silver. Arabian gold. Tiffany platinum interlocked with rubies. There was a Lorelei in Retta.

'Of course,' she said thoughtfully, 'you have to take on board that your sister won't fancy the idea. I mean, I *am* a total stranger to her – though I believe she does quite like me. And of course there's your dad, who will have the traditional pink fit.'

'I know. But I thought . . .'

He had betrayed himself, and she laughed outright.

'You thought I could cope with him. Of course I can. He won't be nice to her to start with, will he? He'll huff and puff. But I shall shut him up. Avril is the important one – and that baby, naturally. Do you think she'd be happy with me? I'm like curry. One can't eat it every day.'

'I did,' he said. And they were both surprised.

During lunch, which actually was cheese and apples but washed down with some excellent red wine, they talked ways and means. Rick explained his sister's reasons for not wanting to go to their mother.

'Because she's devoted to the violent husband? Yeah, I can see that would be a trial. I've never met my predecessor but she does sound the sort of lady I always imagine her to be,' said Retta amiably. They were eating in the kitchen. She paused, wine bottle in hand, put her head on one side and said dreamily:

'Isn't it peculiar, Rick, how the old rules still hang around? There are a great raft of older people who find our sex mix-ups dire. I mean, they *mind*. They keep the commandments and so on. When they're all dead, what'll happen?'

Later they went back into the garden, and Retta told him

what she was working on, three pieces about famous wives.

'Not husbands. The trick is how do men cope when women earn much much more than they do? There's this male pride. A need to be The One, in capitals. They don't like it. They really do not. I lie to Gerry about how much I'm paid. Always have.'

When she asked him about himself he talked mostly about his friend returning again to the Temple rooms. Retta brushed the complaints aside.

'Pooh. You're thinking about sex. The guy goes away weekends, doesn't he? Most people do.'

'I am not thinking about sex.' He was cold. 'Work needs space.'

'Oh, bull,' said Retta. 'You and I both work on planes and trains. Who are you kidding?'

When he was leaving he tried to thank her.

'It's terrific of you to help Avril. If it all turns out impossible, I mean if . . .'

'Don't be a *fool*. I'm her stepmother, aren't I?'

When he let himself into the flat, both his sister and the child were fast asleep. Avril lay in a leather chair, her legs drawn up, the attitude awkward, pathetic. The baby in his drawer – Avril had placed it beside her – looked far more comfortable.

Rick stood staring at the sleeping girl. She looked tired, and the hideous bruises on her face were like smeared dirt. He remembered her at seventeen, eager and talkative and rash and lively. What do men do to women? he thought. What do they still do? Unless a woman is strong, like Retta, must she necessarily be a victim? The idea repelled him. But he did not think, she is the closest being to me in the world and needs my protection. He had a sense of relief that he had palmed her off on their stepmother.

'It's very kind, but I'd better go to Ma.'

'*Avril.*' Guilt made him angry. 'You said yourself that Ma will be certain to try to force you to see Hugh. Retta is on your side.'

'Dad won't be.'

Rick sighed loudly as Avril picked up Teddy, who was making sucking noises. If Rick was annoyed, she was ice-cold. But she had to face, all the same, exactly where she was. It was only too clear that the baby could not go on sleeping in a drawer. And she supposed her stepmother – whom she scarcely knew – would be better than a mother who always went on as if Hugh was perfection and she, Susan, his representative on earth. Convinced that her father would be worse than unpleasant, she was still forced to choose his home rather than her mother's. For the moment at least.

'Retta says she can cope with Dad,' said Rick, reading her face.

'You've got it all nicely settled.'

'Don't be like that.'

'I'm not "like" anything. I'll ring Retta. But not in front of you. I'll do it from the bedroom.'

She went out, baby and all, and presently Rick heard her pretty, light voice. Listening and tense, he heard her give an unwilling laugh.

When she came back she said wearily:

'Retta says we can come this evening. I shall need a taxi. You may have gone by Underground but I won't have Teddy squashed in the rush hour. If you don't mind.'

Rick supposed he deserved that.

Brother and sister talked little during an overlong, traffic-jammed taxi ride across London. Even supposing Avril, who had not forgiven him, had been willing to talk to him, it wouldn't have been possible. Teddy was having a crying jag.

My God, thought Rick, as the little creature howled and doubled up as if in agony. My God, how do women cope? What was even stranger, why did they want to? Avril was busy picking up the baby, putting him against her shoulder and rubbing his elderly hunched back. Then she put him down on her lap again. Then she rocked him to and fro.

The howls went pitilessly on.

At last, worn out by it all, he went to sleep just as the taxi turned into the Richmond cul-de-sac.

'We're here,' said Rick heartily. He sprang out and the cab driver helped with Avril's small zip bag. After Rick asked the driver to wait – he was already set on returning fast to work – brother and sister went up the path to the neo-Georgian front door.

But it was already open, framing a figure in white. She rushed out, kissed Avril's bruised face and, sounding to Rick totally out of character, began to exclaim with warmth:

'I'm so glad you decided to come, Avril, I've been dying to meet the baby. Can I have him? Oh, isn't that the dearest little button nose.'

She seemed unaware of her visitor's bruise-dirtied cheeks and crooned over the bundle. While not lifting her head, she said to Rick:

'Dump the case in the hall. Avril and I will fix things up later. Staying for a drink, Rick? Or do you have to dash back?'

There was irony in the remark, and he heard it. It was not the world's most welcoming invitation. He said quickly that he was afraid he had work to do. He stood for a moment at a loss, wondering if he ought to thank Retta again. But both women, discussing babies, were moving away from the front door towards the sitting room. His sister did glance back to say briefly, 'Thanks for bringing me.' It was cool, and Rick felt guilty all over again.

He went determinedly up to them, muttered something to Retta and kissed Avril. By back luck his kiss landed right on the bruise, and she winced.

'Oh, sorry, sorry.'

'No, I'm sorry for making a face,' she said. 'See you soon.'

He left them, walking light-footed to the waiting taxi. Free to feel guilty in peace.

Chapter 12

Retta slammed the front door and asked friendly questions. Avril said might she go upstairs to feed the baby?

'Of course. I see you're not one of the Hollywood lot; we're now getting it in the UK too, I notice. Women baring their breasts and feeding their babies in public to annoy movie directors or anybody else who happens to be about. Showing off, I feel. History says Vanessa Redgrave did it at a dinner party years back, deeply embarrassing the guys there. Come on up.'

Alone in a large, well-furnished room with windows overlooking the garden, Avril fed the baby. She remembered Fiona Leveaux had said she must try not to have disturbed thoughts when feeding, or the baby would know.

'It's the same with riding,' said Fiona on another favourite subject. 'People think you can daydream while you're riding. That's tripe. You have to stay in touch or the horse won't co-operate.'

Obeying the advice to woman and horse, Avril concentrated on the hungry, sucking child. Then settled him in what looked like a brand-new cot in a corner.

Retta breezed in.

'Got everything you want? What a f . . . silly question. Of course you haven't. Do you like the cot? I got it in Richmond this afternoon and they actually delivered it. Never been into a kids' department before. Isn't it dinky?'

'I think it is beautiful.'

Retta gave her a quick look and sat down on the bed. Avril began solemnly to unpack the two T-shirts, pants and clean tights in her zip bag. She put them into a large empty chest of drawers by the window.

'It's so good of you to have us.'

'For God's sake! I *want* to have you. It's a real treat.'

Retta went over to the cot and stood, arms folded.

'He blew a bubble. Rick said he slept in an empty drawer in the Temple flat. Did he really? I couldn't believe my ears.'

'It was OK. It made a sort of bed.'

Retta gave Avril another of her looks; Avril knew very well that her own expression was hangdog. She ought to make an effort. She was shattered still.

'Nov, Av,' said Retta, 'I am going to nip down and get us a drink. You can have half wine and half water. There was a piece in our paper a few Sundays ago, by my rival who has gone all mumsy and will do these gynaecological bits. She says wine and water is OK. And when I get back you and I had best make a plan on how we play it with your dad. I haven't rung him with the news, by the by. Thought it better to let him arrive to a *fait accompli*.'

She regarded her visitor's horrified face.

'Come on, Av, he can't eat you. You've got me. The new stepmother. Which reminds me, talking of mothers, step or otherwise, you'll have to ring your ma. Rick said she hasn't been told.'

'I only told Rick,' said Avril unnecessarily.

'I get the point. It's tough dressing up facts for parents. I haven't met your ma, but I have an impression she is shockable.'

'Very.'

Loud sigh from Retta.

'Avril, do turn round. Stop behaving as if you've brought trunkfuls of clothes and have all this unpacking to do. I say,' amused, 'you didn't half leave everything behind. Not to worry. I shall enjoy going down and getting your things for you. I'm sure you'd prefer it to be me? Do you think I might frighten your husband?'

It was impossible even in her countryless and bruised state for Avril not to smile.

'Out of his wits, I should say.'

'Oh good.'

Retta sprang up and went to the door. Then paused and suddenly said:

'You aren't thinking of going back to the bastard, are you?'

'No.'

'Good. I was afraid, to be quite honest, that being an RC and all that you might think it your duty to patch things up.'

'I'm only a Catholic now and then,' said Avril, without a trace of irony.

'Like the rest of them. But it sticks. It sticks.'

There was a pause. Retta was still by the door, still wearing the bright, penetrating look of good journalists. Sentiment no part of it. Perhaps a little humanity. Mainly curiosity.

'Has he hit you before, Avril?'

'Years ago.'

A pause.

'You stayed then.'

'Yes.' Avril thought for a moment. 'We hadn't been married long. He was so sorry. And I believed him.'

'And were still in love with him.'

'I can't remember.'

Retta did not believe her.

'I expect you were,' she said, vaguely enough, and then, 'I know I'm distinctly not one of those marriage guidance counsellors, but I've got this thing about men who hit women. Don't go back. Don't think of it.'

'I won't. I don't. Because of Teddy. That's why I left. In case he hurt Teddy.'

'Oh, the noble mother figure,' said Retta satirically. 'Thinking about the baby and not about yourself. No good, that. Women have got to think about themselves. I do. Talking of which, I need some Aussie Chardonnay.'

When she had left the room, Avril had a pause. She gave her head a shake, as divers do when they emerge to the surface, shaking the water from their ears. Retta soon returned, a bottle and glasses clinking on a tray. She sat down again on the bed.

'I suppose,' she was unashamedly interested, 'you think it was the devil's worse luck that your husband found out.'

'I gambled. And lost.'

'It's a gamble women are taking all the time. Too easy if you're sleeping with two guys in the same month. Then there is this interesting puzzle, which of the two is the dad? I gather it wasn't like that with you.'

'No. I found out I was pregnant before I went to St Vincent.'

'Can one ask who the guy was?'

'My boss. He was nice,' said Avril.

Retta was secretly amused at the indifferent voice.

'Looking at your poor face, it's a bloody good thing, it seems to me, that your husband did find out. So you can be shot of him,' she remarked. 'Aha, that's Gerry's car. Now we have to face the might of the Royal Navy's biggest guns. Feeling brave?'

Both women had stood up in the same movement, and Avril heard her father's cheery voice shouting from the hall:

'Sweetheart? I'm back.'

'Just coming, Gerry. Got a surprise for you.'

It was twilight, and Retta had already lit the sitting room lights. Gerald Vincent at the drinks table turned round expectantly.

When he saw his daughter, the smile was wiped off his face. He goggled.

'Yeah,' said Retta, taking Avril's arm. Avril herself was rooted to the floor. 'Here is your daughter come for a stay, baby and all.'

'Oh. Oh good,' said Gerald, with forced heartiness. He immediately recovered from his disappointment. 'Where's Hugh?'

'Well, Hugh isn't here. In fact it's only Avril and Teddy who are staying,' said Retta brightly. 'And if you are wondering,' she added, for Gerald had by now taken in his daughter's appearance, 'what the hell has happened to Avril with that damned great bruise she's got, your charming colleague in the Senior Service clouted her across the face.'

She handed him the news as she'd handed Avril a drink.

'My poor girl!' Gerald, shocked and embarrassed, did not know what to say next.

'Let's sit down,' said Retta, steering Avril over to the sofa and sitting down beside her.

Gerald remained on his feet, legs apart, a man keeping his balance on deck in rough seas.

'Avril, shall you tell him or will I?' Retta asked.

'You, please,' said Avril, speaking for the first time.

'OK. Perhaps it'd be better since it isn't my horror story. Gerry, this is not exactly the case of the battered wife. Well, sure, Avril *is*, but why is the real point. Hugh hit her because he'd just found out that the baby is not his.'

If the carpet had started to speak in muffled tones, if an apparition had come floating in from the garden and pointed its skinny finger at him, if the entire roof of the house had flown off, leaving them exposed to the sky, Gerald could not have been more staggered. He had begun drinking his whisky before she started to speak and now gave a sort of splutter. Some of it went up his nose.

He began by saying, 'Do I understand—' and then changed it to 'Let me get things right—' and again, 'Are you telling me—' He finally finished:

'What you are saying is incredible.'

'I'm sorry, Dad.'

'You are sorry! Do you mean to come here to my house and tell me—'

'Oh, Gerry, do shut up!' exclaimed Retta. She lounged over to him with her long-legged stride and put both arms round his waist. He recoiled, his handsome middle-aged face blank with shock. She continued to imprison him.

'Leave me alone, Retta.'

'Gerry. You've got to cut out those reactions, they don't

wash any more. I'm sure they did once, but they're gone. It is no use, it really is *useless* for you to huff and puff. Avril got banged up and when she flew to St Vincent she did mean to tell Hugh, I'm sure, but then she didn't. One way and another it was what I remember in my theatre-reviewing days is called the bed-trick. She thought Hugh would believe Teddy was his. So he did. That's the point, my love,' she finished, releasing her husband, who was ominously silent. 'The filthy thing now is,' she went on, returning to Avril and the sofa, 'when Hugh Brett believed Teddy was his flesh and blood, he bonded with him. He was the perfect father. Then when he found out the truth, he knocked your daughter down and disowned the baby. So here she is. Staying with us.'

Gerald put down his glass.

There was a curious silence. It had melodrama in it. It resembled in its quality the terrible and destructive emotions of long ago. There was Retta, watching her husband, her head back, and there was Gerald, torn between disgust and outrage and the weakness of being in love with a woman twenty-five years younger than he was. And there was Avril. At the mercy of both of them.

'So we're going to look after them,' finished Retta.

Gerald gave his daughter, just then, a look like Medusa's.

'I see I have no alternative.'

'You'll be crazy about Teddy,' said Retta. 'Wait till you see your grandson. His nose is like a lump of putty.'

Gerald Vincent was already in bed when Retta, who had decided to have a bath, came to join him. He had an open book in his hand; he was reading Sherlock Holmes. It was a sign which both his wives had discovered meant he was angry. Poor Susan Vincent used to feel miserable when Conan Doyle was in evidence. Retta merely stretched out a hand and gently took the book from him, closing it and putting it on the bedside table.

He looked at her. His face was set, nose prominent, mouth folded so thin that the lips scarcely showed.

'You had no right, no right at all to make such a decision without first consulting me.'

'So what would you have done?'

'Washed my hands of the whole dirty business.'

'Washed your hands,' she echoed. 'My God.'

Retta was never scandalised in a tough and immoral world. But she could still be surprised.

She walked back to her dressing table, pulled out the stool, sat down and swivelled round to face him. She clasped both hands round the satin knee of her pyjamas. All Retta's nightclothes shone in colours of grey or cream like clothes made from mother-of-pearl. Her husband, his expression making him look more than his sixty years, sat like a judge on the bench. She said coolly:

'I'm ashamed of you.'

'What did you say?'

His voice was so harsh that Retta's red eyebrows shot up, touching her hairline.

'What are you saying?' he repeated, his voice grating. 'Don't you know what you have done with your – your sloppy sentimentality ... your ridiculous feminism that ...' Words failed him. 'How dare you invite her here in such circumstances? There will be an unpleasant divorce, it is just the sort of thing the newspapers ...' He started again, still furious. 'Am I to be put in the position of conniving with a woman who tried to pretend her bastard was . . .'

He had no chance to finish, for she ran across to the bed and put one pale hand across his mouth.

'Shut up! Just shut up! Don't you say another word or Avril will not be the only woman this week to walk out. I mean it. I'm ashamed of you. Do you know that you're terrible?' He easily dragged her hand from his mouth, but she continued.

'Don't you even breathe that you are shocked. Shocked! Your poor daughter is in bad trouble. She's your child, for fuck's sake, and she's homeless and the man she married is a shit. Now what you and I have to do is to look after her.'

Silence.

Retta pulled off the loose, gleaming pyjama trousers, wearing only the shimmering top. Naked from the waist down, she climbed in beside him.

'How did you sleep?'

A red head appeared round Avril's door. It was eight o'clock, dull-skied and damp. Avril was feeding the baby.

'Not too well, I'm afraid.'

'Poor you. Still upset?'

'No. It was Teddy, he was awful.'

'Oh, the wicked monster,' crooned Retta, coming over to pat the bald head. 'It is his new cot; he thinks pink bows are sissy and I agree. I'll get blue ones instead. Will that suit you, Monster?'

Retta's voice was not pretty and rarely soft. Even when crooning to a baby it was a kind of croak.

The sound of a plane broke the morning calm and roared overhead.

'Bloody things. They use Richmond Bridge and Kew to show the silly f . . . s where they are.'

She wandered over to the window.

'My grass needs one more cut before winter.'

Avril was patting the baby's elderly back. With the bald patch and fringe of dark hair, back hunched, he resembled an old monk. She shifted him to the other breast. Retta now returned and was critically studying her stepdaughter's bruises. They had not started to fade.

'I must get you some witch-hazel at Boots. Lovely smell, hasn't it? There's something I want to say. Don't look worried. Stop looking like that, Avril. All I want to say is don't expect your dad to be civil at first. You know him better than I do, but I guess we have different viewpoints. I mean, you still respect him or think you ought to. I'm not sure I ever will. But give the poor bugger time. I know he's sixty, but sometimes one might say a hundred and sixty. He keeps reverting to being disgusted of Tunbridge Wells. I suppose rules and stuff hang on if you're in the Services. Did you notice that? Good grief, I'm a tactless dope, with you black and blue from the fine old English traditions. Now. To start with. Not another word about leaving here or thanking me or anything else daft like that. Just because your father doesn't yet know how to behave. And don't start thinking that maybe you'd better go to the Cotswolds and put up with your ma's lectures. I should imagine she's a keen one for the rules too.'

'Almost more than Dad.'

'That reminds me. Stiffen the sinews and ring her this morning. The big issue, Av, is that we *want* you and Teddy. Your father doesn't know it yet but he does. As much as me. Poor Gerry,' she added, showing her large teeth in a grin.

'He hangs on to one rule of behaviour but excepts himself. What about extramarital sex with me? He is still on about Queen's Regulations for other people. And he gets really thrown when the Regs are broken.'

'He looked so horrified.'

'Flummoxed would be more accurate. Do you know, Av,' said Retta pensively, 'I was trying to get what that reaction of his last night made me think of, and it seems to me he was rather like a man whose car is always waiting for him at the door. Down the path he goes, climbs in and drives off. One day he walks out, *thinks* the car's there and sort of climbs in. No car. He lands on his bottom.'

'Oh, Retta.'

'So he's got to pick himself up, hasn't he? Now, I've had this terrific idea. About getting your bits and pieces back from the Dorset ogre.'

Retta's awkward simile was not far from the truth. Gerald had indeed landed painfully on the ground. He had prided himself from his youth on knowing right from wrong, and even when he cruelly wounded his ageing wife and took in her place a woman with the elixir to make him young again, his conscience did not give him a hard time. He and Susan had not been happy for years. A clean cut was best, thought Gerald, like a surgeon. Deeply in love with an odd, clever girl who ruled him by her sex, scarcely believing his luck to have won her, he tried to behave well to his ex-wife. He settled more money on her than he could afford or she needed. He helped her to move house, having previously toured Oxfordshire with her to find her a new one. He telephoned her so frequently that in the end Susan told him to stop being sorry for her.

It was to Susan Vincent's credit – she had a practical, day-to-day approach even to sorrow – that she had now made a sort of life. Gerald's too-obvious concern and the pity she sensed beneath it got on her nerves. He was released not because of his virtue but because she had guts. Recently Gerald felt he could concentrate on the questionable right to be happy.

Until last night.

In the final stages of his Service life, he was working at Greenwich on the Navy's organisation for pensions. He liked the work, it interested him and he felt good about it. Every morning he drove across London towards the City at scarcely half past seven. All the Richmond gardens were still full of autumn roses, which even the traffic fumes could not spoil. This morning he opened the car windows and the sliding roof. Above his grey head was a soft, matching sky.

The traffic on the Embankment slowed to a crawl. A stop. A crawl. The beautiful old house where Dante Gabriel Rossetti and his family had lived, giving parties and keeping kangaroos and peacocks in the garden, stared at him with a dusty face. Whistler's house too, where, gloomy and inscrutable, he had painted symphonies. And up a side street had lived the serious Scot Carlyle. Paintings and poems, history and legend had been here, part of English life now covered in London dust. While alongside the street senselessly crammed with cars, each containing a single man or woman, the river flowed unburdened with craft.

Gerald did not notice the traffic's chaos or the river's watery liberty. He was absorbed in his own thought. It was not only life and death, goddess and skeleton, who sat facing each other at their eternal game of chess. Youth and age did the same. From the moment last night when he had

begun to make love to Retta she had won their game. That
game. She always would.

He had always been a confident, conventional man,
much liked, as Hugh was, by his own sex. As for women,
Gerald needed and despised them. He did not admit to that
second feeling, but it was in his bones. His manner to
women, particularly to the sharp-eyed Retta, showed it. He
was attentive in an old-fashioned way. He held back and let
women chatter, pretty creatures. He opened doors. His
masculinity was enhanced by rugged looks, and Gerald's
certainty that man was the superior animal and this was
what Nature intended was the source of his strength. Like
a fragment of plutonium which heats of its own volition, it
had glowed in the centre of Gerald, making him the man he
was. But when after over forty years of authority he fell
deeply in love, Retta put her hand straight through his
ribcage to clasp the glowing stuff. She was the thief of what
had been Gerald's self.

Chapter 13

The telephone makes cowards of people, thought Avril. It certainly did of her. Not being able to face the incredulous silence followed by the tinny questions of her mother, she did not ring after all. She wrote. But the careful letter arrived too late, for Susan had already heard the news; Gerald, inevitably, had telephoned. It had been a balm for him to share his outraged – and at Richmond his now concealed – emotions with Susan.

In answer to Avril's letter, Susan replied. Yes, she had heard 'from your father'; she thought what had happened 'very dreadful and you cannot expect me to give you any kind of sympathy'. Susan didn't suggest they should meet. She did not ask after the grandson she'd been so proud of. Apparently her principles were more important than Teddy.

At Richmond Retta said that by the by Avril would want to go out now and then, though she realised she would need to rush back for whatever feed was due; meanwhile, to give her some time off, she and Gerry could certainly mind the baby.

216

As usual Avril began to protest and Retta to pooh-pooh. Even Avril, none too bright at present, saw that her stepmother was enjoying her role of champion of the oppressed.

Following the offer of minding Teddy sometimes, Retta came out into the garden where Avril was sitting on the lawn reading her father's *Times*.

'I'm just off. Back around six, I guess. Lots of stuff in the fridge and Araté – Retta's young Spanish help – 'is going to do Teddy's ironing. Teddy's had another conquest there.'

She sat on a nearby chair and added casually:

'It doesn't take too long to get to Dorset, does it?'

'You've rung Hugh!'

'Sure have.'

Avril had an inward struggle. She realised that Retta had meant it when she'd said she would go and fetch Avril's possessions. The idea was practical. It was charitable too. But oh, the grating sensation of all this taking and taking.

'I thought I'd lug along two of Gerry's beat-up old Navy cases; I found them in the attic. They're good and large. Tell me where your clothes are. Usual places? Wardrobe and chest of drawers? What about Teddy's stuff?'

'What did Hugh say?'

Avril's voice was thin.

'That he'd be there to let me in. He sounded sniffy. I put on my office voice and,' she chuckled, 'there *was* a moment when he sounded quite alarmed.'

And you, thought Avril, are delighted with yourself. Beyond protest, she described where everything was. Teddy's clothes in a small room, it had been the spare room, of his own. As she said that, Avril remembered when she was pregnant and had papered the little room with a

217

pattern of ducks and ponds and bulrushes. As an after-
thought she said:

'Could you look out my painting stuff?'

'Of course. I remember Rick did tell me you paint.'

Retta had produced a tiny Psion organiser to take down
some of Avril's answers. Fine. More keys chattering. Then
with a salute and a 'Wish me luck,' she was gone.

Avril knew that what her stepmother was bent on doing
today was the only solution. In any case she couldn't have
stopped her; Retta's charity was commanding. There were
times when Avril almost preferred her father's coldness. He
scarcely said good morning, and when he did speak to her,
never more than a few words, his manner was so icy that she
had begun to think it rather comic. She had even wanted to
giggle.

Retta always said later, 'He'll get over it.' But will I?
thought Avril. There was a glass wall cemented now
between herself and her father. Can somebody stop loving
you because you do not keep the rules? Perhaps that is what
happened to me with Hugh. He refused me a baby. He slept
around all the time. So I did not love him any more. And
then *he* stopped loving Teddy because Teddy wasn't his.
Love, thought Avril, is nonsense really.

It was strange to think of Retta going to see Hugh, whom
she had never actually met. There had been social telephone calls after Hugh's return from St Vincent when
Teddy was only a few weeks old. There had been chappish
conversation between Gerald and Hugh; a get-together had
been planned. Hugh, always sociable, had been enthusiastic about the idea. They would drive up to Richmond
taking the baby with them and stay the night with Gerald
and Retta.

But it had never happened.

And now Hugh was about to face the sort of woman he simply did not either rate or understand. He will be thrown. Self-conscious. He'll dislike her very much.

Retta knew little of the West Country. A city woman, at home in London, New York and San Francisco, not a stranger either in Rome or the South of France, she'd never had a reason to drive westwards. She was very taken with the lonely countryside as her small open car advanced into Dorset. She admired the patrician old houses which here and there, too near the road, stood behind yew hedges. She crawled in and out of country towns. She was relieved when there was a motorway or a dual carriageway. At last she arrived in Avril's village, slowed down and looked about for directions.

A fat man in working overalls was coming towards her wheeling a motorbike.

She stopped the car and leaned out.

'I wonder if you could tell me where Fuchsia Cottage is?'

'You caan' miss 'un,' he said, pointing with one enormous oil-stained hand. Retta listened intently to his instructions but was so intrigued by his appearance that she forgot every word. His fat cheeks were tight across his face, he looked like an enormous polished apple, and his Dorset accent was almost incomprehensible. He repeated:

'You caan' miss 'un.'

Retta thanked him and drove way. Luckily further down the lane there was a small thatched cottage, exactly where he'd pointed, and sure enough on a low iron gate was the name lettered black on white. Just as Avril had described, Retta found she could lift the gate sheer of its hinges to open it. Why, she wondered, hadn't they got it fixed?

She parked the car out of the way round the corner, the exact spot where Keith used to leave his car for nights of love.

Carrying the two capacious cases, Retta loped up the path between lavender bushes and a few very late-flowering roses, some of which had been dear to Avril. If Brett isn't here, I won't be able to get in. Damn, why didn't I ask Av for the front door keys? Ah well. I shall just sit and twiddle my thumbs, he's sure to turn up eventually. There was a kind of terrace in front of the cottage, and some deckchairs. She dumped the suitcases and was looking about when the front door opened.

And there, tall and personable, and quite a knockout in looks, was the husband. He had returned from barracks expressly for this meeting. Like all men who have worn uniform for years it suited him extraordinarily well and gave him an almost absurd film-starrish glamour.

'You must be Hugh,' she said sociably.

He took in the gawky visitor, red hair artfully cut to look slightly untidy, the usual jeans and a T-shirt lettered with some silly message. He said a stiff how-do-you-do. He scarcely moved his lips when he spoke, which gave an odd effect. It was Hugh's habit when dealing with men on charges or impertinent waiters. He opened the door wider and stepped back for her to enter.

Retta marched in and fairly dumped her bags on the floor. She knelt down, snapped open the suitcases and looked up at him expectantly.

Hugh remained near the door as if making sure of an escape. Like someone faced with a nervous dog, Retta could sense he was afraid of her.

'Funny time for us to meet. First and last, I shouldn't wonder. I suppose Av's clothes are all upstairs? I'd better start on those.'

'Indeed,' through immobile lips. She still knelt, regarding him with an unabashed raking glance. He felt impelled to say:

'Did you bring a list?'

'Sure did.'

'If there's anything you can't find, I will be in the garden.'

Off with you then, thought Retta. Does he always talk like that or is it embarrassment and alarm? She knew a man could be physically brave and still be unnerved by a woman. What frightens him is this thing we can have, she thought. And can use against them. I'd best put him out of his misery. She darted a slight grin at his back as he was leaving, but he didn't see it.

When she began to carry the suitcases to the bottom of the stairs he turned round.

'Let me help.'

'I can manage, thanks. I'll just leave them here.'

She was already going up the ladder stair. Hugh hesitated and then went out.

Sitting on the terrace, he could hear the invader banging about up in his bedroom. The acoustics of Fuchsia Cottage were bad; there wasn't a room which had its own silence. Alterations carried out during the years when ancient houses were robbed of their thick inside walls, and staircases torn away and rebuilt, meant a banishment of intimacy. Walls which had kept secrets for hundreds of years disappeared in brick, lath and plaster dust. With the front door open, Hugh could follow Retta's movements,

221

drawers pulled open, cupboards slammed. He felt insulted. His wife had sent this woman to ransack his house. And what a woman. He couldn't bear her London voice, the vulgar hair, worst of all the knowing manner; she was like a man who nudges you in a pub. Her stare was impertinent. In her eyes he saw all the knowledge of his disgrace and Avril's lascivious past. She knew Avril had attempted to deceive him into believing her bastard child was his. Most of all he saw in the woman's expression the knowledge that he had lost his temper – Hugh's euphemism for hitting Avril in the face.

The window upstairs clinked.

'Swim things?'

He got to his feet, went into the garden and looked up. Elbows on the windowsill and framed in the tiny Elizabethan window, Retta leaned out.

'Av doesn't seem to have any swim things.'

'Try the cupboard in the bathroom.'

'Cheers.'

The head disappeared. More dragging and slamming and one or two mysterious bumps. Then footsteps on the ladder stair. He could not remain still a moment longer. When he went into the cottage he could not believe his eyes. Retta had pitched all his wife's clothes over the landing; the sitting room was inches deep in dresses, raincoats, trousers, jeans, shirts, scarves and scattered shoes and boots. She had managed to chuck the underwear into a separate heap which he narrowly escaped stepping into. Bras and knickers, nightwear, tights, leggings patterned with roses. On the top was a peacock-blue swimsuit he had bought Avril one after-sex morning at St Vincent.

Retta clattered down.

'Thought I'd pack down here, it's easier. I haven't done the baby's stuff yet, but it looks as if I won't have enough luggage. Have you got a couple of zip bags I could borrow? I can send them back later by carrier. I'll pack Av's stuff now. Better keep Teddy's separate.'

'I suppose,' he said with freezing politeness, 'you need help.'

'Well, to be honest, I think you should. Considering,' Retta flopped down on her knees like a pious Catholic at mass, 'all this is your fault.'

'*I beg your pardon.*'

She was folding a dress and didn't look up.

'Don't bother to deny it. We both know it's all your doing. You and Avril could be having a perfectly normal life this minute, a sensible life too. Husband, wife, baby. If you hadn't hit her. And worse still, if you hadn't turned against that cute little Teddy.'

In a muscle-stiffened tenseness, controlling his voice with difficulty, he began:

'I prefer not—'

'To discuss your private business with a stranger.' She scrabbled more clothes together. 'Why not? You're going to discuss them with a solicitor, aren't you? Tell him the gory details. And as I know them anyway, and so, I may add, does Avril's mother, her father and Rick, what's the big deal about me mentioning what happened?'

He wanted to escape. To get into his car and put miles between himself and all this. Another part of him for a moment would very much have liked to strike her. Having hit one woman with dire results he saw it was one way to settle a score. It had a filthy satisfaction. But something in Retta Vincent, something clever, jeering and antagonistic to the Hugh Brett who never failed with women, kept him there. He actually picked up the blue swimsuit, folded it and poked it into a corner of the rapidly filling suitcase. She accepted the gesture and they continued to pack in silence until the floor was clear.

She then dragged out her organiser and began to tap and click.

'Ah. Forgot those. Her painting things.'

'What?'

'Your wife paints,' patiently. 'Remember? She didn't tell me where she kept her stuff. Where would it be?'

'I have no idea.'

She gave a sarcastic laugh and went upstairs, but was down again almost at once. He was still standing adrift in the centre of the room.

'Come on. You must know where the painting things are.'

'And if they're so important she must have told you.' He was very sharp.

'Well, maybe, but apparently I didn't make a note about it. Could they be in the kitchen?'

'Of course not,' he snapped.

Retta ignored that and padded away. A few moments later there was a triumphant shout.

'Brilliant! It's a real talent of mine, finding things in weird places. They're in the kitchen cupboard with the sweeper, *and* in a bottom drawer. God, what a mess. Give me a hand, will you?'

Hugh was silent in sheer surprise as he helped her to disgorge a cupboard into which he'd never looked once since moving into the cottage. The weekly help used it for cleaning materials, but it also smelled strongly of turps.

Retta dragged out boxes of oil paints, jugfuls of brushes, canvases (some damaged); then, opening the deep drawer at the bottom of the cupboard, gave a loud whistle.

Crammed into it were canvases. She pulled them out one by one and carried a pile into the sitting room, too intent on packing to stop and look.

'We'd best wrap them up. Find me a sheet, will you?'

He fetched a clean sheet in silence and helped. He did not look at the canvases either. The studies of apples, cherries, the cream jug, the hazelnuts in a dish. All were shrouded, ignored, packed in the sheet. Then he found a black plastic garden bag. Retta decided against the bottles of turps.

'They'll stink out the car boot. I'll leave those.'

She sat on the cases one after the other to close them. It wasn't easy.

'Now for the baby. Do you happen to have some spare bags?'

'Yes.'

He went into a downstairs cupboard and produced two smart navy-blue canvas bags bound with leather and almost new.

'Great!' she said. 'Leave them down here. I'll go up and get his things.'

He did as he was told. He was nerved up for baby clothes to come flying through the air to land all over the floor, but Retta appeared very soon, her arms full of minute garments, blankets and shawls. On the top of the pile a felt duck was wobbing, and under one arm, carried with difficulty, an enormous pack of disposable nappies.

She flopped down on the carpet and opened the first of the travel bags.

Hugh, again, helped. Like all naval people he was neat-handed, and now and again refolded something Retta untidily shoved into the bag. When the job was completed, she finally squashed in a teddy bear. She was still on her knees and Hugh bent down to help finish the packing. He was not a man to kneel. He fastened the zips and the little brass padlocks with a click. Then straightened up.

Retta scrambled to her feet. In her hand she held the blue and yellow felt duck. She sniffed it. It had the wonderful smell of new babies.

'Thanks for the help.'

The steel thread was gone from her voice. He picked up the heavy suitcases and the plastic bag that contained the canvases.

'I'll take you to the car.'

'It's parked on the right. OK. I'll bring the bags.'

'Can you manage?' he said with his automatic courtesy.

Retta said amiably that baby things took a hell of a lot of space but weighed nothing.

In another silence they went out into the clouded afternoon. It was Hugh who loaded the luggage into her open car, taking time to wedge and rearrange.

Retta stood swinging her keys on a thick gilt chain decorated with a jewel-studied R. She said suddenly:

'I realise it is none of my business. You were quite right to object to me discussing it. Bloody nerve. You mustn't think me too prejudiced. Too much on Av's side.'

'But you are.'

'Of course I am. But I despise one-eyed people incapable of seeing the other viewpoint. I don't expect we shall meet again; it seems unlikely, doesn't it? Will you answer me just one thing?'

When he did not reply, she took it for agreement.

Like an actress who chooses her own dressing room for a meeting as the place where she is in command, Retta climbed into her car before she spoke. He opened the door for her and she hopped in. He shut the door firmly. She didn't start the engine but turned and looked up at him where he stood.

'The thing I want to know is not about Avril. I'm not asking you about her and I have scarcely, I might add, asked her about *you*, though I did advise her to steer clear. Other people's sex lives are their own. What I really want to know,' she added, looking at him with real curiosity, 'is about Teddy.'

He said nothing.

'Teddy,' repeated Retta, raising her voice as if he were deaf. 'The baby.'

'What are you saying?'

It was most odd. His handsome face had become quite natural while they had shared the job of packing. He had looked human. Real. Rather nice, she had thought, in that over-handsome way. Now it was again as stiff as a board.

She started the engine, which roared and then settled to an idle purr. She squinted up at him; he was against the light.

'What I truly cannot understand, what hassles me every time I try to make any sense of it, is how you went off the baby. It's . . . it's incredible. I mean, you loved him, for fuck's sake. Avril said you were bonded to him, you said the poor little bugger looked exactly like your grandfather. How could you just . . .?'

'*Be quiet. Will you be quiet!*' he almost sobbed, and rushed away towards the house.

She made a face as she drove away.

Poor sod, she thought. Pride, I suppose. He can't accept

that Av slept with another guy. He can't forgive her, it was the ultimate insult to himself. So he's lost that baby and he minds.

But Avril and Hugh both knew this was not so. If to be a father can engender a flood of possessive love, an emotion so strong that it is filled with passion, to discover that after all the little being never grew from your seed can dry up the love as if you had poured acid over it. Hugh did not love, miss, care for or desire the child. The very idea of it – the baby was never 'him' now – revolted him. He hoped he would never see it again.

With Teddy in his buggy, Avril was in the garden inexpertly knitting when she heard a footstep on the short flight of iron steps leading from sitting room to garden. She was startled. Retta was early. But instead of the lanky figure of her stepmother she saw her father. When he, in turn, saw her, he went straight back indoors. She guessed he must have gone to consult Araté, as to when Retta would be home. He tried to avoid asking Avril direct questions. Avril knew the Spanish girl had gone home.

She waited for him to return, her heart beating slightly faster. I must not let him upset me. Bad for my milk. I must keep calm.

He reappeared and walked across the grass.

'Where is Retta?'

He sounded, he looked, very disagreeable.

'As it happens,' said Avril, 'she has gone to Dorset.'

'To *Dorset*?'

'To pick up my things,' said Avril patiently. She thought, really, men are so stupid sometimes. Why else?

He had taken it in and after a moment, more disagreeably than before, 'And why didn't you go, pray?'

That did it. Her nerves left her. She said bitingly:

'Really, Dad, you are appalling sometimes.'

The elderly blue eyes glared.

She spoke fast and loud, angrier with every word.

'Yes, you really are. I believe Retta thinks the same about you as me but obviously doesn't say. Why do you *suppose* she decided to go in my place? Do I have to remind my own father that Hugh smashed me in the face? Do Royal Navy wives,' she stared back at him, 'usually return meekly to violent husbands who will succeed next time in knocking them senseless? Who, pray, would send for the ambulance? Your precious Hugh detests me. For being unfaithful, sure, and don't bother to say he's right. *He* slept around from the first few months after we married; God knows how many women he's taken to bed. I had an affair with one man. Just one, OK? And weren't *you* unfaithful to Mum a number of times before your affair with Polly and then the final split? What I am asking is where is the difference between you, Hugh and me?'

Faced with his daughter's accusing eyes, he was literally unmanned.

'I can't talk about this . . .'

And like his son-in-law at almost the same time of day in Dorset, he escaped.

Avril did not enjoy her victory. It tasted bitter. She had never said a crude or angry word to her father in her entire life, not during his miserable divorce, not ever. Her own words, not his expression, set her trembling. She had to walk round the garden two or three times. She felt sick. She gave a positively scared jump when a hand was placed on her shoulder.

It was Gerald.

'Dad, I'm sorry,' she burst out, just as he muttered very low, 'Dear child, I am so sorry.'

To their astonishment they embraced.

Retta giggled when Avril asked her about her Dorset visit.

'You never told me he was so fanciable. That was a turn-up for the book. Cross as two sticks most of the time, but attractive if you like that sort of thing. I suppose you did. Madly.'

'A hundred years ago.'

Retta giggled again. She had done her stepdaughter a favour and felt fond of her.

The late autumn was a curious time for Avril. Her father was kind to her again in his reserved way. They had never been close, so that had not changed. He simply returned to treating her as he used to do, no longer as if she were a fallen woman. Retta was up to her eyes in work, appearing on TV, writing splashy pieces. She was often home very late and occasionally demanded that she and Gerald should go away for a weekend to some expensive country hotel. Avril didn't mind. She spent the weekends peacefully enough. Richmond suited the baby, who flourished, stout, noble and happy.

She was touched when a letter in familiar scrawling writing arrived with a Dorset postmark. It was from Helen.

'I rang the cottage to invite myself to tea. Your husband said you're in London. He didn't give me time to ask for your address, he was in a hurry. I imagine you and that marvellous baby are having a short hol so I decided to send this to your father's (got on to Directory Enquiries!!). I remember you once said he lived in Richmond. I am putting a large *Please Forward* on the envelope and *do* hope this will reach you. Longing for news of you and Teddy.'

There was also a call from Susan.

'How are you?' began Avril's mother too brightly. 'I'm staying in town with Mary Lockton. Doing some shopping and getting my hair cut. Would you like a cup of tea at the Berkeley? Sorry not to give you notice sooner but this trip was rather out of the blue.'

A somewhat automatic laugh.

'I haven't got a baby-sitter, Mum,' said Avril baldly.

Susan laughed again, though Avril did not see the joke.

'That's all right. Mary and I lunched there yesterday and we noticed a child in a carry-cot in the lounge. No one seemed to mind.'

Was this her way of indicating that she wanted to see her grandson again?

Teddy was turning out to be what Retta described as a Buddha-baby, a phrase she'd picked up from an article in her own paper. There were, said childless Retta with authority, two kinds. The big babies, good eaters and no trouble. 'Philosophers. Buddhas.' They were often quite late at sitting up, crawling and so on. The other kind crawled at five months, did everything early, were lively and energetic and didn't believe in too much sleep. They drove their poor exhausted parents mad.

'I'm sure Teddy's a Buddha. You're in luck.'

Living up to his reputation on the bus to Knightsbridge, Teddy snoozed for most of the way. He was still dozing when Avril arrived at the elegant hotel. Her mother caught sight of her across the lounge and waved.

Immaculate in cream-coloured linen and pearls, Susan offered a cheek to be kissed. Avril put the weighty boy gently down into her mother's lap. He slept majestically.

'I'd forgotten how small his nose is,' said Susan critically.

'Oh, Ma!' exclaimed Avril in a loud voice.

Susan shushed her, glancing at nearby guests. The baby, who was nobody's fool, then woke and gave her a knowing grin.

Tea went better than Avril had expected, but it had its tricky moments.

'Dad and Retta are being very kind.'

'Yes, yes. Your father has told me where you are staying,' said Susan, breaking in to avoid hearing any more praise of her successor. 'But the important thing, Avril, is for you and Hugh to meet. You must talk it out.'

'What on earth for?'

Susan shut her eyes for a moment.

'Your father and I think it might be possible to effect a reconciliation.'

Oh they do, do they? thought Avril. She had to re-settle Teddy, who had begun to slip lopsided on her knee. He blew a reflective bubble and Susan leaned forward to dab at him with a spotless scented handkerchief.

'Ma,' said Avril, again loudly, and then seeing her mother's pained expression and the proximity of a handsome waiter, lowered her voice.

'Ma, forget it. I am never going back to him.'

'He might be willing to . . . to come to terms with what happened. He might very much want you to return.'

'Have you spoken to him?'

Susan looked self-conscious.

'Well, he did come to see me. He was in quite a state. As he told me – we went to the Mill, you remember how he likes it? – as he said to me, he simply doesn't know what to do for the best.'

'It's easy enough. Forget me.'

Susan was not as disapproving or even as persuading as Avril had feared. She was rather reasonable, even if she was on Hugh's side to the death. Avril, eating a small eclair, wondered whether to tell her mother about Hugh's affairs. She decided not to use dirty weapons. Sure, she had used them with her father, but that had been fair enough at the time. Yet she had slightly regretted it later. And, her mother would so hate to hear about the sexy past.

When they said goodbye Susan actually said, 'Come and stay. Bring the baby.'

Avril thanked her and tried to look and sound grateful. Privately she thought it was probably a ploy. Susan was capable of springing Hugh on her.

When not being what Retta called mumsy at home in Richmond, Avril, as of old, escaped into paint.

Chapter 14

Avril's life, rich with a baby, was poor as a mouse in everything else. Her only talent was the painting, and it was crazy to imagine she could make any money at that. Who would buy her pictures? But she was now painting in her spare time whenever she could manage it. From the first week of her arrival, after having rescued her stuff from Fuchsia Cottage, Retta was interested.

'I really like your pix,' she declared, having lugged the black plastic bag upstairs and helped Avril to pull out the canvases, which she then arranged all over the bed. 'Who knows? Maybe Gerry and I have got a Cézanne on the premises.'

Avril looked appalled.

Humourless old thing, thought Retta. I do wish she'd brighten up. Maybe a solemn face is what you get when an artist comes to live with you.

It was Retta's idea to convert a glorified garden shed by the side wall into a studio. Gerald helped with the white-washing and carpentry and a local man came in to replace the worm-eaten floorboards. Gerald bought his daughter an efficient if roaring oil heater. Both he and Retta were pleased to see Avril, when the baby was asleep, going to her work place.

'Now she's got something to think about,' said Gerald.

Retta, a work fiend, agreed.

One afternoon, ostentatiously knocking on the open studio door, Retta appeared.

'Sorry, I know you loathe and despise interruptions except by Teddy. But I've had one of my brainstorms. I met a guy last night at that party Gerry and I went to. Guess what? He's got a gallery in Knightsbridge.'

'So?'

'Come on, Av. I'm working at home tomorrow, I can baby-sit. You can manage to be out for two or three hours in the afternoon.'

Hating every minute, and with seven or eight canvases in Retta's largest briefcase, Avril set off the next afternoon for Knightsbridge again, this time because she hadn't the guts to refuse. Her father and Retta had been so gruesomely encouraging, it had literally been impossible to tell them she wouldn't go. That she had no faith in her work. And, most shameful of all, that she did not even know if she could bear to show her paintings to a professional. It had been the choice of two cowardices, and the worse had been to refuse the couple beaming at her with such goodwill.

'I called up the man, his name is Quentin Streatley, and told him you'd be along,' said Retta. Golly, thought Avril, you do push. 'I shall throw my shoe after you for luck. Our picture editor always does that.'

Retta pitched her shoe accurately and painfully at the departing Avril.

Tourists were seething round the Scotch House, their

backpacks so gigantic that twice Avril was edged into the gutter. The gallery was more or less opposite Harrods. It was not small and its windows displayed large Matisse-style paintings in acrylics. Prancing figures in pink and blue.

A tall man with a narrow head advanced towards her.

'I brought a few things,' said Avril awkwardly.

'Mrs Brett? Retta Vincent phoned.' He was cool as he moved out of earshot of a customer and went to his desk, with Avril following. She opened the briefcase. Just then a young woman in yellow, wearing an unseasonable Impressionist straw hat ringed with artificial daisies, came into the gallery. She was pretty and Sloaney.

'Hi, Quen,' she said. 'Here are the extra three for the show. Sorry, am I interrupting?'

She smiled at Avril from under the brim of her hat.

Avril did not enjoy the next ten minutes. The girl produced, from a real portfolio, three paintings which she arranged on the desk. Leopards gazing into mirrors. Zebras travelling in palanquins. Girls with crowns of flowers – looking much like the painter – emerged from rivers to beckon otters or, in one case, a naked-ish man.

'I like the texture of the water, Rachel. That fish, the trout, is so dappled. Excellent.'

When Avril left the gallery she had never felt so demoralised in her life. She had been terrified by Hugh's cruel blow, and fear had made her escape. She had been rudderless and desperate. But this was different. She felt diminished.

Too upset to notice where she was going, she climbed on the first bus, and only well after it had moved off did she realise she was going in the wrong direction, not homeward but towards Piccadilly. The bus rumbled past the great artillery memorial, its tragic bronze soldiers standing or lying dead in seething traffic. The green of Green Park went by. At Bond Street she got down. Retta had recently said, 'Why don't you pop into Fenwicks if you have a second. Take a look at the new season's stuff and treat yourself to something new to wear.'

On her stepmother's lips had been the offer to lend her, which meant give her, some money. God, I'm not yet as poor as that, thought Avril. There was some money left in her account and Hugh must be made to give her more, surely? She would ask Retta if she knew a solicitor.

A man coming towards her down Bond Street stopped to look in Asprey's window. Something about the bulky figure was familiar; she had a sudden arrow-stab of recognition.

'Michael Silver!'

He spun round.

'If it isn't the girl from St Vincent. How nice. How very nice. It must be a year or more, surely.'

He actually seemed glad to see her, thought Avril, still suffering from Quentin Streatley.

'Can I offer you a cup of tea?'

'But aren't you at work, Michael?'

'Good question. Yes, I am at work. I'm casing Bond Street and having a look at my hated rivals. I can finish the job tomorrow. Is tea a good idea? And is it rude to ask if that briefcase contains paintings? You see, I still remember you're a painter.'

'Not yet I'm not,' she said with assumed insouciance.

'I recollect you said the same thing in St Vincent. The point is, are you on your way to a gallery?'

'Just come from one.'

He rewarded this with a friendly look.

'And you didn't enjoy it. So what about tea? We could go to Claridges and see if they still saw away with violins.'

Despite a twinge of guilt about Teddy, Avril found herself settled in the impressive place. Michael Silver said how glad he was they had met again. Iris Lawrence-Scott had given him her address, but there it was, he still kept his old commandment about not contacting the married women of the world.

Avril let that go. They talked without reserve, sharing the distant place where they had met – it was pleasant to have something so beautiful and so unlikely in common. He did make her laugh. She had forgotten how different he was from the other men she knew well: her buttoned-up father, her restless brother, the well-mannered womaniser who had been her husband.

Moving on from the St Vincent talk he said:

'So you and Commander Brett are now comfortably settled back into the Dorset country? And you're in London to sell a painting or two.'

'My husband and I have separated.'

It seemed to pull him up.

'But Iris wrote to me something about . . .'

'Me having a baby.'

He waited, and she added clumsily:

'Having a baby doesn't necessarily mean till death us do part.'

'I see.' He didn't, though. Then he said straight out:

'This means you're no longer in my mustn't phone category. Can I ask you something, Avril?' She liked the use of her name. 'And don't say,' he went on, 'it depends on what I ask.'

Affected by his male admiration, she smiled.

'OK. Ask away.'

'Might I see your paintings? You wouldn't let me see a thing at St Vincent.'

'Because I didn't have any there.'

'Ah, there was the back of an envelope. And I remember you denied even being a painter. Well? Could I take a look?'

Old tunes from long-since demolished theatres played softly; people arrived and left, kissing hello or goodbye in the fashionable way. For a huge room it felt curiously intimate. Avril opened the briefcase for the second time in an hour and took out her canvases.

Michael Silver examined them one by one while she watched in some despair. Looking at them, she knew scarcely one of the paintings expressed the thoughts she'd tried to make them say.

'I like the phlox. It's phloxier than stuff in gardens.'

Pause.

'You use layers. And you distort. I remember that habit in the sketch on the envelope. I like this one a lot.' He had spent most time on a still life of some figs.

'So you took these to a gallery this afternoon. May I ask which gallery?'

'Quentin Streatley's.'

'Wow! That prick. Sorry, but that does describe him. Look, why don't we pop into my gallery when you've finished that scone which appears to be choking you?'

They left the hotel and walked down Davies Street, and he explained. He was now part-owner of a gallery off Bond Street. He had bought in, as it was called, six months ago. The owner-founder of the Cogent Gallery had sold him paintings in the past and had talked about getting somebody new to share the work.

'He knew I was always interested. And as he's now semi-retired, he persuaded me. It wasn't too difficult.'

'I thought you were in banking.'

'So I was. I got sick of it. Money, money, money. A lot of people seem to have gone off their heads making the stuff. Don't think I object to money, Avril. I want to help our gallery to make some, of course I do. My brief is to use my business connections; we're keen to sell our pictures to some of those huge banks and offices the size of Grand Central.'

Michael Silver's Cogent Gallery – the name amused her – was smaller than Streatley's. The window was occupied by one painting of a horse, a barge and a river. Inside, the walls were hung with paintings by the same artist, riverish, watery, evocative. A girl at a desk was talking to a possible client. Girl and customer looked as if a sale was in the air. Michael gave Avril a wink.

He took her out of earshot and said in a soft voice:

'Now, I'd like to try and sell the figs. And the phlox, and these still lives. What do you say?'

When she gaped, he laughed.

'May I keep them for a bit? To see what happens. If they do sell, and I am not unhopeful, I shall want more. Have you any more?'

She muttered that she had.

His terms, he explained, were the same as every other gallery around. Fifty-fifty. Whatever sum the painting sold for was divided in half. Did that sound all right?

Avril was beyond anything but a nod.

He walked with her to the door. Then remembered that

he did not know her new address or telephone number.

'Just in case I have any news.'

She floated towards the bus stop in a state of idiotic euphoria.

Three days later he rang to say he had sold both the figs and the phlox.

'Any chance I could take you out for another tea, say Sunday? And see more of your work?'

'I can't get out again, I'm afraid. My stepmother was baby-sitting last time and she's away at the weekend.'

'Could I come to you?'

He arrived on Sunday afternoon after her father and Retta had left to visit some friends of Retta's. Avril was glad they were not around; she hadn't yet told them about either Michael or the paintings. She felt superstitious.

She was buttoning up her shirt after feeding a now-intoxicated Teddy when she heard the bell. Keeping the baby as near as possible upright so that he wouldn't get the hiccups or be slightly sick from overeating, she went to the door. Michael Silver, hands in pockets of a pale linen jacket, was surveying the front garden.

'Thumbs down for hydrangeas. This one's on its way to take over Richmond. Is this your baby? Magisterial. Does he like cars? Friends with young ones tell me their offspring are car-mad and moan if put into their buggies. I do vaguely remember Toby liking car rides, but he was five.'

'Teddy loves cars. But would you like to see the work first?' she shyly asked.

'Tea first. When I am full of Vienna biscuits I shall be more receptive. Do you know the Orangery at Kew?'

He talked all the way to the Lion Gate.

He was rather intrigued by the girl and her stout,

241

snoozing child. Divorced five years ago, he was over the first crippling blow of being deserted by the wife he loved for a man who was old and rich. He still suffered from his loss of the little boy. Women for him now were only casual encounters. Avril Brett was something different.

It had been no surprise to him when *Still Life with Figs* sold fast, followed by *Still Life with Phlox and Cherries*. He kicked himself for not asking higher prices. He had an idea that A. Brett could be a discovery.

She was also a mystery. What had happened to her since St Vincent? Why had she left that good-looking stuffed-shirt husband in the RN? Iris Lawrence-Scott had said Hugh Brett was the most attractive man in the hemisphere. Had that been the trouble?

'What we'll do,' he said, paying at Kew's Lion Gate, 'is walk across the grass – it hasn't rained lately – past the various follies, the Temperate House – we might call in on the way back and see a tree from the Himalayas – and have tea in the Orangery. It's cosy there, warm too.'

Avril had rarely been to Kew. She and Teddy spent their time on the towpath along by Richmond Bridge. Michael Silver led her across grass thick with fallen leaves. Avril took in the colours, ranging from vivid cherry crimson, through yellow, tan, down to dark-veined brown. As they walked, the leaves made a pleasant swishing noise round their ankles.

They went by the empty follies where Michael said George III and his queen must have drunk hot chocolate, and down long, straight borders, flowerless and asleep in the cold. Finally they came to the Orangery.

As he'd promised, it was cosy. He found a table and they settled down to tea and Vienna biscuits. Teddy, soothed by

warm indoors after cold winter air, dropped off again, true
to his Buddha reputation.

'I feel very positive,' Michael said, breaking a biscuit in
half, 'about your paintings. How about the way the figs
were gobbled up? Let alone your phloxy phlox.'

'You don't think maybe it was just a flash in the pan?'

He laughed outright.

'Are we having false modesty this afternoon? I see I'm
still with the girl who swore in St Vincent that she wasn't a
painter at all. You're a painter all right, Mrs Brett. And
happily one who now belongs to our gallery. Anyway, we
can talk business later.'

He leaned over and gently picked up the baby's foot.
Teddy's bootee had fallen off and it was bare. He looked at
the sole.

'Isn't it a marvel to think that little foot has never
touched the earth.'

'Yes it has.'

He laughed. 'You're being literal. I mean it has never yet
carried his weight.' He stroked it lightly, and the tiny foot
flexed up and out, rather than clenching as an adult's foot
would have done.

'Lovely,' he said, almost to himself.

Since Helen's gushings in Dorset, and the short time that
Hugh had been a real father and Retta's brief 'Isn't he
sweet, must dash,' few people had admired Teddy. Avril's
mother had been detached, unlike that first week after his
birth. Her father never admired anyone much – aloud, that
was. Michael Silver spoke as if he actually liked babies. Or
was he a man who set out to charm? God, I've had enough
of those, thought Avril. When she looked at him she
couldn't guess what sort of man he might be.

But the afternoon was happy. The baby woke and Michael took them to look at the Canada geese. When they were home in Richmond, he asked if he could go into the studio.

'Don't hover, Avril. I'd really prefer to look around on my own. Could you take yourself off? Does that sound rude?'

'Yes. I'll go and change Teddy, he needs it.'

When the baby was in his cot nearly an hour later, she found Michael Silver in one of Retta's chairs, sitting staring into space. It was getting quite dark.

'I like them,' he said. 'Especially the flowers and fruit. I think later we might give you a small show. You seem to me to have done a great deal of work. So. It seems I've found a new Cogent painter.'

'Oh, oh.'

He looked at her quizzically.

'That gives you a buzz, doesn't it? I remember feeling like that occasionally in banking when I made a packet. It won't last.'

'Oh yes it will!' declared Avril wildly.

Gerald and Retta exclaimed and congratulated when they heard the news. Retta said that before Avril had that show in Bond Street she would write a piece about her. Gerald said, 'Well done,' as if Avril had just won the class prize at school. There was no chance to tell Rick, who was in Washington again. Dutifully Avril telephoned her mother, who sounded unflatteringly surprised. When she had said goodbye, Avril was ashamed to feel she did need somebody to admire her. To be as excited as she was.

She rang her old office.

'Avril, how lovely! When are you coming home?' cried Helen. 'Any chance of seeing you?'

Avril hurriedly explained that she was still staying with her father for a while. And Helen, true to form, said how Gerald must worship his grandchild. With the conversation now switched on to the channel marked Happiness, Avril told her about the paintings. Helen gave her everything Avril had strangely hungered for: delight and admiration, genuine, generous pleasure in Avril's good fortune. She was so busy being pleased that she did not again ask when Avril was coming back to Fuchsia Cottage.

Ashamed and assuaged, Avril then took the baby for a long, thoughtful walk along the towpath. The air was cold. There was a chilly mist. She felt glad to get home, tired and thinking of tea, when Retta dramatically appeared the moment she entered the house.

'I've been listening for you. Guess what! Your husband rang.'

Avril's face literally blanched.

'I told you. I don't want to speak to him.'

'Yeah. Well. I did mention that. But he was rather pathetic, to be honest. I mean, really nice. Said how badly he wants to see you.'

'And I don't want to see him.'

'I am sure you don't. But he begged me to tell you.'

Avril sat down on a chair in the hall. She did this in a sudden dropping movement, reminding Retta of a movie when birds were being shot, poor things, on the moors. Like them Avril fell, riddled with lead.

'I suppose I shall have to.'

Rarely on the honourable side, Retta sighed.

'It's only fair. Something important to discuss, he said.'

'I don't want to see him,' repeated Avril. God damn it, thought Retta, she's scared.

'Look, Av, have a sense of proportion. He can't eat you. He can come here and Gerry can do his man-to-man pouring out the Scotch, and then you and Hugh can go and walk round in the garden if it isn't pouring with rain. Or Gerry and I will sneak off to the kitchen. It'll all be very civilised. Perhaps he wants to fix up the divorce.'

'I hadn't thought of that.'

'Stop looking doomy. If you play your cards right, you'll get some cash out of him. About time. And don't, repeat don't, mention you are selling your paintings.'

As it happened, and by bad luck, Retta's plan for providing moral and physical support came to nothing. She and Gerald were invited out to a concert on the evening which Avril, speaking to Hugh for the first time since she had run away, arranged. Retta wanted to cancel their outing but Avril was determined that she shouldn't. It made everything too heavy, made it seem in some way an interview for the whole future, a thought she couldn't bear to contemplate.

With calls from Michael Silver and the business of putting Teddy to bed, she was busy when Retta and Gerald left the house. Teddy, full up and in a good mood, went off to sleep at once. A baby in a thousand.

She went downstairs and out into the now-dark garden. Although the frost had long ago cut down the tobacco plants, they still stood like white ghosts, and she momentarily seemed to smell them. She went into her studio and stood for a while looking at an unfinished picture: scarlet pears and a pewter mug with beech leaves. Pewter was difficult. Finally she returned to the house and tried to read the *Evening Standard*. It was full of broken promises, broken reputations and broken hearts. At last she heard the bell.

And there he was, handsome, tall, erect, and armed against her. I am the enemy, am I? she thought. You'd be scared if I was Retta.

She brightly asked him in, took him to the sitting room and offered him a drink from Gerald's generous tray. Hugh said he would like a whisky.

'Do sit down.'

'Thank you.'

There was the sort of pause, thought Avril, you see in films set in the law courts. Who was the prosecutor?

'You look well,' he said. He didn't mention Teddy. As if he would.

He sipped, then put down his glass, and she saw that his expression, his face, was stiff. It was like that when he was at a loss. The easy, sexy Hugh was absent.

'I may as well get to the point. I'm here to ask you if you will come back, Avril.'

Her reaction was one of sheer surprise. It slightly improved the atmosphere and he said mildly:

'Didn't you think that possible? I never asked you to go. You simply made off. After our row.'

'Is that what it was?'

'Look. I am truly sorry for what I did. It was unforgivable, but I'm asking you to do just that. Forgive me. I never should have struck you. I had had a shock.'

'Yes. I know you had.'

'After all,' he was reasonable, 'no man could have taken what you told me that night without being pretty upset. I say it again. I'm deeply sorry I struck you. I'm here to ask for a reconciliation. We must try and remake our life together. I am sure we can.'

She sat looking at him like a fool. She was wearing a dress Retta had lent her. It was pink. She never wore such a colour and in Dorset, except for the office, rarely wore a dress at all. Trousers. Jeans. She looked desirable. Girlish even. Possible. He managed a smile.

'What about my baby?' she finally said.

He was ready.

'Yes, I know that must worry you. That I wouldn't be prepared to take on another man's child. However, I am. My name's already on the birth certificate and nobody knows the truth except your family, including Rick, whom I've talked to a good deal. He has been a great support over this.'

Bugger Rick, thought Avril, what's he got to do with it?

Hugh came towards her. She still looked at him, hypnotised, and strangely he put out both his hands as he used to do at Fuchsia Cottage and pulled her to her feet.

'I'm offering you and the child a home, Avril. That isn't nothing, is it?'

PART THREE

Chapter 15

The studio was at the back of the house, and although Edward and his sister always yelled, 'Mum, I'm home,' when they came back from school, Avril rarely heard them. She kept the studio door shut and in any case was deaf to interruption.

'You worry me, sweetheart,' said her husband. 'You don't even hear the front door bell. Suppose the kids or I lost our keys; we could stand ringing at the door till kingdom come.'

'You could go and phone from the little shop.'

Avril invariably jumped to her own defence. And defence from interruption was what she was determined to have.

Edward gave his customary shout when he came into the house from a late session at school, where they were rehearsing the Easter concert. He sighed noisily at the perfect silence, looked around for his father or Imogen, no sign of either, and made his way through the house, which was flooded with March sunshine blindingly reflected on the river's surface outside. Through the kitchen was the annexe built by his father as a studio for Avril. Edward banged on the door with the flat of his hand.

'Mum. Me. I'm coming in.'

He was tall, gangling. He had spots on his neck, however carefully he scrubbed and creamed it; he chose his own clothes and somehow, even when they were new, he looked as if he'd grown out of them. He showed no trace yet of the man who in a handful of years was going to take over the lanky boy. He had fits of shyness. Fits of helpless laughter.

'Coming in to have some tea?' he hopefully asked.

Avril was bent over the table; she still did not use an easel. She dragged herself unwillingly away from her work.

'You've been at it since Imogen and I went off at nine,' said her son accusingly.

'You sound just like your father.'

'Yeah.' He looked delighted.

'OK. OK. I'll come and have tea.'

She had, he noticed, that myopic look. Her eyes had not yet focused back from staring at the square of canvas.

Edward was at his best with his mother; his father's mild and teasing sarcasm were often felt by his son to be the acme of cruelty. Edward relaxed with Avril. He had no gift for repartee; his twelve-year-old sister had this in spades and could keep up with her father, using digs and thrusts of her own.

Leaning against the long wooden shelf on which Avril propped the smaller finished canvases, her jugs of brushes and the messy-smelling tools of her trade, Edward remarked:

'Guess what? An old guy came up and talked to me after the rehearsal. Very chatty. Knew all about me. It was a bit weird.'

'Perhaps he's a friend of Dad's.'

'No. I said that. *He* said the one he knew was you.'

'Perhaps he's bought a picture.'

'No,' said Edward positively, shaking his rough fair head. 'I asked him that too. It was peculiar, I mean he was. So *interested*. Kept asking me questions.'

He made a face.

'About me?' said Avril, surprised.

'Sorry to disappoint you,' said Edward with his loud laugh. 'They were about me. How long I'd been at St Paul's. What I was good at and all that stuff. He did go on.'

'And?'

Edward seemed taken by the story of the nosy stranger.

'And that's all really. Oh yes, he said he may come to the concert. Said one of the masters had invited him today or something, and told him I play drums. Maybe you'll meet him there.'

'And what's the name of this admirer of yours?'

She was still cleaning her brushes.

'I forgot to ask. Funny guy, though. Like a detective. I say, I could do with tea. I'll do it, Mum, but hurry because I'm going to make a heap of toast.'

Avril left her work and shut the door on a whole day. Marguerite Duras had once written a play Avril had read, with a beautiful title, *Whole Days in the Trees*. She often thought, that's me. When she emerged from the hours of concentration she felt tired, pleased and dissatisfied. What a lot of work was disappointment. She wandered into the kitchen where the heart of family life beat most strongly, drew up a chair to the table and sat watching Edward busying himself with toast and taking spoonfuls of honey from the pot.

Her forties, the age dreaded by women who have been

beautiful, had added character and a limited success to the uncertain charm of the younger Avril. She was now a pretty woman with an air of contentment, of poise. Her black hair, worn short, still curled naturally; she had put on some weight and was no longer a waif, just as her face had lost the interesting pallor and prominent actressy bones. In one thing she was unchanged. She still wore her oldest cords to paint in and still believed they brought her luck.

Imogen arrived just then, minutes after her brother, and during tea the two began the usual argument.

'You shouldn't eat chocolate biscuits as you've got spots,' said Imogen with pity. Her own skin was flawless.

'You shouldn't either. You're getting a double chin. She looks like Marie Antoinette, doesn't she, Mum?'

Avril waited for the pay-off – 'And look what happened to *her*' – but Edward instead, seizing the *Evening Standard*, decided to read bits out loud:

'"Twins shared the same toy boy . . . Tea lady assisted in the operation." Which'll you have?'

'The operation please,' from Imogen. 'I love them.'

The two exchanged a smile.

Avril left them, arguments boringly started again, and went up to her bedroom, wishing her husband was home. Shall I ring him? Have I got paranoia? She didn't ring, but stood looking out of her window at the river in the spring light. She never tired of the river, from the day her husband had bought the house and brought her here without telling her in advance. Edward had been Teddy then.

While he had still been the Buddha baby, the peaceable godling far removed from the gangling boy downstairs, Avril had married Michael Silver. His way of asking her had been a casual:

'What are you doing every night this month?'

'I don't know . . .'

'I should have said every night this year and the next and so on. Do it with me.'

For the first time in her life Avril had been offered for by two men. Her un-divorced husband who wanted a reconciliation, and the owner of the gallery where two pictures of hers, her very first sales, had been snapped up within days.

Her stepmother couldn't help being fascinated to see Avril, at this important time of her life, havering. Retta had begun to like Hugh Brett, although she'd remained loyal to Avril and still called him 'that bastard' occasionally. But then it changed to 'that attractive husband, Av'. Hugh's spell had worked on Retta, who had taken no antidote and soon found it difficult to think of the elegant man sprawling in the sitting room as a wife-beater. 'Come on in, Hugh,' Retta would say at the door.

Avril's father was cordial to him too, and it looked as if Hugh would win his campaign to put himself in the right. His attitude to the child was noncommittal. He would ask after him, 'Going on all right?' but only when Avril's father and Retta were present. And they always were, since Avril avoided seeing him alone.

Michael Silver waged a very different campaign. He visited her studio, conferred and criticised her work, and sold three more paintings. It was a measure of his belief in her that he decided the Cogent could introduce her as one of their new painters and do it with a fanfare. A show.

There had been something else.

Retta and Gerald had been away one weekend and Michael had come to the Richmond house; he had shared

Avril's supper. And they made love. Avril enjoyed it intensely. He was as sexy as Keith and as skilful, but something happened which, looking back later, she realised had been the most important thing in her life apart from Teddy's birth. She and Michael had been in her bedroom lost in their first sex, silent, coupled, when Teddy began to wail. Returning to sanity, Avril mumbled:

'He'll stop in a bit.'

Michael smiled and went on making love.

But the baby did not stop, and Avril's bliss began to leave her. The child's cries grew louder and angrier; Teddy was working himself into a rage. He no longer cried, he screamed, the noise piercing Avril like so many thrown daggers.

Michael stopped lovemaking and looked down at her.

'Poor scrap. He is in a tizz.'

'Oh darling, I am so sorry.'

He rolled to one side; she scrambled from the bed and ran to the cot, where Teddy was crimson in the face and sweating. She picked him up and walked him up and down the room. The cries stopped, but only if he was on the move every minute. When she finally thought he had gone to sleep, she crept over to the cot, but even as she leaned over to put him back in his place, Teddy started to cry loudly. Don't think, said the little creature screwing up his face, you can get away with that.

Michael lay in bed stark naked, hands behind his head, watching with amusement.

'What a little sod.'

'If only I could just get him to drop off . . .'

Let me have a go. I like babies.'

He padded over, took the child and began to walk as she

had done, round and round the bedroom. His arm was strong, he slightly bounced the small hot bundle as he moved, slightly bounced and rocked, and sensing this was not his mother the baby stared up at him balefully with short-sighted eyes. Avril crouched on the bed. She too was naked. Adam and Eve, long after leaving Eden.

'It's so kind of you, Michael, but let me . . .'

'I'm not giving him back. He's cross-eyed trying to keep awake. Come on, buster, you're worn out. More turns round the room? OK. Up to the window. Now to the left. Now gently up to your cot and don't start snuffling, you know when you're beaten . . .'

His voice was low. The big, fattish, naked man padded round, murmuring to the bundle in his arms, and then crept, step by step, towards the cot. Very slowly he replaced the child.

Perfect silence.

He climbed back on to the bed.

'Now. Where were we?'

One minute later the wails started from the cot again. Avril and Michael looked at each other for a moment, then laughed.

Michael Silver married Avril after a divorce in which Hugh, suddenly reverting, at first tried to defend and then refused Avril a penny piece. She discovered – 'What an innocent you are' – that the gallery, though her new husband's obsession, was by no means his only source of income. His father, Joseph Silver, had left him money, and his great-aunt, Rachel da Silva, had left him more.

'It's our Jewish blood. We're good with the cash. And as a race, you must have noticed that we are uxorious. Now

I'm your husband, I intend to drape you in jewels and Gucci.'

She was quite shocked at his extravagance.

He also insisted that the baby should take his name by deed and adoption. It was all done correctly and fast; as time went by and their circle of friends increased, nobody remembered – most of them did not know – that Edward was not Michael's son. One or two people thought the baby had been adopted. Others that Michael and Avril had produced the boy before they married. Three years later Avril had Imogen and the family was complete. Apart from her own family and Michael himself, not a soul knew that Edward Silver was in actual fact the son of a Dorset solicitor.

Avril forgot too. Imogen was like Michael 'but prettier,' said her father, who had turned the family into the solid lump of closeness which Avril needed. Michael was right about being uxorious. The lazy-seeming, cynical-seeming shrewd buyer of pictures, the man never averse to pretty women, was a husband in a million. What luck, thought Avril. How did it happen?

Avril's well-being, her happiness, only sometimes shot through with fears at the sadness and terror of the world, was strangely disturbed by Edward's story of this 'old guy' at school. She couldn't forget it and wondered why it worried her. For some reason she did not speak about it to Michael when he came back from the gallery that night. He was thoughtful – in other words worried – by the present lack of sales. His partner had retired long ago and Michael's life was at the Cogent or at home; it was the gallery which bothered him.

The morning after Edward's encounter at school, he

hurried down the towpath and crossed Hammersmith Bridge to join the flock of youths very like himself walking to school, while others, small and tall, were delivered by their parents in cars. Imogen, as neat as Edward was awkward, had bossed her father into his car and been driven off in comfort to her own school. Avril went into her studio.

But not to paint.

She picked up the telephone.

'Retta?'

'Hi!' Fifteen years since becoming Avril's stepmother had left Retta more or less unchanged.

'I wondered if we could meet.'

'Let's do lunch.'

'No.' said Avril. 'I mean yes. I mean both. I need your advice. I suppose I couldn't see you today?'

Retta had not lost, together with a figure nearly as thin as Edward's, her journalist's curiosity.

'What's on?'

'You know I hate the telephone.'

Retta's sharp ears picked up strain in Avril's voice; she said breezily:

'Why don't I drop by before lunch? I've got a date at the Ivy but I could stay half an hour before I need to leave you. Is that,' she added, 'long enough?'

Retta was punctual. Her fault was being early when time, which she treated with respect, was on her side. She banged loudly with the doorknocker of the Upper Mall house a good ten minutes before Avril expected her.

The two women kissed briefly; it was an embrace as natural nowadays as the kiss of peace at mass. The weather was bitter, sleet was blowing across a river the colour of steel, and Retta wore a rakish black felt hat. She dragged it off the moment she came into the sitting room.

'It's Moscow outside. Thank God your central heating is blasting away; Gerry has fits of being a miser. Do you know he actually creeps over and turns it down in the evenings when I'm watching TV, hoping I haven't noticed. Have I hell.'

She squatted on the floor by Avril's false gas fire, warming her over-ringed hands. In her late forties she was unchanged except for little lines in her vivacious face. She had managed at forty-one 'by the skin of my teeth' to produce her only child, Avril and Rick's half-sister, a crinkly-haired little girl, Lizzie, now eight. Retta was devoted to her but slapdash: she left Lizzie with nannies and sent her to an expensive school; she worked, then swept the child off to fantastic outings, theatres, even a weekend in Paris. The little girl was dazzled by her mother but it was Gerald, long since retired, who was Lizzie's slave. With him the child was a despot, which Retta thought a comic turn.

At times Retta's vitality made her seem a girl still. At other times her character showed; she might have been over fifty. The hair was still dyed but a deeper copper. She favoured Indian earrings. Avril's appearance, understated and none too tidy, paled beside the Titian fizzer.

'Come on, Av. Why am I here? Don't keep me in suspense.'

Without the old hesitations and self-deprecations Avril told her about the man at school.

'Well, of course it's Hugh!' exclaimed Retta.

'That's what I think.'

'Imagine. After all this time. How *odd*, Av. Quite the opposite of what usually happens. I mean, adopted kids can't resist hunting out their natural parents; you remember the piece I wrote? I had some amazing letters afterwards; the kids all had this intense curiosity. What were my real parents like? Where did I come from? But a parent seeking out a long-lost kid must be really rare.'

She was deeply interested.

'Retta, Edward is *not* Hugh's child.'

'OK, OK, not technically. But he's got his name on his birth certificate, even though Michael legally adopted him. Anyway, Hugh was your husband for years and he could have been the natural father. He thought he was for a few weeks.'

She continued to think aloud.

'I bet he's turned into one of those childless men one meets occasionally. Divorced and now totally a bachelor, selfish as can be and boring with it. Two or three drinks and he pins you in a corner saying, Where did I go wrong?'

Avril was alarmed and annoyed.

'It's all very well for you,' she snapped. 'We aren't talking about *Lizzie* meeting somebody who is not even her natural father and upsetting her. Anyway, Lizzie's a little girl, not a teenager.'

'With all those hormones boiling away. I know. Edward's very like that at present, isn't he? I'm being a heartless bitch again, sorry. But you must admit it is rather riveting. There is only one thing for you to do.'

'Tell him to back off.'

'Exactly. And fast. I should do it today if I were you. Before he turns up again at St Paul's.'

'But I don't know where to find him!'

'The Navy, surely.'

'Retta, I tried that right away. He left nine years ago.

You're the sleuth, you're good at things like this. What do I do next? I looked him up in the phone book, and do you know there are *over two hundred Bretts* in London alone, and Hugh's got about three first names. I don't remember which is his real one, the official one I mean. And he probably doesn't live in London anyway. He never liked it.'

'Naval Club? United Services?'

'Even if he is a member, you know that without me getting his initials right they wouldn't tell me. Places like that pride themselves on being sniffy.'

'True.' Retta frowned. She thought in silence for a while, pulling at her hair. Suddenly, 'I'm mad. Of course. Your brother is the answer.'

She was pleased with herself. Her memory – Gerald called her a walking library – was one of her vanities. Years ago she had made a mental note that Rick Vincent kept up with all his acquaintances. She had noticed it knowing it might be useful, and anyway, she did exactly the same thing. Not from sentiment but because the more contacts a journalist had the better. The wider it could make their research. If you know who, you know where to find out what.

'I can imagine Rick keeping in touch with your ex, can't you? They always liked each other. And Rick wouldn't forget that Hugh was rather knowledgeable about the services. Not only the Navy but all three. I remember Gerry said that.'

'Do you think,' said Avril, 'I'll get the address from Rick?'

'It's your best bet. Look, I must dash. Come to dins next week and see Lizzie. Your half-sister, as she often points out to me, is getting to be good company. Really funny sometimes. And a treat to look at. OK? And don't you dare forget that I want to know what happens about the mystery guy from the disgraceful past.'

Avril's brother was no longer the golden boy; at times he had the feeling that he hadn't fulfilled his promise. It was true that he did well now from books as well as journalism, commanding good advances for subjects which took on the current issues of the day. He'd become an expert on the tortuous world of international finance. He knew a good many financiers. But he had no contract with a paper and he missed the buzz. Working for and by himself made him occasionally morose.

Rick had married and lost two wives in the space of six years. Second-time divorced with a spoiled son from wife number two (he scarcely saw the child), Rick lived alone near the Royal Opera House, in an expensive flat converted from an old fruit warehouse. Avril rang and asked if she could come and see him.

He said of course, come along and I'll give you some tea.

The horrible weather had worsened; the afternoon was a mixture of white and grey, thin snow turning into slush before it had time to settle. The boutiques in Long Acre were empty, colourful and sad. Avril rang Rick's outside door, heard his voice on the intercom and the door clicked open. She climbed a steep stone stair. He was waiting at the top.

'You're quite a stranger,' he said, leading her into his main room.

It was enormous, stretching from one side of the building to the other. Once it had been piled with crates of scented oranges. From floor to ceiling there remained two huge supports of thick iron, painted white, which gave the place a distinctive character. But here the distinction ended. The two vanished wives had each attempted to cope with Rick's disorder. Now, liberated from women, he had let rip. Books were piled all over the floor, scores of old newspapers stacked under the windows, papers thick along the work-bench which had once been a carpenter's. He cleared some papers off the sofa and she sat down. The room felt chill. Was Rick getting their father's habit and turning down the heating?

While Avril's looks had altered over the years, Rick had not improved. He was thin and washed out. There had been a time when a tan had suited him; he had used a sun-lamp, but he had given that up when his second wife left him. He was paleish olive and his face was drawn. He had more lines than he should have for forty-nine. Retta maintained that every line represented a battle with one of his wives.

More human when he smiled, he made her some tea in a mug which had seen better days and asked after her children. 'And Mike of course.' He was behaving well and his sister knew this was because he was having a conscience attack. He had not seen her for weeks and weeks.

'Have you see Ma?' she asked him. This was one link he never lost.

'I took her out to dinner in Oxford. She was in goodish form. A bit of rheumatism. She went on about the garden, I'm afraid.'

'Of course she did,' said Avril, smiling. Her own daugh-terly visits to Susan happened quite often because Michael took charge. He liked Susan and showed it.

Rick then asked Avril about her work. He should have

known better. She had often told him there was no answer to the question, even when kindly meant. Did one say, 'Actually, I am painting some out-of-season plums and the skin of the things has got all wrinkly'?

She firmly asked him about *his* work and was told about an article on the illegal sale of church treasures. When he stopped talking, she put down the mug.

'I want to ask you a favour.'

'Thought you might.'

'So you think that's the only reason I come to see you?'

'Don't be so neurotic. No, I don't. But you're a practical soul. Or have turned into one.'

'True. So. I am looking for Hugh.'

He looked up at that so fast that it was almost laughable.

'For Christ's sake, what for?'

'Something I want to see him about.'

She had made up her mind not to tell Rick what had happened. Her brother was contrary. He was not like Retta who got the feminine point at once, the worry of an ex-parent making an appearance in the life of a sensitive teenager. The man must be told to go. To leave them alone. Threatened even? Avril was not sure how she'd do that but she felt strongly that she could. But Rick, she remembered now, had always taken Hugh's side. Even to the extent, astounding as it was to think it now, of suggesting an abortion.

'What can you possibly . . .?' he began. She interrupted.

'Look, Rick, I'd rather not discuss it at present. It is no big deal. But I do need to see him and Retta suggested you might have his address. So could you give it to me?'

'I'm not sure I've got it.'

There was something in her brother's voice which she

had known from when they were children, something
defying her to say that he lied. Something which, implying
doubt, was his way of refusing her.

'You could at least have a look.' She knew that to show
her annoyance would get her nowhere. She waited for him
to switch on that computer. It still surprised her that people
kept their addresses not in an address book but in a
computer where some genius had invented a device which
by an accidental touch could obliterate all the friends in
your life.

'I'll look if you insist,' he said, shrugging. He reached
over to a shelf where books, folders, papers, letters were
piled in a Rick-like mess. A brown leather address book was
hiding under some old copies of the *Spectator*. So he did use
a book after all, she thought. She now expected him to flick
through it and say – sorry, when I transferred the names
from my old book . . .

Before he could say it, before he had even opened the
book, the telephone rang. He picked it up with a charm-
less:

'Yeah?'

Whoever it was, he changed his tone at once.

'Hang on, won't be a moment.'

He shuffled a few papers, gestured vaguely in Avril's
direction and left her, holding the phone to his ear. He
sounded cheerful. A new girl, I'll bet, thought Avril.

When he had shut the door of his bedroom – it had once
been a minute office leading into the warehouse spaces –
Avril heard her brother say:

'Mirry . . .'

She grabbed the address book, flipping furiously to B.

There it was. Brett, Hugh. Astonishingly enough an

address in Islington. She pulled out a biro from her shoulder bag, scribbled down the address on the back of her chequebook and replaced the address book exactly where Rick had left it. Then made herself look relaxed, feet under her, reading an early edition of the *Standard*. Rick's call was short.

'Sorry, Av.' When he came back his voice had a lift and he gave her a real smile for a change. He offered to make her fresh tea, which she refused, and said quite affectionately:

'Sorry I can't help you. I suppose I can understand if you don't want to tell me why you would like to see him. None of my business. Look, change your mind, do let me make fresh tea and let's talk properly. I meant to tell you Ma is very approving of you and Michael these days, and really boring about Imogen.'

When Avril drove away from Long Acre it was the rush hour. But the jam did not worry her. She slowly negotiated her way towards the City, round St Paul's, and then as the traffic seized up entirely she studied her A to Z. There it was, St Ethelburga's Square. She worked out the direction, and drove on as the traffic began to move again. The sooner she saw Hugh the safer.

His wish to meet Edward again was not going to be a one-off impulse. She wondered how he had discovered where Edward was at school and again realised that her brother had provided the answer. Hugh would scarcely bother to go to the school, find Edward, chum up with the boy and leave it at that. After all, his name was on the boy's birth certificate; to the law he was Edward's natural father. He must have some plan. To come into Edward's life, even to extend some claim upon him. Her heart was in her throat at the secrets which must come out. Edward believed he was

Michael's son and Hugh could have no other design but to say the boy was *his*. How could such a lie be nailed without making things worse?

Speaking to Edward at school yesterday had been Hugh's act of possession.

For a woman whose character was naturally mild and peace-loving, Avril had moments of rage. Michael Silver knew this, although they had never been turned upon him. They filled her now with energy, firing her veins and making her heart beat faster. She was eager to confront the man, warn him off. Again came the idea of threats. I suppose I could use his past, she thought.

St Ethelburga's Square was astonishing. In a London destroyed first by bombs fifty years ago and then by money, there still remained whole areas of Islington with graceful eighteenth-century houses, Adam doorways and lofty windows, iron railings which Churchill hadn't stolen, and here and there, on blank walls kept so, formal figures in studied attitudes of Grecian grace.

Facing a couple of these, in a narrowish, elegant street leading into a square, Avril parked. There was the house. It was not as freshly painted as its neighbours.

She locked her car, walked up two worn steps and rang.

She waited.

At last a footstep.

A tall man opened the door.

The years had treated Retta fondly and Rick harshly, but they had not touched Hugh Brett. Like all ex-servicemen he had been taught to stand upright as a boy, to hold himself well – this physical discipline was one of the reasons time was at bay. Still handsome, his looks were dated and so were his too-perfect clothes. Even his shoes.

He treated his own surprise with a laugh.

'Avril, as I live and breathe.'

'Sorry to turn up like this without ringing you. I won't keep you long.'

'Come in, come in, you mustn't stand there freezing, you will catch pneumonia. They say there will be more snow.'

Inside the house he switched on more lights and took her into a double drawing room where a real log fire smouldered. He pulled an easy chair close to the hearth and smiled at her.

Avril, nerved up, excited, resolve running through her, was scarcely conscious of distant noise, a blast of music and some shouts. Hugh had just begun to say, 'What can I do for you?' when the door burst open and a boy of about ten, with a mop of curly dark hair and wearing black jeans, came rushing in.

'Dad! Mum says if you don't be quick the toast'll *congeal* and Emma says you've got to help with her dire maths and Cassy and Sam are being foul to each other as usual, they'll go on forever if you don't come down . . . Oh, sorry!'

He broke off, grinning.

'Boz!' shouted a woman's voice from somewhere. 'Did you tell your father it's ready?'

A woman entered the room; she, too, broke off when she saw Avril.

'I'm so sorry. I'm interrupting, and so did Boz, who has no manners. I'm sure he just barged in. How do you do?'

Her smile and manner had a sort of saintly slowness, not unlike that of Avril's old friend Helen. She wore a long, pre-Raphaelite, sixties-style dress and her fair hair flowed.

'Avril, this is India, my wife. And my son Boz. This is Avril.'

'We've heard all about you,' said India Brett, taking Avril's hand in a warm clasp. 'You're the painter. I took Boz to one of your exhibitions at the Cogent. He wants to paint and we so enjoyed the show.' She added an invitation to come down to tea.

'When Hugh and you have finished your chat, do stay. In this cold weather I always believe a good tea is absolutely vital.'

She shooed the boy out of the room ahead of her, and through the open door came a chorus of children's voices.

Avril heard herself say:

'Four.'

Hugh looked modest.

'Yes,' he said. 'Rather a quiverful, wasn't it? It is very pleasant to see you after all this time, Avril. Now, what can we do for you?'

Avril, whose thoughts were as chaotic as the sounds coming from the basement, stammered:

'My son Edward said he had met somebody at his school, St Paul's. A man came over to talk to him, and when he told me, I felt sure it was you.'

The change from the raging determination of a few minutes ago to this tame sociability struck her. Hugh said no, he had never been to St Paul's. Was her boy doing well? He slipped into parent chat.

'I imagine you thought I'd be interested in the school on Boz's account? Perhaps Rick told you about my eldest? Of course everybody knows St Paul's has a magnificent reputation, but we couldn't manage it, I'm afraid. Not with a gang like ours.'

He gave a sound rarely heard in modern families, the self-congratulatory laugh of the father with a large family.

'Now. Tea. No, you must stay, please.' Overriding Avril's protests, 'India really admires your work. When she discovered,' he was unembarrassed, 'that you and I had actually been married, she bombarded me with questions about your painting. She was shocked when I had to confess I remembered so little.'

Avril was taken down to a basement noisy with children as handsome as their father.

Sleet was still falling when she drove home. She felt battered by the high spirits of four young Bretts and the hospitality of two adult Bretts all bonhomie and broad-mindedness. During an elaborate tea – cinnamon toast, sausages, crisps, home-made cake – Hugh mentioned that he'd left the Navy some years ago, after Boz had been born.

'Hugh works as secretary to one of the Navy's big charities,' said India, giving her husband a serene look.

Avril vaguely recalled Hugh's private money, but wondered if he was well paid. Jobs like that sometimes were. Glancing at India, she was willing to bet that he was.

Hugh had chosen for his second wife – or *been* chosen by her – an earth mother. India Brett created and bloomed in an atmosphere of noise, demands, jokes, arguments, clothes needing to be mended or lengthened weekly, children to be hugged or scolded, mystery colds, epidemics, and ghostly pyjama-ed figures materialising by her bedside to say hoarsely, 'Mum, I've got earache.'

Avril's own life had contained some of these things, but not on the grand scale of India Brett's. There were nearly four years between Edward and Imogen. In many ways Avril had escaped the expense, the exhaustion and the fun.

Driving home she marvelled that India had succeeded

where she herself had so pitifully failed. How had that saintly woman, serving two entire loaves of cinnamon toast, coaxed or forced Hugh into fatherhood? No wonder India was cordial. She had four trump cards in that bread-and-buttery hand.

Two days after Avril's visit to Islington, Edward came into the studio again after school.

'Guess what? That guy was around again. I saw him talking to my housemaster, and then he came over and said old Wellman had told him I was a vital part of the jazz group at the end-of-term show and that he happened to be jazz-crazy himself. So he's coming to the show. He said he would see us both there. Oh yes,' Edward was at his vaguest, 'sent his love.'

'Who sent me their love. Who *is* this man?'

'Mum,' patiently, 'I told you last time, I don't know. Said he was from the long-gone. Thought that was quite funny. He laughs a lot,' added Edward.

Avril was still working on the same out-of-season plums. She'd had to go to the supermarket twice to replace them. The plums came from Israel and still retained splodges of soft whitish bloom. Now, losing concentration, she blurred the edge of one of the plums in the foreground. And swore.

It was all the fault of the gormless boy fiddling with her pinboard.

'Surely you remember some of your old friends,' he had the gall to say. 'And no, Mum, I didn't ask him his name. It would have been really rude. Tell you one thing,' he was eager to be helpful, 'he's jolly fat.'

Chapter 16

The Easter term at school had been chosen as a suitable occasion for a concert. Prize-giving was the big do at the end of the summer term and included various exhibitions of the pupils' work, as well as the school cricket match. The Easter concert was to give pupils and parents a touch of frivolity.

Edward was a jazz and blues maniac, with an encyclopaedic knowledge ranging back to his favourites in the 1950s. Muddy Waters, John Lee Hooker and B.B. King came streaming out of his room, as familiar to him as the up-to-the-second groups worshipped by his sister. His CDs took up four shelves in his bedroom, and Imogen was forbidden to borrow one. Much she cared. She had no time for that silly old stuff, she said. But she admired him. Three and a half years older and inches taller than she was, Edward was something of a hero. However, she drew the line at his rehearsing the drums. She hammered on his door, shouting:

'Have mercy!'

'Shut up!'

'That's what I'm telling you to do.'

Their father negotiated the peace. Edward was allowed to rehearse from six to seven and Imogen, a big favour, given Michael's study in which to do her homework. The study was at the other end of the house. On the dot of seven Edward must stop.

Edward agreed sulkily to the new law, and Imogen, pretty and pert, took the kitchen timer with her into the study. When it pinged an hour, she was out of the room and up the stairs to Edward's door like lightning.

In this familiar atmosphere, safe now that she knew it had not been Hugh coming out of the past, Avril's anxiety cooled. She had a brainwave. Edward said the man was fat. Who else could it be but her old enemy Peter Huskisson?

Huskisson had actually turned up last year, to her difficult-to-conceal dismay, at one of her private views.

'Remember your old pal, Helen? Met her at a fête; she told me you're quite a big name now!' he boomed deafeningly, looking round. He laughed as if the idea tickled him. But later she heard him loudly enquiring prices from Michael, and later still saw him actually buy one. The smallest. Michael told her afterwards that Huskisson had bought it 'because he read about you in the *Observer*, and the picture was an investment'.

It would be just like him to send ho-ho messages, and like him too to chum up with the housemaster. He must have a son he wanted to get into the school and thought a connection useful. She traced how Huskisson could have found out that Edward was at St Paul's. Surely from Helen once again. They kept in touch still, long letters folded into Christmas cards. Helen, married and also with a son, loved family news. Affection came winging up annually from

Dorset carried by harp-playing angels.

No longer alarmed by a spectre-like Hugh about to make her son unhappy, Avril felt strong enough to tell Michael.

Both children were at last in bed and Michael, reading Zola, had his feet up on the sofa. The wind was satisfactorily howling across the Thames and the false fire satisfactorily pretended it was real.

She sat down.

'Can I interrupt?'

'Do. This bit's very dark.'

He observed her across the space between them.

'Something to do with your painting?'

'Not this time.'

'So what is it, sweetheart?'

His voice had a smile in it.

She told him about the man at St Paul's.

'When I heard, I had this awful idea that it was Hugh.'

He was listening with attention.

'Come to make a claim, you mean?'

'Yes. Something like that. I kept thinking Hugh had never had kids – after all, he'd never wanted them – and now he might begin thinking . . .'

'Indeed he might.'

And then she told him about the Islington visit. She thought he would laugh, but he didn't. Instead he said thoughtfully:

'So he turned into a father after all . . .'

'And how!'

'And the man at the school wasn't him.'

'Michael, I'm sure I've solved the mystery. You remember Peter Huskisson?'

'The guy from your office whom you couldn't stick? And

who bought the little picture of the flowerpots? How could I forget him?'

'It's him. I know it is. Exactly the sort of thing he'd do, always one for the main chance. I'm sure Helen told him where Edward's at school, and he thought an introduction handy.'

'And doubtless remembers you're quite celebrated.'

'Darling, I'm not.'

He laughed out loud.

'How many times have I told you we won't have the false modesty? Av, you do look tired, you've been working too hard. You've got shadows under your eyes. Come here and have a cuddle.'

Before they turned out the light in the bedroom, he said:

'Sorry I shan't be at the concert. I'm hanging the new show, damn it. And Edward's such a demon at those drums.'

When Avril and Imogen were sitting in the smaller of the two school concert halls, Avril kept looking round to see if she could spot Peter Huskisson. She raked the rows of seated parents with eager eyes to see if she could discover the pig-like face. There were many parents: middle-aged fathers, wives whose good clothes were certainly making their sons and daughters groan pityingly. No sign of Huskisson that she could see.

Imogen's eyes were stars when she saw her brother on stage.

'Doesn't he look great, Mum? I mean, really great.' The little girl fixed her attention fiercely on Edward who, distanced by the rows of the audience and a big swathe of parquet stage, had an unreal dignity.

As for Avril, she enjoyed the jazz and felt proud of Edward. But she couldn't help wondering when she would see Huskisson, and whether he would be quite as awful as he had been last year.

The concert ended, the applause was loud and long, the group disappeared carrying their instruments. In Edward's case he could not manage four drums alone and Imogen exclaimed longingly:

'Oh Mum, can I go and help?'

'Darling, he will be with his friends.'

'But I know them *all*.'

'OK. But don't be a pest. They'll be excited and might not have time for—'

'They always,' said Imogen firmly, 'have time for me.'

Avril was inclined to agree with her. She had turned to pick up her coat and programme when a voice said:

'Hello, Avril.'

She started and looked up. A man was standing beside her. A man with thick white hair, a round rosy face and a smiling mouth which turned up at the corners.

'Keith!'

'That's me. You haven't changed one bit. How do you do it?'

She felt winded. Her hands, clutching the programme, began to shake like the hands of an actress holding a paper or a teacup and attacked by stage fright.

She managed:

'So it was you.'

'Edward told you I'd met him?'

'He said somebody talked to him.'

'And you guessed, of course.'

How could she tell him the truth? They began to walk

together towards the adjoining room where tea was being served. No sign of Edward or Imogen. Avril was alone with the past.

The fact that he looked so much older and his manner was so exactly the same affected her. She went on shaking slightly. Not from emotion and not from sexual memory. It was plain fear.

He looked about for a seat and found two folding chairs.

'Shall I get us some tea?'

'I don't want any just yet, thank you, Keith.'

'Neither do I.'

He leaned back. His weight, his fatness, made the chair creak loudly.

'I'll break it if I don't look out. I did that at a supper party recently,' he said, grinning like an overweight schoolboy. Then the smile vanished.

'I suppose you are wondering what the hell . . .?'

'Yes. Yes I am.'

He fixed her with faded blue eyes.

'Did you hear that Sally and I divorced last year?'

'No. I hadn't heard. I am so sorry.'

It was the old Keith just then, talking of his wife. He did not look at Avril but at his own loss.

'Yes, it was bad. Pretty bad. She left me for some bloody Canadian academic she met at one of those conferences. It was in Montreal. Do you know,' with emphasis, 'we had a long-distance divorce. Can you imagine? She simply never came back to the UK at all.'

'I'm so sorry,' she repeated. She could see to talk of it still upset him, yet he wanted to. It was both a pain and a relief. He gave a sigh.

'Funny thing, love, isn't it? I really loved Sally. Now I

realise she only put up with me.'

'I'm *sure* that isn't true.'

A change came into his face, brought about by Avril's vehemence and concern. He said more cheerfully:

'No, it isn't, is it? I guess I just said it to hear you contradict me. We had good times, Sally and I. Years and years of good times.' He went on in his good-natured way, 'I'm afraid I'm a bit of a sentimentalist. Always was. I suppose,' he lowered his voice, although the crowd, as crowds do, was now swarming to a distant table where the food and drink had been set out, 'I suppose it's my sentimentality that brought me here. Made me seek out our son.'

The two words froze the marrow of her bones.

'Keith, please . . .' And then, in the stupidest fashion, out came Imogen's often-repeated phrase, 'Have mercy.'

He turned in his precarious seat and looked at her for a long pause.

'Are you afraid I would tell him?'

'Of course I am.'

'I wouldn't, Avril. I swear it.'

'You wouldn't be able to resist it.'

'Of course I would never tell him. You have my word. It's just . . .'

He looked across the room. In the distance they saw Edward's loose-limbed, awkward figure. He was talking to Imogen, both of them shaking with laughter.

'It's just that I never had a child, you know. Sally wouldn't at first. And then she was too old, to be perfectly frank.'

Avril had a long moment of thinking – you wanted to kill that boy over there. You sent me money to do just that. She didn't speak.

'What I was thinking,' he tentatively said, breaking into her silence and looking at her with uncertainty, 'what I was hoping is that you would let me see him now and then. You and your husband – you married again, of course, Helen told me. I mean ... couldn't you say I was a long-lost godfather. Godfathers usually disappear when children are six or seven years old. I know mine did. Has Edward a godfather?'

'No. He disappeared.'

'You see? That's what I hoped. I mean, if I could come and see you and your family when I'm in London. Business brings me up now and then. I'd like that. I'd be so grateful, Avril.'

He was looking at her intensely. She returned his look without pity. He saw it. Felt her thoughts. He said in a voice so low that she could scarcely hear:

'Don't refuse me. After all ...'

The words died.

'You were going to say, after all, I am his father. No, Keith, you are nothing of the kind. Michael, the man I married, is Edward's dad. He was the one who carried him round the bedroom when he was a baby and crying. He sat a whole night with him when he had earache. I know that's clichéd. The truth is clichéd. It was an accident that you and I made that baby. It was sheer chance. Or perhaps I made him and stole him from you, I've often thought that's what I did. But never say you are his father. That is pathetic, and it is not true.'

He grimaced.

'I know. Damn it, I do know.'